Douglas Oliver has published five books of poetry, of which the much-praised satire on modern Britain, *The Infant and the Pearl*, is included in the present volume. His collected poems, *Kind*, were Peter Ackroyd's choice as poetry book of the year in *The Times* Christmas Book Supplement for 1987 and the novel *The Harmless Building*, now published in a revised version, received critical acclaim unusual for a small press edition. *Poetry and Narrative in Performance* (Macmillan/St Martins) is his technical study of poetic prosody and its links with the mental experience of reading narrative fiction. He has been a journalist and a lecturer and is well-known in Europe and America as a performer of his own poetry. Married to the poet Alice Notley, he currently lives in New York.

By the same author

Oppo Hectic
The Harmless Building
In the Cave of Suicession
The Diagram Poems
The Infant and the Pearl
Kind
Poetry and Narrative in Performance

Douglas Oliver

THREE
VARIATIONS
ON THE THEME
OF HARM

selected poetry and prose

PALADIN
GRAFTON BOOKS

A Division of the Collins Publishing Group

LONDON GLASGOW
TORONTO SYDNEY AUCKLAND

Paladin
Grafton Books
A Division of the Collins Publishing Group
8 Grafton Street, London W1X 3LA

A Paladin Paperback Original 1990

The Infant and the Pearl first published by Silver Hounds for Ferry Press,
London, 1985; also in *Kind*, Allardyce, Barnett, Lewes, Sussex, 1987.

An Island That Is All the World is published here for the first time;
individual poems have appeared in *The London Review of Books*, *Partisan
Review*, *Fuse*, *Archeus* and the collected volume, *Kind* (see above).

The present version of *The Harmless Building* is an unpublished revision
of the original publication by Grosseteste and Ferry Presses, London,
1973.

The Infant and the Pearl is reprinted in this book by arrangement with
Allardyce, Barnett, the publishers of Douglas Oliver's collected poems
Kind (1987). *Kind* is available in the UK from Allardyce, Barnett,
Publishers, 14 Mount Street, Lewes BN7 1HL, and in the USA from SPD
Inc, 1814 San Pablo Avenue, Berkeley CA 94702. Paladin, Grafton Books,
and the Collins Publishing Group are grateful for permission to include
this poem in the present volume.

Cover photograph by Susan Cataldo

ISBN 0-586-08962-4

Printed and bound in Great Britain by Collins, Glasgow

Set in Caledonia

For Alice

Contents

THE INFANT
AND THE PEARL
(1985)

for Jan, Kate and Bonamy

I

Lying down in my father's grey dressing gown
its red cuffs over my eyes, I caught sight
of Rosine, my pearl, passing out of my room
one night while a dream passed out of the night
of my nation. What a robe she was wearing! Brown
and sinewy, lion colours in the doorlight;
she turned, Laura-like, on her face a light frown
to be leaving, not reproving but right-
lipped, reddish hair loving the dead
facial centre: virtue could've kept her
had I enough of it, though I dreamt of it.
In my grey gown I would have gladly slept by her.

I was wrangling in my grey gown, full of wrath
as the door closed. And I felt close to me
the paternal cloth quietening, the rough
flannel lie flat in darkness; if even the
diagonal doorlight had been cut off
in the night of my nation, if even the
much-hoped-for Rosine had just had enough
of the dream – a fragment of light finally
dying in the room – well, the realm in my
closed eyes came alive with one colour:
the rosy-red pearl, so rich and womanly.
I shuddered in the grey for I should have slept by her.

Pearl, whose rose grey gleams
with infant hints in the hinterland
of my dreams, as when any poet dreams
of a lost pearl – some principle refound
only by resting on a gravestone! Rosine's
the mother of policy, priced beyond
our suspect neo-patriotism. She seems
in my nights to radiate reddish beams
as if whatever our actions she gladdened
our unseen selves, while without her our
conscious selves are immeasurably saddened.
In my grey gown I would have gladly slept with her.

The self that shines in the greying sunshine
of the immediate is actual, though it is
not all that is there. The feminine
is numinous in my masculine: it isn't nonsense
to picture a pearl placed on a shrine
inside myself; on the swirling surface
is Rosine's reflection which, as if she's been crying,
half turns away, ashamed where her mercy's
judged socialistic, too soft for justice.
For the dream isn't Margaret; the pearl's true minister
would be as lustrous as Rosine is . . .
In my grey gown I would have gladly slept with her.

My thinking greyed; the vision eventually
flickered in half-sleep – then Rosine had fled,
a fastidious foe of the tin pan alley
serious, powdered, severed head
of Margaret, whose self serially
repeated, televised, pearlized, and reported
ten times, tampered with immediacy.
An empty voice in my empty head . . .
and sexual absence inhabiting my bed . . .
like a vacuum in a vacuum, except for the
cuffs on my eyes, recall of red . . .
I shuddered in the grey for I should have slept with her.

II

A grey light dawned and on the distant
hills that I dreamt of lay a city of disdain
circled with steel walls, with silent
spires like warheads, in which one pane
gleamed in bleak agate; an arrogant
city above countryside that a murrain
seemed to have hit: a hoar-frost land,
medieval, the poor and the mighty again
in the chivalric hierarchy, but no golden chain
of charity joining them, just the martinet
reign of chance ruling commerce, in whose train
come prosperity, perils and probably regret.

The hills, though, were free, free of disorder,
hills of privilege, of prerogative governance,
a régime arising from the ruins of order:
lording it over the lean shires; once
the same Britain, now they were Britain's border,
an encircling supreme around happenstance.
And I was a new-style, a knowing dreamer,
though a grey friar flying over foetid expanse,
whose unfortunate fields were unfertilized by Providence;
where medieval was modern and where Margaret
ruled without Rosine, true mercy, while Chance
bred possible prosperity, perils, or regret.

In this landscape of chance, all at once a Churchillian
ghosting of blue graced the hills' far clothing,
yet the soil near at hand rotted, and the sillion
reeked. Brother ploughman ploughed with loathing,
knowing some were making a million
out of the serving classes and saving
their compassion like credit, crowing at each minion
the slogan, 'Supply and Demand,' mouthing
the language of natural law, laughing
off as nonsense that 'natural', though Margaret
legislates, is Chance, and legalizes nothing
but possible perils or probable regret.

In my dream I dreaded those hills, for they meant
a journey through ruins to a winter horizon.
Two whole epochs half merged, a convent
looked like a failed factory, the device on
its gate a graffito against unemployment,
as if nuns would denounce anyone who relies on
the medium, money, to act as agent
of *arete*, allowing self-love to alight on
the back of social like a lion with flies on
intent to rape. The resolve of Margaret
is rare, but lets flies randomize on
Britain's prosperity, bringing perils or regret.

The hills receded as I ran to them through
a badly-enervated wood, environmentally
ill, i.e., thin trees were into so-so,
leaning away from each other. And the lichen
was the same as my flaking psoriasis – so
the dry edge of my heart had evidently
infected both flora and my face with psycho-
somatic, fallacious sickness. Silently,
across a noisome stream, a blue Bentley
awaited me. I could tell that Margaret
might be in it by its pennant. It was empty, but apparently
proffered prosperity, perils or regret.

III

In such dreams the river kills time, and regret
faces those who fearlessly dive in:
they don't drown like Leander but like the Pearl Poet
awake no hero, having hoped for a life in
Eternity. There was *timor mortis* in this rivulet,
green as grimy greenbacks and striving in
vain to meander. Though I didn't forget
that time is money, the time half alive in
all currency couldn't thrive in the current. 'To connive in
cutting down cash flow,' I reasoned, 'takes vision.'
And the Bentley had a beckoning glove in
a doorlight grainy blue-grey like television.

If the stream smelt stagnant, the blue saloon
had tyres whose walls would keep white for ever.
But shouldn't I stay safely on my own
side, pure because purposeless? For wherever
the Bentley was bound, I was bound pretty soon
to ride out of reality altogether,
like a puerile *Private Eye* lampoon.
The car's petrol compartment cover
flipped open on the flank. That 'come hither'
glove waved in the window with derision.
From the front emerged a gnomic chauffeur,
his livery grainy blue-grey like television.

The chauffeur's blue suit was of airy weave,
a half transparent screen through which the trees
ghosted. We might honour Airey Neave,
but this was more Saatchi (or Saatchi), who said, 'Please
come over to us, Sir; it's a short step. We've
a special personage waiting and she's
both your will and your way.' Flashing his teeth,
he unlatched the rear door and I crossed dead leaves
to join him, jumping the current, ill at ease
to enter this Bentley – a betrayal of socialism.
There was still no-one inside, simply voices
in a light grainy blue-grey like television.

'Are you blue spirits spirits of Tories?'
I asked as I whoofed into an English hide
seat. 'I thought these Bentleys had lavatories,'
I joked as the voices whirled confusedly. A wide
arm rest fell down for me and my worries
dulled over. The foul air outside
was, inside, as fragrant as fairy stories
and the chauffeur was bending down beside
my door, fuelling the car with Countryside
Stagdeflation Mixture from the stream. My decision
as we started was a gentlemanly raid
on a drinks tray in the blue-grey like television.

Why the air was so blue Christ knows!
I wasn't swearing, wasn't sipping 'Cure us, Howe',
that blue liqueur once imbibed by bibulous
bankers; but the gin glowed blue and through
the air curled blue billows
of writhing, polaroid shapes; a shadow,
a scent, beside me. 'She comes and goes
like this,' crackled the chauffeur. 'The video
reception in here hasn't been how
we like it.' 'You mean my imagination
is persuaded,' I said, 'that our premier's now
just a grainy blue-grey like television?'

IV

The blue bonnet with its proud little 'B'
for Bentley or Britain coasted like a boat
under the barren boughs. 'Hitachi
have fiddled with logic control and come out
with what you'd anticipate, adjustable futurity,'
chuckled my driver. 'It's the actual's antidote,
the future replayed in the present, jitter-free:
a revision of what hasn't happened. What
we do is this: we project into spot
x, say your dream, a futurity reader
function that monitors the future mote
in your eye and the beam in the eye of our leader,

and replays a replica leader onto the screen
of the present, holographically if we have
to.' (In the front passenger seat came the sheen
of a thin, televisual figure, a grave,
black-coated man assembling.) 'Do you mean,'
I replied, 'it's really her replica? What of
the actual Mrs Thatcher?' 'Actual, in a dream?
Have you taken leave of your senses? We save
the actual for believers. You'll have to behave
as if all responses are real.' 'But we need a
true guide to the future, not a TV wraith.'
'In *your* eye – not in the eye of our leader.'

The leader herself 'switched on' – I suppose
you'd say – beside me, though with some 'tearing'
of her upper torso towards me, the nose
angled aggressively, though the whole was caring
in demeanour despite being dislocated. I froze
in panic at such a celebrity. She was wearing
a pearly suit, not silver-rose
pink, since sadly we seemed to be sharing
a black, blue and white world. But the bearing
of the front passenger meant a man for the media
to deal with delicately: a Joseph for dreaming
and descrying dreams in the eye of his leader.

But Sir Keith, staring round at his leader, somehow
altered and became Adam Smith! And
Smith turned into a stockbroker! 'How – ?'
The broker broke in: 'Of our band . . .
except those engaged on defence . . . anyhow
of the rest the centre is me; I stand
for the essence, the mechanical entrails of video-
age Tory. I take it you intend
to ask about Howe. He's in the boot,
where we want some solid weight. Indeed a
colleague on Foreign in this dream's contraband.'
And lambent the beam in the eye of the leader.

He lied for his leader: 'Where misery *is*
it's incurable. There's no cure for our ills
where the land isn't fertile. This
you yourself would say. Your sort tills
poverty's ploughlands. It's paralysis,
dead seed sown into soil that kills
it twice over.' I told him: 'You must miss
on your video half what I *will* say: that spoils
our discussion. Let's not scorn all the skills
of free barter; but chance – that's the breeder
of this mess. This national murrain muzzles
me; and so does the eagle eye of your leader.'

V

In lieu of the leader – who vanished, smiley-eyed –
that essence, the new Adam, that *éminence grise*,
turned icily, like a teacher who's tried
n times to explain the economic freeze.
'Look through the window at the world that has died
under your sentimental socialism. The Tories
have the perfect pearl, our policy.' Beside
me the seat shone, so that the trees
took a gleam from the glowing. I saw poverty's
sad spirits amid the slim trunks.
'Whose ghosts are these?' 'Whose? Oh, aren't those
the idle, the dull, the deprived, the drunks?'

To muddle the dull and the desperate and indigent
argued not that anyone had an arrogant heart
but that gentlemen are gentle and generally so eminent
they propose Sir Pretentious Privilege, Bart –
this stockbroker, ally and co-agent
of the merciless morals of monetary art –
to act as example, an astute accountant,
to a meddled-with nation. 'We must make a start
somewhere,' he said. 'The prosperous have first part
in the likely prosperity. Let the lower ranks
labour for it; and let *them* live apart
from the idle, the dull, the deprived, the drunks.

Liverpool's slums, Lambeth's . . . the dull haunt
our labour markets; they must live monastic
lives until the industrious, the investors, the brilliant
and expert haul us on stretchy elastic
towards wealth.' We whisked by the scant
foliage; finally the faint tick
of the Bentley puttered through a gap; the pennant
waved in an autoroute's wind; then as quick
as changing channels, we chased in fantastic
acceleration along the high banks
of the motorway, meditating our majestic
escape from the dull, the deprived, the drunks.

'Those who are disloyal, dull or leftist
can't be argued with,' came the down-my-nose-
pours-contempt-for-the-wet-collectivist
tones of the broker. 'Any true Briton knows
the Battles of Brixton were a left-wing ameliorist's
feeblest hour: first he allows
free rein to the rabid immigrationist
and, then, terrified at race tension, throws
borrowed money at the fighting that follows.'
'Are you a peggiorist, then?' 'That's the punks
and sick-minded. Only we *cure* the sorrows
of the idle, the dull, the deprived, and the drunks.'

The dull concrete didn't narrow with distance
as parallels ought; with no vibration, the v-8
lightly-stressed engine gave no sign of advance
down the blind, hurtling roadway. At this rate
we travelled on, talking as in a trance,
while false video reception made us late
though on time with each ready response. Then a giant's
soft pantomime hat appeared over the exit
sign to a services station. 'Wait,'
shouted this hirsute hitch-hiker. If my monk's
robe was threadbare, his fustian was fit
for Idle Jack, Dull Dick, and stage drunks.

VI

This was the dull giant, *Want* – Idle Jack
would prove his partner – he was gasping for air
in his ill-kempt heights, coughing with cardiac
troubles from carbohydrates, a ragged tear
in his doublet, bearing a child on his back.
Sir Pretentious huffed as we passed that despair:
'He can't compete: he hasn't the knack
of self-mobility; in our mercy we care
for the weak but wet-nursing by welfare
won't solve his problems: our priority is the average . . .
to upper-average; and afterwards care
for Giant Number One of those named by Beveridge.'

A 'Diversion' swept us into a giant slum
area where drifts of ancient dirt
stirred in the curbsides and soiled every room.
Beside high-risers, kids called as if hurt
in their gullets; one gaped as aghast as a dumb
man mauled by a lion; a militant squirt
of spit from another in an infant's nihilism.
His mother's broad bottom bustled her skirt,
plumped out on poverty; like an incestuous flirt
she cuddled a skeletal grandmother, savage
in extreme *Squalor*. The Bentley took a spurt
past Giant Number Two of those named by Beveridge.

We drove by a dried-out fountain, its giant
stone basin wreathed in weeds. As our
Bentley stole past the Job Centre's spent
offerings, cat-calls were coming from every colour
of ethnic minority: dusky Moslem, defiant
PNP Blacks, punks with purple hair,
red Irish, brown Indian . . . in fact, every tint
from China to Cockaigne crowding round to pour
an inner city scorn on me; a spinning flour
bag carried right through our ethereal carriage
walls, while I smiled wonderfully as though saviour
of *Idleness*, Third Giant of those feared by Beveridge.

'Regrettably, a number of giants roam
our land,' groaned the broker. 'All born identical.'
But a baby giant, abandoned by adultdom,
sat by the roadside ahead, a shackle
like a criminal's on his ankle. He was one on whom
innocence and incapability impose an immutable
Buddha face beaming; for Down's Syndrome
which places in eyes such a permanent chuckle,
had kissed him with mercy. My passing, meanwhile,
threw dust on this infant, *Ignorance* – at the edge
of welfare, you may meet the mild eyes of the mongol,
and of Giant Number Four of those named by Beveridge.

We passed into putrid smoke, the pageant
of giant abuses perhaps over; a stupor
engulfed me; I eyed some effulgent
steam leaving my lips like a super-
luminous illness; an inner irritant
penetrated my lungs from the pea-souper.
A hospital portal loomed up: 'No patient,'
read its sign, 'admitted unauthorized. We recoup a
part of our expenses from private groups.' A
nod from the broker: 'It's not just the rich:
better to combine against *Disease*. We have BUPA
to fight Giant Number Five of those named by Beveridge.'

VII

Inside the pollution a police sergeant spotted
us and stopped the blue Bentley, not on Sus
for we were above suspicion. We started
gliding from the slum as he guided us
out on the freeway toward our allotted
destination – Steel City – as detritus
blew free from the bonnet. But the cuffs
of my gown were wet with blood. Worse,
my mind rained into my heart at my callous
and inactive embitterment. Empty pity
made me shrink from the broker or return mute animus
as from Hazard Country we sped to Steel City.

Blotting the blood with some Baldwin-era Hansard
pages that I found in a fresh folder
beside me, I began inspecting the tarred
surface vanishing fast under us; from old
repairs and bumps, the Bentley bit hard
on a shimmering grey straight; it yelled a
gale, tyres roaring, as we raced toward
that shining city on a far hill's shoulder.
Past crumbling factories, or convents far older,
we kept after that upland vision, whose clarity
depends on distance; it grew colder
as from Hazard Country we sped to Steel City.

'To hazard a guess at the thoughts in your head,'
cautioned the broker, 'if we could only create
jobs out of thin air, then we would' – though as he said
this he was speaking out of thin air, that
is, he'd become a mere shadow and ahead
of me seemed out-of-synch in his video state:
fast rewind, flutter, cut dead.
'May I explain for a moment: we get
jobs that last when a definite delivery date,
price, and goods we produce fit the
needs of our customers . . .' I stared at his seat,
as from Hazard Country we sped to Steel City,

for he too had vanished; the old Hansard file
lay open and I almost believed that Baldwin
himself was now speaking wonder woman style:
'I'm not the one who's responsible when
people in jolly good jobs strike . . .' At this denial
something glinted on the English hide seat between
me and the door: a dull whitish pearl
of the size and opalescence of a spring onion,
newly shaped. The chauffeur shot me a grin.
'It's an old disappearance dot from TV
history. It's our warrant, our will to win,
as from Hazard Country we speed to Steel City.'

On the hilly horizon of Hazard arose
a non-liberal city of stainless steel
tilted toward us, trembling like a spring whose
destruction wrought outwards but whose real
rage was central. Dante's rose
had been superlative, swift and still,
but this was more like the maze of Minos,
chief justice of chaos' capital,
its centre fixed in the fierce free will
of capitalist entrepreneurs, its peripety
a doorless wall against the weak. Yet still
from Hazard Country we sped to Steel City.

VIII

Ascending to the capital of Hazard Country,
I saw cornfields spread out like sandpaper squares
beneath us. A little Britain; its boundary
encompassed by my eye; an island of cares
made solvent by oily seas. Our Bentley
halted by a high city wall that Bill Sirs
would have been proud of: steel, polished to buggery,
a stainless satin finish like 'Where's
the flaw in perfect polish?' There was
a 'magic eye' in the mirroring precipice
of metal, one blind to paupers and borrowers.
My false pearl paid the price

of entry: its falsity educated the 'eye'
whose photons suddenly thought themselves wrong,
misled by the selfishness of mirrors and by the lie
of bad timing beamed at them along
the rays from the wrong pearl, reflected by
the steel. The wall opened; we slid in among
shining shops and de Chirico sky-
scrapers. We could hear the ringing song
of Christians in a metal cathedral, whose long
curve of steps climbed to the iris
in a door like a lens, where loitered a throng
of girls. Their false pearls paid the price

of entry to false fame. They were snapped up by a
huge Canon – the camera, that is, –
formed like St Paul's. Though I seemed a friar
in my gown, I was actually more of an atheist
but was snapped by the iris and came to in the choir.
That lot were journalists and looked even less honest
than me: silk-suited, silk-faced like a Blackfriars
drinking den after deadline, their diarist
eyes on the swivel. I was intoning some eucharist
hymn about salvation without sacrifice
of the class system, hyped by a sensationalist
press whose false pearls paid the price

of entry; and I was now a newsman as false
as any on the Street. Steely light
slanted past slotted columns, for the cathedral's
were like camera spools, splendid in spiritual night.
The congregation in black, except for the girls,
who were lambs round the altar rails and wore white
Princess Di wedding dresses. 'Sundry earls'
heiresses,' I assumed, seduced by the sight
of the sub-Royal served up to write
about in some gossipy piece paying lip service
to Royalty as spectacle, rubbing up the right
way an editor's false pearls, the price

of my entry to by-lined falsity. The Bishop,
from the Diocese of Deference, had been
round with the wafer course already; the cup
approached and although awake in a dream
I closed my eyes and supped a sweet syrup
while conformity cooed overhead and the canteen
passed onward. I sensed that to sup up
such class sentiment was an unclean
act and I was heady from it. I had to lean
on a neighbour for support. Yet I felt nice,
full of hauteur, high on decency – but obscene,
for my false pearl paid the price

IX

of entry. A false sun in the soaring
metal cupola melted the manifold
of my dream-time; the dome, speckling
like some television wipe, spilt gold
coins which cascaded down into crawling
heaps. Those valuable virgins, bold
at this privatization of spiritual striving,
tore off their muslin and – like me, taking hold
of the coins – jammed them just where old
Danae discovered you could day-dream a fuck
from hard money. My self-image swelled
as I left and strode out on the Street of Good Luck.

Ego inflation on that egoists' street
was for wealthy Members only it was only too evident.
Two jobbing brokers blanched at my state.
'I thought we were working on nought per cent,'
spluttered one of those experts, consulting his slate.
On a farther hill the proud 'I' of Parliament
arose by the river and its tower had a great
Wheel of Fortune for Big Ben, as if government
meant ruling the City, the Exchange and the Mint
by the hope that a fall of the hands on the clock
would land on lucky six; a hell-sent
inversion of values on the Street of Good Luck.

Behind me, a section of street sank in
as the phony cathedral collapsed, amortized
in its own sinking fund of spiritual in-
solvency. The girls staggered out like squised
cats – Chelsea cats for they'd shed their muslin
and appeared Zandra'd up for supper, apprised
of liberated fashions to feed the famine in
their Tory hearts. Not truly politicized,
they scattered, hoping some husband-sized
financier would be waving a wallet so thick
that female and funds would fuse in a high-rise
high-yield stock on that Street of Good Luck.

Stalking the street, erect with that stuff
about royalty and religion and ready
to fornicate with Fortune's feminine staff,
I loped after a likely lady,
friar though I was and wearing such rough
clothing. Her carefully-cut Rasta-thready
blonde hair, her wily nether half
filled me with: sex = self-will = speedy
orgasm = self-aggrandizement = 'Steady
on, I am the dreamer and can dream up success that's worth more than a wallet. Already
you've gathered *my* gold on the Street of Good Luck.'

The next bit's a mystery: mistreating a woman
– not even the abuse of another's soul –
hadn't any tie-up with Tories; but the terrain
of chance, of Steel City, and the whole
theme of false values now ran
through my loins like lust; I stole
up behind the blonde, crowed like a bantam,
didn't go for a posterior goal
but entered her top to toe. A coal-
blackness blotted out her silk back
and I reeled in an utter reversal of role:
all good turned to bad on that Street of Good Luck.

X

On that street sex was one-sided and sterile,
an inversion of self-image on its own image
as Dante was drawn through the dark navel
of Satan. My face froze frig-
idly like a demonic id whose idol
is itself in its stony enjoyment of rage.
My stomach tried to turn over to tell
me it was a happy puppy, but the passage
turned me entirely, eventually to emerge
at the woman's front, facing her, faint
with despair to have done such self-damage.
She said softly, 'Follow your Saint.'

In the following instant I thought that the fortune-
hunter's blonde hair had
become a rich red and that Rosine
herself, whom I'd been hunting, now stood
before me, her russet robe a ruin,
her face all frowns, her fair eyes sad
at the vicious violation of virtue in
my pretended acts of love, my perverted
rape of the rosy pearl whose red
was talismanic – a truth without taint.
In this single instant I realized what she'd
suffer if I followed the feet of my Saint.

For my blood flowed upward to beat on the barrier
of the spiritual; and I saw into Rosine's soul –
it screamed like an oyster in hysterics, the inner
sanctum slimy. But a shining idol
lay within the lining, tiny, dreamier
than Buddha; it was the beaming baby mongol,
Ignorance. Immediately, I felt calmer.
The rosy saint of all sexual, all social
polity had appeared in her soul. The pearl
seed of her Socialism was this subnormal infant.
The soul was screaming, suffering my evil
violation, but the voice said, 'Follow your Saint.'

All I saw was her soul and, following that, Rosine
herself couldn't be dreamed of concurrently:
just this jewel, this joyful, serene
jot of the former giant, though ignorantly
deprived, become all I desired, the divine
baby-being in non-being. Fervently,
I sought to stabilize the ignorance, but the scene
was blurring. As it blanked out, the Bentley's
silver-blue sidled up silently.
Inside was the silky-backed blonde, her serpent-
like Rasta-threads wreathed quite reverently
into saintly halos, so that 'Follow your Saint'

meant 'Follow this Medusa'. My mind
was still bathed in babydom, but
the woman awaited me. She was some kind
of secretary now, all pencils, sorting out
parliamentary papers. I was an M.P., my suit lined
with plum-red – the gown had gone – ; no doubt
I was Labour – of the lunched-at-Locketts, dined-
at-Whites variety, never without
this personal assistant, and set up to spout
for party and people, proud that Parliament
had seduced me. I sat down beside her to scout
out a refuge from innocence, from 'Follow your Saint'.

XI

We followed the river to Fortune's Wheel
and its Parliament, then down an underpass
with metal surfaces, spinning like a steel-
coiled worm-hole through time, whereas
we held steady as a spaceship in a special
effects catastrophe. My secretary was
proffering my Order Paper as though political
protocol prevailed in whirlwinds. Pompous
because the Bentley was mine now and because
the main motion before the Parliament
was mine also, I stared in surprise
at the annoying frivolity of an amendment –

'annoying', as I was aiming at a veto
of Margaret's money measures with a motion
of censure: 'That this House has no
confidence . . .' and so on. The Opposition
leader would come first, but a clever cameo
performance, well-reported, would promise me promotion
chances: just my luck if some shallow
ass threatened our forcing of an election,
wording the anonymous, a-logical alteration
that: 'Parliament places no confidence in Parliament'.
As if one could *confidently* call into question
oneself? An annoyingly frivolous amendment.

Lost in the annoyance I was hardly aware
we'd been grounded in a gravy-brown, gothic
décor. From the car door a corridor,
panelled in oak, opened an honorific
progress down a carpet in the Commons. My career
was poised on the pure *realpolitik*
of the day's debate. The doors to the Chamber
were pulled open by the body politic
of the Sergeant at Arms and I saw seraphic
gleams of light. But a grey garment
floated by me and I almost forgot to think
of my motion and its annoying amendment.

Annoyance gone, I saw my grey gown
sported by an old M.P., pass by us
en route for the opposite lobby. My own
feeling was I should follow, that impulse
being stopped by my secretary – she'd shown
me my speech draft. I stuttered, 'This is serious:
who was that man?' 'Well, he's been known
from here to eternity as "Father of the House",'
she sneered. 'But Shinwell, who's a scrupulous
Lord, is no sell-yourself Socialist bent
on crossing the Commons in a confidence crisis,
when we're up against such an annoying amendment,'

I argued, anxious instead of annoyed,
for the 'Father' had resembled my father,
drained and grey, descended to that void
from which he waits for me to remember
him in dreams. Through the doors that candid
light reminded me I was a Member
of the assembly, one unable to avoid
being beckoned by ambition. To enter
the Chamber changed me entirely. A sheer
bombardment of light blazed on the Government
side where *I* was! All was wrong. But whoever
had added the previously annoying amendment,

XII

could annoy me no more. The light
that flooded the Government side of the Floor
shone from a white world opposite
whose crystal cliffs crowded the shore
of a fast-flowing stream. This was the trite
stream of time that I've talked of before,
unusual here in issuing in spate
from sluices set under the Speaker's chair.
The Commons was cut in two: the corps
of M.P.s from all parties packed close
together on the Government benches, and that gladder
kingdom whose cliffs were clear glass.

The glassy surfaces gleamed with fragmentary
mirrorings of all the M.P.s, as we peered
at a cliff-like façade like a stacked factory
for industrial ice whose cubes reared
up winking in sun from an unseen clerestory.
And the sun was Switzerland-warm; it speared
across narrow alleyways, silvery-rosy
as a laser lancing through weird
chunks of Turkish Delight. It cheered
my heart, empty as that heaven was,
for the normal confusion of the Commons had cleared
in that other kingdom whose cliffs were of glass.

Like a Douglas Oliver look-alike
the Speaker dreamily searched our side
and 'recognized' me, which although autoscopic
for both of us, deepened the dark divide
in myself. I stood up to speak,
conscious of the stream swirling through the wide
middle-ground of debate, a dike
between self and supreme. I couldn't decide
what stage we were at in the motion, but I'd
read Aaronovitch on the A.E.S.,*
so I started magnificently, like a sinner who defied
a heavenly kingdom where the cliffs were of glass.

I glossed over Margaret's giant, *Inflation*:
wages were hiked when unions pushed
hardest; this, helped by a hapless nation
whose purchasing exceeded production, pushed
up prices; then the pound's depreciation
pushed up import prices, and that pushed
up not just prices but the expectation
of price rises to come, which pushed
up purchasing demand – then the wage push would
renew: it was 'who pushed who', if alas
you plumped for the policies the Tories had pushed.
I called this across to that kingdom of glass.

Each glassy fragment flashed a vignette
of some vinegary visage beside me, famous
in Cabinet, Shadow Cabinet, Bennite,
or SDP-Lib circles; so as
I explained the monetary answer, I expected
the common Commons mix of raucous
attack and counter-attack; and yet
reflected in facets of the bevelled surfaces
was a sort of solemn, sourpuss
musing, like orang-outans *en masse*,
except for the pearly premier's face
quizzing me hard from the kingdom of glass.

* Alternative Economic Strategy

XIII

I lambasted the class basis of this blatant
war on workers, those job losses which
were a deliberate disciplining, with decadent
fiscal fiddling to facilitate rich
investments abroad and to add to arrant
social disparity at home. 'We must switch
to expansion, power-sharing with the potent
multi-nationals, a new package
of nationalization . . .' Bennites and Aaronovitch
had proposed planning agreements, provision
for welfare, etc., but I stopped, such
a woman I saw walking in the unworldly kingdom.

The windows of that world shone as they opened
at her passing; her compeers in the sans-pareil
surely hid in the cliffs, their heightened
purity transparent: Rosine's apparel
was royal red, a red brightened
by the crystal country which, like Campari
running through ice, her progress reddened
as she turned and re-entered my reverie.
Like the lost lioness – not the Tory
roary British lion but a better emblem,
a more lithe, love-like beast – she
walked shoreward in that unworldly kingdom

to confront the Commons from the world of clarity.
I recognized Rosine the way you'd recognize
your lover's look in union as a unity
if you won your way inward to where her eyes
have sent contrary signals to the quiddity
of single sight. She doubly symbolized
both lioness and pearl: lioness in agility,
pearl in the setting of an immobile paradise
made active by her movements. In medieval guise,
she'd denote Mercy, the divine *donum*;
secularized, she was Socialism, this wise
woman walking in the unworldly kingdom.

She stood by her world's steep shore,
her red raiment baubled with pearls;
others hung in her tawny hair or
braceleted her wrists; a rope of those jewels
gave her gown a girdle, and she wore
sandals as sparkling as a little girl's.
Many wanted to join her, whether
rightist or leftist, but the rapid whorls
of the river ran between us. The curls
of her head were adequate coronal for the Common
People's royalty; yet nothing so regal as
this woman walking in the unworldly kingdom.

Her speaking stole through our world with a spatio-
temporal delay: I definitely heard
her but what I clearly came to know
was the voiceless knowledge of some quick word
that grips my attention as I gradually go
off to sleep – voice and knowing not severed
like the temporal tricks of the Bentley's video
yet knowing a wit-stroke behind the revered
word. And I ached to be whole-hearted
about it and always encountered the phantom
time-lag between the truths uttered
by this Saint walking in the unworldly kingdom

XIV

and my world. 'The unpopulated whiteness
surrounding me,' Rosine reluctantly began,
'casts light from an ideal land – the place
where I'm exiled, since your exiguous island
won't pay the price of the pearl. It's of less
value when removed from the Real, but I can
stay for a few years only in a virtueless
nation, or mated to some magniloquent man
whose ambition rides high on the alternative plan
of the T.U.C. Don't you see
your unfunded promises could prove falser than
the false pearl of the premier's policy

that you've spent so much spite in politically blacking?
Did Labour, with Wilson, show the down-the-line
courage to win on the wage front? Did Jim
Callaghan grapple with a single, genuine
solution to the seventies' gradual slacking
that the radicals didn't reject? To undermine
is *so* bloody radical that it leaves all the rootless attacking
the roots.' 'Order!' roared the Tories. 'Resign!'
roared the radicals. 'This isn't our Rosine,
this isn't Socialism.' 'This isn't even seemly!'
countered the Conservatives. And some: 'It's a sign
that there's more false pearls than the premier's policy!'

'Virtue is vulgar; there's no politic
pretension of phrase in my prescient domain
where the voice of the poor is the voice of the rich
as high in aspiration as the Harrovian,
Oxbridgean, Union Soc., wealth-thick
velvetone of a Commons status-vulgarian,'
retorted Rosine, with uncommon rhetoric.
'Until you can also condemn the also-ran
horse-tail-wagging-the-head, trade-union-
inspired, internecine, leftist sycophancy
in a style fit for it, the state is stuck
with a Tory for pearl and a falseness for policy.

The warm heart, when weak, is politically unsound
and even Conservative Christian courage
like that of your father is sounder. He'd have found
it spineless the way you welcome the wreckage
of monetarism, omitting to mention that, drowned
in liquidity, the whole western world sees that wage-
based, spend-your-way-out platforms are bound
to fail eventually. A fine rage
you pretend at Tory "cuts" when your page
is blotted with careless schoolboy accountancy!
It's the people have paid for your go-brokerage
which has lacked the pearl, some policy

of courage. The policy pushed through by your premier,
though bad, was believed in. Not yours. But
no, you resist these thoughts, thinking them far
too unradical, and you undemocratically undercut
the roots of all politics by packing the Labour
echelons with economic dreamers; and the electorate
is supposed to think wishes are pearls. Where are
those who will learn the lesson? Not
Tory cruelty – fight that – but if a vote
goes monetarist you must work for it, until mercy
mists the eyes and the majority doubt
no longer that the pearl is false. Her policy

XV

then, through the premier's persistence, will police
the State back to Socialism, for it's who's who
looking after who's who, what's called "extremist" –
though it lets the poorer half learn what you're up to:
not a gentleman Tory gerrymandering consensus
by wooing the affluent worker to a "something blue"
morganatic marriage, where all marital status
would go to the "wet" Tory spouse.' This view
of Margaret and her monetary ministers was too
benign for my Bennite belligerence. I rose
to interrupt and Rosine withdrew
by walking the shore, her sandals in the shallows.

'Shall we allow this Socialist spirit,'
I asked, 'privileged in her palatial,
ice-cold dawns, to disinherit
her followers in this forum with her unreal
centrism?' (The side of her skirt had a tear; it
was as if my words whipped age on her, a weal
of grey skin was scored where the cloth parted.)
I went on: 'We're worried about real
incomes, real indigence, really unequal
national shares; no soft-nosed
kindness to all comers, no universal – '
She stopped on the shore, her sandals in the shallows.

'The centre's not shallow,' she sighed; 'all you said
lashed at my flesh, made my heart fail
and my spirit grow old; when the Grail has fled
the grey creeps over the realm, yet you rail
against any national unity naked
enough to bear offspring, for you a betrayal
of a Marxist revision that would wed red to red
in a bed become barren. Believe this: the Grail
is a mystery for *me*, a union of male
and female in fruition. Maybe something glows
in a centre of birth, very deep, a changed soul . . .'
She stayed on the shore, her sandals in the shallows.

Shallow water wet my feet
while the same water wet hers which wore
the wavelets like colourless footwear – fit
galoshes for such sandals. The more
I gazed the quicker time's oar beat
down a river running without a roar.
She let me look at her; the glassy light
that shone across from that crystal shore
cast a greying glamour on to the floor
where the Commoners crowded together, our rows
frozen into silence, our stillness the sculptor,
as she stopped on the shore, her sandals in the shallows.

'These shallows,' she said, 'show us the way
to judge the extreme; it's only one edge
or the other of the fast-flowing play
of the river purling between us in a passage
so swiftly exact that nothing can stay
its course; it careens by the clear verge
of my world like a wasting away
of potential perfection. The ideal cannot purge
your chamber of Thatcherism: no thaumaturge
can cure a thaumaturge. Follow those
who keep to the centre current of courage.'
She spoke sadly, her sandals in the shallows.

XVI

Beyond the shallows the stream's sinews
wrestled beneath black gum:
what was so swift was still, whereas
the depths drove ever onward. Dumb
and motionless, the M.P.s seemed to muse
like beached oarsmen bum by bum
under the balcony beams of a boathouse
– for the cutting-off of the Commons gave it some
such affinity with the river flow. From
afar, I saw a steely sheen,
a patina on the profile of the TV P.M.,
as the river ran so rapidly between

Rosine and this premier – not iron as the Press
allege but an adman's alloy of steel
and pearl. If a TV's phosphores-
cence fails, satin-finishes steal
into brightness and burnish the bones of a face.
So now a gathering greyness gleamed in the pearl
features of all our faces – yes,
faces of steel. Furthermore, the ideal
heroine was altering, ageing, in my still
enfeebling dream. The facial skin
of Rosine was begrimed with grey in a gradual
decrepitude. The river ran rapidly between

us and, at the age-lines that ran through the ashen
remains of Rosine's once-rosy appearance,
I was horrified; in my hot heart I began
to examine at last that excessive reliance
I'd placed in attacking the Tories; and
it came clear I was caught in a frantic trance,
one in whose heartless debates no woman
premier had acted; only the adman's
lying image. I looked askance
at the steely leader and knew what I'd seen
was no Thatcher but one of my own dream's creations.
Then the river ran so rapidly between

Margaret and Rosine that my eye ran with its
depths and returned reluctantly to the red
gown by the shore. But the garment's gussets
were growing grey; the colour had fled
from the skirts, and, scattered in singles and bits
of girdle, the pearls pebbled the bed
of the river. That fair face in fits
of ageing altered before my astonished
gaze. The gestures were jerky in the pallid
robe: the regal form of Rosine
shrank and her straight spine doubled
as the river ran rapidly between

the cracked crone, who ran cackling back
from the shore, and me, her ashamed supporter.
Those crystal cliffs had become grey rock –
the sempiternal as senile. The Thatcher
followers shone brightly as they sat stock
still: heads still steel, their suits a
polished pearly sheen; each back
mirrored the front in a vice-versa
as if *ego et me* might be sister or brother
twins, like meaning *all* you mean
mightily in a worship of will without a
blemish. The river ran rapidly between

XVII

those rivals and the crone, Rosine, who ran,
doubled, into a darkening, door-like cliff;
and it cracked apart and closed again,
its granite surface shook as if with
the honour of receiving her. Once a heaven,
that aged world was no longer worth
a dream; the stream had grown Stygian,
its waters oily, full of offal, not swift
as before; and the Commons blanked out, because if
the ideal is lost, the real also loses
its iridescence; in the eye itself
a politic blindness, not pearly roses.

In the blind gap between dreaming, my bed
groaned and the grey gown writhed as I tossed
and turned, tormented, since all that I wanted
had waned at the word, 'courage'. I almost
awoke, feeling empty and isolated,
continuing the debate with a departed ghost.
But the dream survives between dreams in the red
furnace within and the black frost
without, this double denizen lost
but refound when the live heart unfreezes
a country's Conservative night at its coldest
and in politic blindness bloom pearly roses.

Blindness of spirit had beggared my vision;
its duration that night I shall never know.
Finally I felt a hand on the crimson
cuff of my gown. I came to, and although
dreaming was blind in the dream. 'Ash on
an old man's sleeve,' someone thought; somehow
the phrase was a parody; for my father's cremation
that I'd attended ages ago
left ashes, not this corpse to clutch at me so
by the gown's red cuff which for me I suppose is
like wearing his heart on my sleeve, as though
in the blindness of ashes could bloom pearly roses.

Yet I seemed like a blind man led by another,
stumbling in sand; and I sensed that the Eliot
thought had been my own thought, for my father
now spoke, in death still a typical Scot:
'Please yourself with all this palaver
about Socialism; the cemetery is certainly not
a Tory stronghold. The truth is, I'd rather
your Socialism shone with your past; you're not shot
of that fatherly honesty, walk humbly but
remember your innocent days; who refuses
his childhood's a booby – and I haven't forgot
your politics, with its blindness and pearly roses.'

The blindness began to clear but I saw
we were stepping through sand flecked with ash
which clung to my feet as we followed the shore-
line of a rapid river. On a rash
impulse, I faced my father before
I was prepared for his pallor and I wish
I had not, for he fainted and fell to the floor.
When I knelt, there was ichor under his eyelash;
he was grey-gowned, red-cuffed, but his sash
was gold. I held him, held him as close as
I could and prayed for his Scottish courage
to place in my blindness a promise of roses.

XVIII

Lightning blinded me; in the thunder I embraced
ash, and would have kissed ash if I could,
for the flesh fell apart into cinders. The past
would not give me kiss for kiss, though the good
in it flurried the ashes into life. Amazed,
for I again wore the gown, I gaped as each cloud
chased after cloud and discharges raced
into the earth where I knelt; I knew that I viewed
swift time from its crystal shore; then I stood,
unharmed, armoured, as it were, in the old
gown but unable to gaze at a new flood
of light from crystalline cliffs flashing gold.

For the littoral was laved with light as a band
of grey-gowned friars gathered by my side
and a company of nuns came along white sand
in processional; I matched them stride for stride
like the past passing, ashen, through the land
of ideals. I faltered, for suddenly I'd
a presentiment that these were post-Falkland-
take-up-the-Task-Force Tories and alongside
Kinnock-clever, clothe-what-you'd-hide-
in-rhetoric Labourites; yet it's lovely to behold
whatever is wise and all were wise-eyed
under light from crystalline cliffs flashing gold.

The women wore veils but once when the light
raked us a face of sisterly reverence
smiled at me. It was my secretary, who in spite
of all that I'd ventured forgave me. Like virgins
entering God's city the nuns crowded tight
together under the glare, grave pilgrims
to a precipice ablaze. Unimaginably bright
a golden axe glanced down from the heavens
and clove the cliffs into two immense
diamantine doors. On that dazzling threshold
played a mongol baby. Its babbling was *Ignorance*
in light from crystalline cliffs flashing gold.

Light went spiralling sideways through solid
clearways of glass as one great door
opened and all walked humbly ahead;
the pearl that provided so signal an honour
was *Ignorance* – and him just an innocent kid!
I took him in my arms with just as much awe
as Rosine had aroused when young and splendid,
and believed I was the baby, he my progenitor.
He chuckled and a cheerfulness I had never before
experienced now entered my heart as his bold
eyes, so sunny, surprised my deep store
of light. The crystalline cliffs flashed with gold.

In an interval of fulgurous light, in an
instant when the baby gurgled, all the glass
scythed sideways. I had glimpses of spun
barley-sugar passages studded with sapphires,
fit pathways for the now-modest procession
of silent M.P.s; but my own progress was
an arc across the immediate, as again
in an instant I was inside the cliff. And found darkness.
However, a window glowed weakly, about as
scintillating as a cigarette lighter when some old
codger won't get its refill of gas.
The light so much less than those cliffs flashing gold.

XIX

Behind me the background was probably lit
by the passageway; I sensed that the M.P.s
came to surround me. Certainly it
was no time to turn round, for a touch on my sleeve
told me my father'd returned: I would forfeit
his guidance if I glanced at him. Giving me his
arm in a kindly way he confided:
'No, you're not to know: she's
not how you remember her. Eh? Rosine's
the person I mean.' He began to mutter:
'A nation must know its own ignorance. Now gaze
where that window glows beyond a gutter.'

In the empty window appeared an elderly
woman whose shoulders were wrapped in a shawl;
her framed face, lit faintly, looked fairly
stupid, her surroundings – a funereal
terrace – were like what you normally
discover old dears in, in all
inner city slums. She hardly
bothered to raise her eyes. Her real
disease dwelt in the centre of the ideal
realm. She was Rosine in Rags, in utter
poverty; in her cupped palms was the pearl.
Her window gave on to a grimy gutter.

Through the window she was as pale as a water-
mark as I made an attempt to cry out.
No voice came. I felt a
constraint round my neck and knew I had not
forgot *Ignorance*. This infant taught a
great truth to me: he kept tossing about
in my arms in anguish as if he thought *her*
his mother. My father confirmed it: 'The proud
and the politic pretend to have policies without
this blessed baby. You'd think such butter
would melt in their mouths. Hold out that wee tot
to the window giving on to that grimy gutter.'

Our grey wall of gowns confronted the window.
I gave up *Ignorance* who without breaking glass
entered the frame and flew to the elbow
crook of the crone, like a handicapped Jesus
cradled by a careworn Madonna. Although
the pearl appeared in his hand, in a pious
iconography of orbs, the whole hollow
conformity of creeds seemed but a callous
response to his slant-eyed saintdom. None of us
dared speak, for the scene was changing: wasn't that our
own ignorance now part of the indigent terrace,
whose windows gave on to the grimy gutter?

The window went cloudy, but then its weak light
reddened like a TV returning to colour,
and Rosine snapped on to its screen with a slight
wobble. She was weeping but young once more,
pearl girdled, gowned in rose-white,
and clutching the baby to her breast. 'Your
sentiment's so easy,' said her voice. 'Right
in the ideal's inner sanctum you prefer
a sort of commercial for Christ or for
the politics of set-apart poverty. This is but a
child, of an uncared-for category; you ignore
that this window gives on to your own grimy gutter.

XX

Now watch the window.' Within my ignorance
just one, unoriginal, ordinary thought
became so obvious it couldn't be nonsense;
the Second World War for a moment had taught
my nation to know that Conservative negligence
of poverty weakened the purpose fought
for. The strike-bound seventies, strengthening the difference
in working class hierarchies, caused chaos which brought
half a nation to claim that their own cosy comfort
was the aim of their living at all. The way down
was leftist but nasty: do nothing get nought.
(I groaned, lying down in my grey dressing gown.)

'Does the dream come to this? A debased King Lear
with a sip of the SDP?' In my anguish
I called this across to the screen. The clear
voice answered me: 'First acknowledge
that the highest human intelligence is a near
relation of ignorance; let language
untwist on your tongues. There's no true idea
of political system; so say so; don't languish
in rent-a-Marx/Margaret rhetoric or relinquish
the winning of wealth to the selfish. Anyone
who works for the poor is the pawn of the rich.
But don't – lying down in your old dressing gown –

lie about serving *this*.' I still stood
in the dream by the gutter among all the grey
gowns as she showed us the child: food
crudded its cheeks; each candid eye
was half closed by the lid giving it a lewd
ogle; the mouth lay wide open with its oystery
slime, a birth-place, both oyster and blood.
The ghost of my father all at once went away
to an immense distance. An intense ray
of midnight from the eyes' centres entered my own
eyes in a black instant of immediacy.
(I gasped as I lay in my grey dressing gown.)

A memory sea that had lain at low tide
in my mind slowly mounted making green
my dense darkness, radiant liquid
filled my vision; somewhere, half-seen
a precious pearl was shining in me; a pellucid
awareness of all that had passed – all that had been
born in me one morning when the mongoloid
eyes of my son stared at me, smiling, serene
in their way – was eerily glowing again, what I mean
by Socialism, that our soul and our selves are unknown
yet unconsciously known in the union between
people. (I lay in my grey dressing gown.)

She said: 'The pearl is ourself in which lies
a rosy reflection of all whom we care for
enough, the Other rendered perfect in a paradise
of our self-love. Unthinkable therefore
to pretend that the poor will profit from policies
whose mercy has greyed in the pearly mirror
of the nation's identity. We should idolize
the giants of Beveridge, make a Britain to cheer for,
a workforce that works for all we are here for
on earth: the self and its soul whether known
in the one or the many.' (My mind full of fear for
that pearl turning grey, I lay in my gown.)

The pearl that lay in the baby's palm
centred all thought and in it my face
enlarged, smiling; I saw the smooth arm
of Rosine round my neck. Then rays
of heartening light, rays of no-harm
shot from my eyes to my eyes. But the space
between us was widening; in alarm
I began crossing the gutter that only grace
can cross. I caught a mere trace
of grey from the gowns, her grave frown,
and awoke in a dawn of our daily disgrace,
lying down in my father's grey dressing gown.

AN ISLAND THAT IS
ALL THE WORLD

In honour of Mona
and those closest to me
whose pasts were involved
with these presents

I have to write some autobiographical things; talk about deaths of four relatives; let myself be sent back by deaths to childhood; then return to a middle age of restless moves between England, Paris and New York, never losing the obsessions which began in childhood. But I hope a much wider question will steal into this: what does it mean to talk of spirituality in poetry when no religious belief lies behind the inquiry? An unfashionable question. Avoiding intellectual sophistication, I shall look at the actual occasions of poems to find, not ways of explaining them, but spiritual sources in childish or adult sides of personality. Literary philosophy cannot escape scepticism or programmatic ambiguity about spiritual issues because we are trapped in the web of language, doomed, it seems, to disbelieve in the unity of self and of artistic forms: along with that, goes a loss of spirit. Such theorists are dangerous guides in areas where the poem, on the other hand, can make evident to the simple-hearted: 'This happened – spirit entered language and simultaneously I perceived such and such sights, spoke such and such words.'

Can't see diesel fumes faze
from tunnels when the night train's
ricketing down, carriage fighting carriage,
on a journey to the past: time in reverse
leaves no smoke trail behind,
memory hurries to the birth of kind.

The train shakes badly near home station
as gales increase, before violent rest
of very beginning, a destination
centred in your life again and again,
perhaps a mother waiting, perhaps a mother dead.
Once there, a white cloth effaces all ahead.

In middle age, before I left England for Paris, I took the late train from London Waterloo to my mother's bungalow in Bournemouth on the south coast. I think of that night's fierce blizzard as shaking the train's silver harmonica: light in its upper holes, a reverberant buzz. My open carriage was deserted, freezing, and smelt of sour saloons and elderly dust. I sank into correcting a manuscript as we pulled out of London and jolted over the wide crossings. An hour or so later we'd picked up to 100 miles an hour. Then a loud bang, almost thwang, snapped a huge spring and we sickeningly slowed; the lights rapidly dimmed and went out. The windows darted with red sparks flying backwards; whiffs of burning wood penetrated the carriage as we went into a queasy four-mile skid. My mind divided between the calmly pragmatic and the curious. Pragmatic: if we hit a train the bench seats might crush me; so I slid to my knees in the aisle as if praying, but not. My calmness seemed premonitory that I was not about to die. Curious: as the skid continued, I compared the experience to a description of a derailment I'd once written. The whole front of the train heaved and bumped about, an angry Leviathan, shifted to the left, lurched downwards with more thumps, and fell into hissing stillness.

With another passenger I headed for the cab; but the driver, holding his head, was already making his way towards us. He had coped well with the tree that had blown in his path and no-one was hurt. Farce took over. After three-quarters of an hour rescue arrived – far too much of it, multitudes of ambulances, police and fire services. As we negotiated the tall carriage step down to the track, a public relations man in business suit stood up on the snowy embankment, his voice fading behind us as we trudged in darkness towards ladders on the slope by the bridge. 'British Rail regrets the inconvenience . . .'. Up top, fleets of ambulances carted us off like invalids to a British Legion hall for tea and biscuits served by volunteers at 2 A.M.

In fiction and dreams I have imagined a train or bus racing through the night; a face appears outside its windows or a rich, calm voice is heard from outside. In this derailment, the fantasy came very near me, a voice born not exactly in the speeding Hampshire countryside but *implied* by my whole life conceived in its unity, yet a voice general enough to be relevant to everyone on the train even if it calmed only me, kneeling there, and almost spoke, comforting me.

When I got home my mother, then aged about 77, told me of the first time my 80-yeard-old father collapsed playing a round of golf (the second time, he died). She'd been in the garden and at the precise moment heard her name called, gravely and calmly, from the kitchen, 'Marjorie'. So that time such a voice spoke.

The innermost voyager

Jetliners climb above the middle air
of spiritual journeys: flying in dreams
is usually humanized and takes the shaman route
of older beliefs. Once, in a train derailment,
I bore my sense of self so lightly it yearned
for those middle heights. Probably, when dying,
we rise above and see nurses acting in perfect democracy.

We'll not romanticize shamans; but whatever
our job or class there can always be some dream train
where we're squashed in by fuzzy-featured companions;
and one is this other kind, a spirit-voyager:
think of a tree bole robed in furs, a wooden bear mask
that nearly speaks. For me, it'd be poets travelling
to a festival, a voice more ancient than ours among us.

We're off to perform our poetry in a noble library,
lodging together, squabbling for bedrooms.
This one in the carriage really troubles us;
he's this great trouble for cleverness,
one who looks as a bear might look if it were a god,
mouth as amused muzzle, head far too large,
blind eyes, great simpleton ears, his suit shaggy.

The carriage wobbles on its bogeys; we spit clever gossip,
exhibit taciturn domination, leftist talk of Gödel's
theorem applied to politics: Fanon's wretched
of the earth will be just that enigma resolved
in the higher social order to come: the talk
soars over famines and floods – hubris like a swank plane
gleaming in the clouds above human geographies.

We're humped about by each other's ambitions.
Frozen Hampshire fields pass by train windows;
there are multitudes of the impoverished
squatting like fir saplings on crusted snowfields,
yellowing sunset as in romance, the figures unmoving.
It's supposed witty to say, 'That view can be resolved
by reference to wider fields of snow, greater poverties.'

Blue-grey shadows mottle this covered heathland
as if a bear's spoor led to whitened hill crests.
The snow's both animal-warm and absolute-zero.
A voice from outside the field of vision, whether
beside us in the carriage or out there in the gliding,
has a warm Hampshire burr, for you perhaps it's female,
for me, the uttermost countryman of my innermost country.

The voice tells how one evening no-one will be safe from cold.
A tree on the line, a loud bang up front, carriage lights dim,
a slowing, windows freckle with sparks, a smell of burnt wood,
and the wrecked express skids four miles with charcoal in its paws.
Then train walls burr terribly but death would arrive
with slow riding and displacement of fear.
Poets would wish their voice warm and fit for such riding.

My middle age seemed new still as a job opportunity opened up in Paris, where, now a teacher, I'd formerly been a journalist. I lived alone in a Paris studio above the hot, roaring Avenue de Clichy. My mother died and then my sister. A time of sea change after years of stability. Daytime, I taught literature; nighttime, I roamed out with journalists, enjoying the free relationship between men and women temporarily established in restaurants and bars. Later I would smoke a cigar in bed, be warmly drunk, and listen to the tric-trac players crowding round cardboard tables in the street; they fought or shouted protest as a pail of water showered down golden in lamplight from flats above; prostitutes conducted their ballet on the pavement; Brazilian transvestites crowded the cafes; then constant traffic accidents, with police, fire and ambulances screaming off to northern limbs of the city. It was a pleasurable time of self-corruption, and I worried about that before going off to sleep with layers of cigar smoke drifting above my old Apple computer.

A friend drove me out for a swim in a disused gravel pit on the Parisian outskirts. From down in the pit's wide hollow, sand sloped up to hairy green crests, the sky so blue it almost came over the hilltop. Inshore, the lake was stained oak colour but out in the centre, wherever sun geometry didn't brighten the surface, the dark colour of a 17th century chest. My companion set off with a strong sidestroke and I liked watching her progress before plunging in and striking up a crawl designed to catch her up. But she was 12 years younger and the cigars had affected my blood. In the lake's centre, I watched her climbing out on the far side; and discovered I was completely out of stamina. For 20 seconds I flailed about wildly or tried to float, which only made me lose precious breath, and I thought myself sure to drown. She was too far away to help. (We found police notices afterwards warning against swimming there.)

It came to me that the mind must have some hidden rescue of its own. There stabilized within me a steady, confident self, which I imagine to be the self I had often speculated about, the unconscious unity of everything we have experienced and incorporated throughout our length of days, an entity that persists, minutely changing, very minutely, as our conscious self goes through its wilder swings of mood. Much modern linguistic philosophy argues this large entity out of all real existence, but I simply don't believe it. A larger self instructed me to let my limbs do the work while *it* lay back, almost entirely uninvolved. After great calm – the panic holding off on the periphery – I realized I had ground under my feet, staggered up the shore, and collapsed, as everyday conscious awareness flooded back.

Sometimes I return to the sea scenes of childhood to seek the origins of whatever stabilizes myself in space and time.

The Oracle of the Drowned

Memory in sea-green with sea-weed grain
of glass as the rearing wave rains briefly
before a lot of bother
on the beach of childhood
and men with a burden file across sand.
Those far-out surfaces are lipped
with transparent phrases coming to mind:
that the real dying happened in middle heights
between the lips and the sea floor.
Remember the swim trunks lost in waters
and the first man in our lives who drowned,
this, now, his cortege from the tide-edge,
the sacred hanging-down of head and arms
seeing that person's white groin
cooked chicken bared near the hook of the ribs
and a shore-line of horrified children
arrested in their digging to gaze
at seas of such corruption as to change him.
His shirt left behind too long on the promenade rail,
always there in our lives, its caked cotton
fluffy-white in its inner wrappings.
The cloth wandered open at nights as we wondered
what a drowning body could say
when its chest became translucent green,
we courted in our minds such corrupt purity,
never escaping but sinking into not
the unthinkable gift of the self to death,
not the sea flash flood in the throat,
but into the oracle of the drowned;
because the oracle of the dying comes to a halt
but the oracle of the dead continues and has humour in it.
We ask the dying, 'How do you go about drowning?'
and the answer comes first 'I cannot – '
then swims in ambivalent vowels
and voiceless consonants in the washing tide
voiced consonants in the last buzz of the eardrum:
'Aah, I am funtoosh, zooid, walway,

wallowing, rows and rows of waves,
a gooooood one, my soooul a sea-mew' –
and we learn nothing but the knowledge of pain,
and the hope of a future from it.
But the gone-dead are beamish and talk to us
from out of memory's hollows and gulphs:
'You, boy, in your Bournemouth bed, be with me now
and I will come to you many years later
still drowned in a medium of green liquid
the water whispering through its lips
as the dark whispers to you in caves or before sleep.
And I was a man and had babies
as you, a baby, will have a man and call him "Father"
and as the drowned will have the drowned.'

After my sister died in her mid-50s from liver cancer I flew back to England and helped sort through her belongings, keeping for myself only one early painting and her art college sketchbook. The colour schemes of her oil paintings had changed from the muted greyish-browns of her student work to wilful yellows, mustards, over-cheerful blues and too-sappy greens, with just a grey wispiness reminding you of her earlier days. I associated this over-cheerfulness with a strain in her Christianity which once, for a shaky month, had become messianic.

Her smile constantly expressed goodness and despite spasmodically-ascetic dieting she got fat. She sought out the elderly, infirm and handicapped to help them. At her request during her psychosis I accompanied her to my local church; she made a point of surrounding an extremely-able wheelchair patient with her care. The sermon dealt with St Paul on the Damascus road, but probably only Mona of the whole congregation fully believed in the story, because she was having visions herself. By being a careful confidant and by discussing the relationship between emotion and vision, I was of some help and, with drugs, she recovered. Years afterwards, she asked me if I'd kept in touch with the wheelchair patient and I snapped that I hadn't.

When she got better, her endless hospital visiting, painting of church posters, and attendance at fetes, her simmering passion for the whole clap-trap of social Christianity, still had slight traces of the month of vision.

The time of her dying lay within her power to orchestrate; she'd been a good amateur actress, a genuinely useful skill at such times. She gathered everyone round her at Christmas in my brother's home south of London. On the Sunday of my arrival from Paris, she and I were still planning a trip to Florence, her first, in the New Year. By Wednesday, she was drifting, I thought with the morphine, and we found a wheelchair light enough for me to wheel her round Florence. By Friday, the whole trip had become out of the question.

At communion, on Christmas morning, her last church service, the morphine had left her mouth dry before the hymn. 'God sent me saliva in my mouth so that I could sing,' she said afterwards. She slid towards unconsciousness because of the poisons in her. I took leave, promising to return on the first flight – I thought she had a few weeks to go and was proved wrong. All she wanted to do was make peace with God: 'You can't help me this time.' Not being Christian, I agreed. She tried to thank me and, as I adopted a jokey expression intended to assert my belief in her energies, added, 'You must let me thank you.'

I never quite understood Mona until a memorial service for her. I can't speak for the 600 other people there, but some psychic gate burst open and we were surrounding her. She had felt at risk of divine condemnation and had found her form of salvation: the path had led through slight mania; but it led, let's say, to heaven, or to a greater deserving of such a place than I shall ever achieve.

These words of the quite awful and sometimes wonderful Ramon Lull hold a clue for me:

Blaquerna enquired of the Truth of his Beloved: 'If in Thee glory and perfection were not that which thou art, what then wouldst Thou be?' And Understanding answered Blaquerna: 'What but falsehood, or a truth like to that of thine, or naught at all, or that in which there would be affliction everlasting?' And Blaquerna said: 'And if truth were not, what then would glory be?' And Memory answered: 'It would be naught.' 'And if perfection were not, what would glory be?' 'It would be that which is naught, or nothingness.'

How does this apply to Mona? Suppose she was driven far into herself by loneliness – having that fatal combination of immense energy, creativity, meticulous memory, emotional inhibition, and occasional long-windedness (a product of the sheer detail of her memory); and suppose this same combination to have been fed by the loneliness. But then, in her isolation fearing divine condemnation, she poured all her denied love into her salvation with such energy that she wrought a highly-coloured goodness, winsome-sweet, religious and eccentric. Well, glory is a necessary part of that, for she aimed so fervently at the Truth in her own vision of it. Though I'm talking to you, Alice, what I'm writing is also set down because of Mona.

Beyond active and passive

'Oh, you are born already!' cries the English mother
in pained surprise to her hanging baby,
as though the finished phrase
had slipped, unfinished, out of an anguish
still continuing, into its adventures.
From before the time when birth was given
babies enter a world of harm.

How suitable for Jains of ancient Bihar
was that Sanskrit middle form,
'I die
unto myself,'
since theirs is a faith of shedding harm
from the solipsism of the journeying soul.

An art teacher, dreamy on morphine, said,
'You can't help me this time,'
as her few relatives
watched her clothe herself for God;
she acted out her death at Christmas
in her Christian counterpoint to birth.
Formerly, having no babies, she became
a little religiously dotty, I'd say,
and cared for the elderly
(who crowded her funeral).
Once, when car licence plates coded divine messages
and every lame man was a messianic sign,
on those Damascus roads she called for help
and, needing little, got it.
Sane again, she refound loneliness and service,
living on diets, calorie balances on the dinner table;
her paintings changed from green-browns of college days
to orange-blues of willed bliss;
she talked minutely of those I never knew,
acted the spirit in *Blithe Spirit*,
and died in her Christian language,
'unto Heaven and unto others':

it was the most normal possible thing to do
in the courage of this isolated heart.
Though you cannot do birth for others
but only give it, she gave death to others
by shedding of its harm;
and I think she wasn't born again but born already.

I angle Mona's sketchbook into yellow streetlight and the pages become bright islands floating in darkness inside our Manhattan bedroom where I'm writing these reminiscences. One pencil portrait shows a beautiful boy either reading or gazing into a gas fire beyond a table and musing over what he has read. The book, dating from 1948 art school days in Bournemouth, was hiding like an owlet in a sculpted bookcase when we cleared Mona's Lincolnshire bungalow. The drawings are of specific drawer handles I remember; an old shoe; a post-war Morris with leather radiator cover rolled up; a South Western Railways coal cart piled with empty hessian sacks and a blinkered Dobbin in the shafts; the beautiful boy dishevelled, braces hoisting short trousers into the buttocks – he's shadow-boxing, gloved up.

The islands are almost still places in memory; but not quite film stills, for I set them in motion, just for a second or two as in a brief theatre. The boy on the chair has a few of his then habitual thoughts; the drawer handle clatters once or twice; the car's starter motor whirrs and begins to catch; punches are thrown but only one or two. These moments once formed the unconscious, vivid present in which our larger self grows and assimilates part of the whole event. Unconsciously, probably, we remember not everything we have experienced but everything we have incorporated into our selves. Because conscious memory is much more selective its moments spread out brief or long and become space-time islands. The island centre is a darkness through which all the islands are linked together. I call it a centre but *also* it's everywhere and without location; it is the immediacy itself. Looking at the sketch, I don't just remember what the boy used to think; I have a shaky sense that I might be thinking it exactly now, in his vivid present, inhaling the leathery-petrol smell of the old Morris, or smelling coal sacks. Simultaneously, my mind enters the darkened areas and a vague presentiment of my life's enduring self comes near to me. My favourite, Stevenson, compares such a self to one of his family's lighthouses:

> So, to the man, his own central self fades and grows clear again amid the tumult of the senses, like a revolving Pharos in the night. It is forgotten; it is hid, it seems, for ever; and yet in the next calm hour he shall behold himself once more, shining and unmoved among changes and storm.

Can anyone exactly enough explain to me why the word, 'shining', is so right in this context?

The beautiful boy could have been my Pharos self, he does shine a little in his island, on the page, under the streetlight in the Manhattan bedroom. I imagine him as reading about a female counterpart, for example, in the *Aethiopian History* of Heliodorus, our earliest classical prose romance. She is Cariclia, discovered by robbers at the beginning where she sits, dressed in white, upon rocks. She stares downwards at her lover's body, lying bloodied and perhaps dead, among the bodies left behind at the tide-edge after a battle. Pirates and robbers carry away such women as Cariclia in such romances; but on her back is a quiver of arrows which we already admire.

The boy as delightful maiden, honest and true

A maid endued with excellent beautie, which also might be supposed a goddesse, sate uppon a rocke, who seemed not a little to bee grieved with that present mischaunce, but for al that of excellent courage: she had a garland of laurell on her head, a quiver on her backe, and in her lefte hand a bowe, leaning uppon her thigh with her other hande, and looking downewarde, without mooving of her head.

Heliodorus

Once I was a beautiful boy and sat on a chair
sketched by a sister in an angry house, but this
before the little bellied grate be fiery,
wireless of fretted wood still silent
before the hand-jobs with the 'here are you' hand,
for I was like a goddesse, sat upon a rock,
grieved with present mischance but of excellent courage,
leaning upon her thigh with her other hand and looking downwards,
this, me, escaped from some measledrome,
discombing the hair, discovering the unruly,
disboying myself to enter story and disobeying my elders,
so to unangrify the house and empty it of radio voices
so to mirror me: I sent a cheerful self-portrait
to dwell in the shadow of a beach
below Bournemouth Municipal College of Art 1948,
to live there privately as if in a secret sketchbook
among the hiding place of birds,
live brilliantly in their flocks,
frocks of flowers on a scattered cliff, frocks for my limbs.
The charming spread of tide spilling spirit gum at the edge
then a fillip and a rush of purpose;
one gull already there before the sky backgrounded its flight.

From inside that breakfast room by the tyrant radio
I threw a stone
so wide in aim it winged the entire Bournemouth Bay;
central, the squat turret of a jetty islanded in shallows
from its post a sea-mark hung of intersecting iron hoops,
an armilla astrolabe to measure altitude of many days.
This also found, drawn in veridian on another page.

We are allowed flattering veils over the scar of misery,
pen wash over coils of sea spun from purpling wires,
colour of angers;
and if my mood can become blue-black Waterman's ink
I will get my drift,
beautiful-chinned, take my place on a chair
in the page of the sketchbook;
it's bound in black, falling apart, *mille feuilles*,
'The kitchen as seen through the doorway'
dishtowel over a ledge, hands mixing an omelette,
dead kinsfolk in lit rooms;
but the seated boy otherwhere minded,
moonlight sweeping adolescent beaches
in blue-black; or on that veridian page:
outline of a dog scratched out,
black-headed gull with only half its head blacked in
standing in runnels by the jetty
and in the reflection its head isn't black at all.

The goldpoint of my own whole life is the sketchbook drawing, where the boy, reading, looks beautiful in the promise of that luminescent moment. Then I know, too, that the boy was beginning the stormy adolescence usual in the 1950s. Not realizing his happiness, he would rage out of his house to go and watch birds on the marshes in Christchurch harbour; in the flight of geese, gulls, herons and smaller wading birds he found the freedom and rhythmic grace that soon were to lead him to poetry and to the mysteries of its stress.

In a poem, each stress is held in memory and perceived as a unity of sound, meaning and special poetic emotion. All durational things on either side of the stroke (the wing-beat) of stress – the length of its syllable, all its sound qualities, what words come immediately before and after it in the poetic line, the whole movement of the line – make us think how weighty or light the individual stress is. The stress centres a tiny island in memory. The centre of the island is occluded; it is the moment when we believe the stress actually happened. We can even strike its instant, a little late, by tapping a finger. If we could bring all those instants fully into consciousness, the poem would become vivid.

We are faced with the ancient question about time: how could we consciously experience an instant of time, when we always conceive instants too late and when an instant can't contain anything at all? Time, self . . . very small moments of self-experience as portrayed in a sketch . . . poetic stress: how can we fill this stroke of time which has no duration with meanings and emotions that have? How can an instant and duration be imagined as simultaneous? It's what Christians suppose to happen in the mind of God.

When we try to bring an isolated instant into consciousness, this mystical possibility doesn't occur, because of the tardiness of our minds. We say: the clock has just ticked, I was this kind of self just now or just then, that stress was weak or heavy by an exact weighting. We make in memory a little working model containing the past and future of the moment and, by mental trick, convince ourselves that we experience that model as a present moment. The models are these mental islands of time; and poetic stresses are the smallest clear and complex examples of them I know.

The Heron

I talk only of voices either real or virtual in my ear;
of shadows, only those that pass over islands' sunny turf
vivid to my eye. But when I come to all my birds,
all I've ever seen, they are too many. I talk of things unseen.

Together, they would pack the sky like moving embroidery
in the white silks, browns and blacks of their great tribe,
endless litters of puppies writhing,
a heavenly roof alive but no progress of flight in it.

Every memory adds to this intricate plot;
starting up redshanks first, and they bank, flashing white,
across a sepia estuary where I felt freedom
in watching their undulating patterns on the air.

They flight down but hold at mid-height: horizontal
stick puppets of the Styx. The black light whitens
with the harmonious wings of swan formations,
the day cast over with their bright feathering.

Behind the swans the sky absolutely fills with starlings
homing to roost as once I saw them over Stonehenge;
gulls flock up and hold there, and brown passeriformes
spring between airspaces and stop on invisible branches.

Millions of birds, crows and daws, teal,
quicker wing-beated than wigeon, among mallard hordes;
swifts print arrows on the pulsating featheriness;
the sky is covered over with the puppy litters.

I can't tell you all the names; I'm worried
about the birds rabbling the sky. D'you suppose
I can avoid even the dusty body of every sparrow,
or every sparrow hawk flipping over a thicket?

Unseen, this nature crowds my mind. If there's pulsation,
it's disturbing; if stasis it's a painting
and all the life goes out; but any sudden switch
between pulse and the static is schizophrenic.

In the foreground of the multifarious flights
one talismanic bird, a heron, lifts to the top
of its single leg and takes off like an umbrella.
Fluff in a corner of the past becomes grey flame.

Its shoulders unshackle and heave, legs become the addendum,
the beak stabs out purposefully from the sunken neck.
It sails. In this flight's brevity,
I find what lives for me among all the dead songs.

Although the same person, the short-tempered boy sketched boxing looks younger than his more beautiful counterpart sketched reading. I'm almost schizophrenic in how I regard the two figures, one aggressive, one peaceful, as if, though they both lived in Boscombe, Bournemouth, the town itself becomes a different mental geography when I set one or the other boy active in memory.

My family's Scottish presbyterianism taught that life held conflicts which boys should face with sportsmanship and that sometimes these conflicts would be moral as well as physical. Two pairs of boxing gloves appeared one Christmas morning in the pillow cases; and that holiday my beefier elder brother and I took to sparring out in the freezing garage when the old Morris car had creaked off to the office. Our strip was grey school shorts and mandatory grey shirt. Within a clutter of rakes, brooms and other garden tools, we had to circle an oil patch that had oozing layers under black cardboard crusts; as I write, the oil becomes the centre of that memory. Too small to win, if I looked like losing I'd resort to biting.

My life-long fascination with boxing and also my fear of the emotions it aroused began then. I would long for the fair to bring its boxing booth to King's Park each August and meanwhile would indiscriminately cut any champ's photo out of the *Sunday Express* and the *Radio Times*.

Nowadays, grandly, I like to imagine a 'philosophy of the knockout', according to which a punch can impose on the victim an experience of an instant without content. The boxing profession generally has believed the Cus d'Amato doctrine reported in Jose Torres's classic on Ali: 'It's the punch you don't see that knocks you out.' But more than once I've read in *Boxing News* of losers who, after a K.O., complain: 'I saw the punch coming but it still knocked me out.' I watched the TV replays of the Dave 'Boy' Green–Palomino world title bout: Green's head was first wobbled by a stiff left hook; so a second, weaker punch could penetrate his unconscious when it was unprotected by will-power. The knockout catches the mind between its tiniest islands, in a moment when the instant has not quite entered memory to be filled with form. If you've ever been knocked out, you know that the K.O. strikes either to our sheer surprise or when we are too weary or addled to have an 'I' in consciousness to defend.

The boy knocked out

If you were four foot six
when Billy Smart's Circus
came to King's Park
post-war
what you did
was get in
the boxing marquee
first,
before the adult crowd,
stand right by the ring wall
on bruised grass,
the tent still dark,
and rest your nose
on the canvas.
That way,
when the lights shone
in a dark forest of spectators
you could watch
a South West England champion,
Harry Legge, his
one muscular leg
and one thin leg
(early polio, gruff men said)
shuffle round the ring
above your very nose
as he trounced a wild
challenger from the marines.
I owe much in poetic life
to Harry Legge,
for the black stroke of the K.O. punch
(it's not always the hardest —
Jose Torres talks of this)
has links
with the white stroke of prosody.
Like this:
In poems
each beat

fills my mind with melody
half there from the past
half there from the future;
but if the boxer's punch
can catch an opponent
mid-mind
before the self has thought
to fill itself with the self
which is protection
the glove hits target
in an instant
almost empty of consciousness:
any moderately hard punch
at that moment
will K.O.
But at the stroke
of the unconscious
what
is the apparently plenary self
which retains control
of your falling body,
stands outside it even?
I have been that boxer. You?
There's been the rhythm of the fight
a flow, beat-beat of punches,
then suddenly the K.O.,
stuns
but spot on time
temporally a pinprick
arriving between the loser's
self and its self
letting one of the selves fall,
the secondary one
that bears will and loyalty forwards.
Slow drift of magical possibilities
a human form moving vaguely,
white
before me,
a white-bodied man glides
above the altar in the tent

a woman in white clothes
glides above the altar
her tennis shoes high above
the grassy tent floor,
the slippery woman comes into my head
my head can't think
of the thing that she says
because she's so white as snow
and I'm a little boy
come in to creep with the white thing
like a huge umbrella
and the umbrella drifts and drifts,
roaring, post-war noises,
I'm a statue little boy
on a sports pedestal
an island of light
round my feet lifts me
I float like a bird-statue
in a billowing marquee;
all is dust, dust,
roaring,
all the tent is stripy,
and holy with the spirit of . . .
the grass is snowy it looks like . . .
the boy in my head
is so silvery-bobbly he looks like . . .
Leave all that, waking up,
on the ring floor
the fallen self forced to be
defenceless like a baby,
awakening from magic
into a simple K.O.
everyone looking down from Paradise
no responsibility for this.
Caught still in my earthly fight,
masochism
to empty the instant of responsibility.

From the pencil sketches I can imagine the cheap red velour of the breakfast table covering, with spiky patches where intractably stained. On it, I'd stick articles and photos of boxers into a grey scrapbook smelling of flour paste and tatterdemalion with old cuttings. The room, but not my scrapbook, is there in another of Mona's sketches, the colours coming to life, the knitted tea cosy loosely fluted in orange and blue on the aluminium pot, the wheezy post-war radio, a particular glass flower vase catching the light, the wooden chairs painted mud-brown.

As I filled in the scrapbook, I'd come across a maverick cutting from Ripley's 'Believe It or Not' strip syndicated in the *Sunday People* or the *Express*. Jain monks in India respect the holiness of reincarnation so devoutly that they sweep the ground before them in case they tread on anything living. Later on I read that at New Year some Jains would send cards even to almost-strangers apologizing for any inadvertent harm caused during the previous 12 months. Of the 2 million or so Jain adherents an unusually high proportion are rich merchants or bankers; a pleasing irony to think that money hurts no-one.

I've returned as an adult to this early obsession with a religion of complete no-harm; it plays a counterpart to the boxer's wilful harming. The Jaina cosmos resembles tiered cake trays with our own world of Jambudvipa in the middle rank between the various worlds of hell and heaven. Each layer of the universe is arranged in elaborate mathematical symmetries: our own world is central in other concentric worlds divided by circular oceans on that same layer, all of it reflecting the rigid central patterning of Jambudvipa. In the middle of our world: the holy mountain, Meru. As well as representing heavens and hells, the cake tray layers also model human psychology, Jaina-style. If we could only pass into the centre of our Jambudvipa we might unify into one conception the temporal continuum of our lives. The map of my childhood would unite with all my adult self-worlds islanded in memory, perhaps at the cost of unconsciousness, or death in salvation.

An Island That Is All the World

'Seven' on the Norman tower of Christchurch,
a precisely topographical beginning
on Stanpit Marsh, sea harbour peninsula,
salt, the marsh birds flake out and curve down;
pain dies away, tail lights twinkle at dusk,
outboard dinghy grumbling through tide race;
mud levels melt at the peninsula's edge,
brown coiling in the soiled foam.

Hidden at first in the central hillock of gorse,
the young mapmaker descends to salt flats, gulls
everywhere for bread on burnished grass.
Boy's hand in red exercise book, his Wellingtons moving,
as the pen, unguided by cartography,
enlarges a shore line
according to enthusiasm's measurements
until the map exists.

Ballpoint on paper napkins, Sidewalk Cafe, Avenue A,
I tell Alice a legend: 'The island was like this.'
But in my head the peninsula of that other beginning,
redrawn in New York, has become a coloured disc
like the Jambudvipa of the Jains,
an island that is all the world, mapped
in an immense platter with ocean blue
enclosed in adamantine ramparts of the rim.

The land disc is divided into three empires
by vivid and diametrically opposed rivers;
and central is Meru's cone with hidden summit.
The spiralling arms of its mountain ranges
wall in open spaces crossed by woods.
Watercourses, forests form exact rectangles:
only in such mathematical countries
could Tirthankaras preach about deliverance from harm.

Descend the holy mountain, follow the map, emerge into woods.
'Why, Alice, these are pines in Jambudvipa
like those in my English home!' Not the peace of the marshes,
I have entered some old kid's conflict,
truant in pinewoods by the English Channel,
stepping through couches of needles,
dusk smoking through the rhododendrons near Stanpit.
Redrawing the map, I take out harm, restart in the centre.

Birdwatching was my escape from family regimen. I kept a detailed card index with sections for: birds seen and habits noticed; nesting; distribution; and, increasingly, citations in literature, especially in poetry. My house was 35 Browning Avenue and the surrounding roads bore poets' names too – Byron, Shakespeare, Wollstonecraft, Shelley – because built on the 19th century estate of Sir Percy Shelley, son of the poet. The whole area of cliffside detached homes was incredibly Conservative, retired colonels and doctors with, across the way, some wireworm-thin, sugar-silver unmarried woman, courageously living on a dwindling income. Shelley Manor was derelict post-war, a dirty-white, rectangular mansion at the head of a little park islanded in the road system. Its rear was a minute wilderness of rhododendrons, sand dunes and pines leading back to the cliff road. I sometimes dream of the park now as if it were the whole of Africa and I flying over in a light plane looking for lions.

In the evening I'd watch owls there, though I was more amused by angering courting couples, since I'd be armed with a torchlight and binoculars. Hiding, I could masturbate in a wary peacefulness. One evening I met a dubious elderly man with money-hooded eyes, who emerged from one of the natural tunnels that form in rhododendrons. Having asked me my school, he launched into a false anecdote about the death of the poet Shelley who had allegedly sailed across the English Channel from Boscombe Chine, to the right of us down the cliffs. The poet and companions had drowned in a gale, he explained; a sodden copy of Homer was found on Shelley's corpse washed ashore in France; and now his ghost haunted the manor, etc. (Shelley died before his son, himself a sailor, bought the estate.) Not trusting the man's intentions, I sidled away. But he did tell me that Stevenson had been friendly with Sir Percy and his wife and that the house had had a private theatre.

I cycled the five miles from Boscombe to Branksome to visit 'Skerryvore', the house bought for Fanny Stevenson by the novelist's father and named after the celebrated family-designed lighthouse. Damaged in war-time bombing, it had been demolished and a memorial garden laid out. RLS spent three convalescent years in the Bournemouth district in the 1880s and wrote more than one masterpiece there, including *Dr Jekyll and Mr Hyde*. For all his own elitist Conservatism, Stevenson has since become my example of how to wrestle with the presbyterian background in a way which restores honour to the parents.

After that, my owl-watching subtly changed: Shelley manor house itself became my memorious object, entitled in my secret mythology 'The Harmless Building'. On a moonlit evening, the walls now a dazzling white and the windows dark rectangles, another imagination appeared possible: it would be for me like the Hans Christian Andersen balcony room in his story, 'The Shadow': a hidden theatre from which streamed light and music and romance. If, as I did once or twice, I climbed through a broken window downstairs into a stinking room full of litter, I'd get instantly depressed and the sounds of the theatre died away.

Stevenson and the Owl

Tonight in New York I'm intimate in poetry with you:
may I take a moment in derelict Shelley Manor,
back then, in the Boscombe Sir Percy let be built?
I constantly see a truant boy post-war.

Beside trees in the park's seawood, pines,
he heard owls and found trees of another
life, branches, declivities, and shades
labelled in a sketchbook, purple, white lights, redder.

My sister's death now jocund. Her sketchbook of light,
medallions of my family drawn in it, the black cover
scratched with fundamental particle tracks.
Inside, a pencilled-in tree trunk falls like a shed door.

I take the truant moment, full of potential poetry,
and wait in the wood's centre, rhododendrons there,
tunnels of them whorling moonlight over the Channel,
sand dunes white as salt, a centre of uneasy savour.

It's not my personal story, exactly, to turn and see
black rectangular windows in the moonlit manor,
a harmless building that hadn't yet lit up with art,
though once Sir Percy acted in his private theatre.

Then the manor seemed small as our garden hen shed,
but an owl in acrid darkness called from its own centre;
it must have fluffed out large round the occulted talons.
Two branches in that wood rub wrists together.

The harmlessness of Jains and the destructiveness of the boxer are emblems of two moments in the finest detail of the poem: sound that doesn't change and sound that changes. For a brief interval the vowel continues unharmed and then its purity is destroyed by a diphthong glide or a consonant. What doesn't change will always eventually bore us, through saturation; yet we seek to limit human destructiveness. The flight of birds is emblem of the movement of the poem, punctuated by its beats – beats in which the interaction of the sound's continuity and change is suddenly grasped by us. A sketch of the child become beautiful is emblem of the static scene of imagination; and the inner theatre of childhood is emblem of the static scene set into brief motion. The grave voice usually just out of hearing when death or calamity nears is emblem of the whole voice that rests at the end of the poem's life and is its final form.

Quixotic obsessions and chance events in my past life cohere into a life's work.

I have gone to fights to write boxing fiction at the ringside while the other, real fight was in progress – just plugging into its energies, not borrowing the factual detail. Through an editor friend I got myself accredited by a London political weekly to cover a European title fight in Rome between Mo Hope, the Antiguan-born British light-middleweight and Vito Antuofermi, the Italian champion. That allowed me to breakfast with the boxer on the fight morning, visit the promoter, see the weigh-in, and, along with other journalists, interview Hope in the dressing room after the fight and in his hotel drink champagne to his victory.

Lack of real assignment left me free at the ringside for experiment; and I tried to take down the absolute continuity of the action, every punch and shuffle, into my notebook. I noticed an odd phenomenon: whenever the action was too fast I would become lost in continuity. Afterwards, I would find that my handwriting had become stuck in continuity of either vowel or consonant too: 'Moo lands a goooooood onnne', an entry would read. 'Faaaa(s)t hooooook frrom Viito'. The intervening punches would be missing.

Hope, since retired through an eye injury, was British boxing's Mr Cool, for he worked mostly to the body. The crowd didn't like him too much, despite his later world title, because after an apparently boring fight, about round ten, the other man would suddenly collapse. Weakened about the heart. Mo was a boxer's boxer. As his manager, Terry Lawless, said:

'He's so deceptive, he's like a sleepy old crocodile, you think he's slowing and then he's got you.'

In round 13 Vito hitched his tufty, damaged eyebrows up a notch and followed through so hard that he sprawled on to Hope who fell into the ropes. The crowd gave it full throat.

Later, Mo leant forwards from his dressing room bench, his right eye swollen and face dripping sweat and shower water on to his knees. 'When he fell over me that time I felt his body on top of me like a dead weight.' In rounds 14 and 15 Hope attacked with such fury that he knocked all questions out of the fight, and won by a T.K.O. But back there in round 13, if you'd been judging by the cheering, you'd have given it to Vito.

When I was the boy pasting up his scrapbook I used to think the cheering like a tune sung by the fight. I remember 1948 when in Belfast Rinty Monaghan took the world flyweight decision off a convalescent Jackie Paterson. As Rinty sang hideously but victoriously 'When Irish Eyes Are Smiling' I recall the crackly cheering that came in waves over our pre-war radio. In fact, as the Rome championship showed, if you could create a tune, a poetic melody, that would express a fight's real fortunes nothing so crude as crowd cheers would do: it would have to be a clear note sung hard, fast and accurately, from punch to punch. On its own, each punch creates no language, just a daze of amazement, an almost-empty instant of cruelty.

A photograph of Mo Hope punching out shows the mask-like expression of a cat looking at a bird. Almost all photographs of boxers landing punches have this: even the Ali snort-lips didn't alter that his eyes were, for once, without audience and direct to target or otherwise rapt and inward. The direct transparency of will is devilish, like a moment in Hawthorne when a man becomes a total stranger, half the face changing from flesh to brilliant red. But this can be answered by the face change of the loser, such as Hazlitt's boxer, Hickman, who '"grinned horrible a ghastly smile", yet he was evidently dashed in his opinion of himself . . . all one side of his face was perfect scarlet, and his right eye was closed in dingy darkness'.

The punch is the moment of change, the snap of the crocodile, devilishly empty.

The Jains and the Boxer

I

The Jain monk would live in unending harmlessness,
shedding karma, confessing, studying for the fasting death.
He avoids quarrels and politics,
may not repair three unmended garments, nuns four,
has rayaharana, the hand broom of wool or grass,
to clear living things from his path,
a cloth to wipe animate dust from his face
and to prevent such beings entering mouth or nose.
He takes care not to walk too far after rain
because life springs up abundantly then
and must not be damaged.
At dawn, he examines utensils and his skin
to preserve tiny souls;
he will not wash limbs, treat wounds or eczema,
may spend hours in immobility save
for involuntary breathing, coughing and physical secreting.
The monk's presence may be scarcely bearable:
the filth (mala) on the acarya Hemacandra
brought his sect the honorary name of Maladharin,
We find such things in the Cheyasutta Mahanisiha,
whose Salluddharana explains contrition and confession;
and whose Kammavivagavivarana
encourages chastity, warns of sexuality and aggressive evils.

II

The boxer imposes 100 per cent will
punching harm into harm in sadistic rhythms.
He's called Alan Boum Boum Minter, Mo Hope,
Rocky This, Kid or Killer That.
His history comes in puffs and spurts.
Listen to the bollocky tights, buttocky satins
of Bob Fitzsimmons in his longjohns.
Since then, all the boxers have fallen,
broken-legged spiders,
Joe Gans 'in his famous fighting pose'

'the old master', said the great Fleischer,
fallen. Patterson's head down
arms wide on the floor,
all fire out, while Johansson
waits in the corner like a fire hydrant.
Straight nose punches.
The Woodcock straight left
Cribb's face a creased bun
his left staggering Molyneux
Teddy Baldock leaning back but flattening Kid Pattenden's nose
Bombardier Billy Wells straight on to Porky Flynn's jaw.
The closed socket of old timers, badly drawn,
like the head of a fleshy screw
a caterpillar trickling down the cheek of Marciano
craze marks on Mills's eye v. Baksi
but you should see the Eskimo eye
of Lesnevich, head in towels, K.O.,
over Mills, 10 rounds, May 1946.
Blotches on the imperfectly inked glyph of Pruden
Walcott's face bringing its forehead crumbling down
in the 'Moment of No Return', said *The Ring*
Treacle round the eye of Cruz
then the crudding round that of Ramos
Chuvalo's face blind, blown,
but that wasn't the bloodiest fight ever known;
some would say 'Harlem' Tommy Murphy
bombing out Abe Attell
the face of Attell covered in shoeblack
imagine that the black is red
just the fixation on red
Pone Kingpetch dethrones Perez
despite a clown's eye made up bloodily
Cooper's eye versus Clay/Ali
the face so grey against the shattered crevice
the light of the game extinguished, turning liquid,
gradually the blood is spent
hollow sockets of 'The Pugilist', bronze,
in the National Museum of Rome.

III

The boxer's sounds interrupt plosively,
while the Jaina vibrate, so repetitive in consonant
that all is almost vowel, a continuous voicing.
We wish for that passivity, the single vowel of wonder,
unchanging reverence for the sacred. But we fall
into Frenchified voodoo sacrifice: the clean blow,
sudden slice at a cockerel neck. It's disgusting
to gain erotic victory at such a price.
The Jains know the flow of time free of harm.
The boxer knows its beat: destruction and renewal.
Poetic music flows, undulates, hits beats.

We never wholly lose our childhood 'immediacy' because immediacy is the beginning of all consciousness. Politicians, boxers, priests and witches know this; they try to gain power over this origin of our identity in their various ways; it's in immediacy and the self-image we glimpse there that our sense of our status and moral worth begin, and the politician's 'freedom' is not the freedom we find there.

Michelet's *Satanism and Witchcraft*, bought from an arcade bookstall when I was 14 or so, describes a village girl fleeing the *droit de seigneur*, who couples with Satan in a wood and swells with devilish vapour; she has a brief reign as glittering quean before torture and ignominy. In Michelet's source, Sprenger and Kramer's 15th century Inquisition manual *Malleus Maleficarum*, a witch is seen in a wood with greenish smoke rising from her thighs. I would think up jokes about the chapter headings: 'On the manner in which a sorceress can transport penises through the air in a matchbox'. Once I wondered if a whispered 'yes' was enough to sell yourself to the devil, and whispered it, and had an immediate stab of fear. Such childishness.

Then it's as if one night in Bournemouth Jazz Club a crowd of beautiful blonde girls came down the steps: post-war austerity ended, Scandinavian language students flooded into the town, Espresso coffee arrived, and the generation gap widened. Adolescent sado-masochism, disguised as an interest in the history of witchcraft, matured into more generous understanding of relationships. A 16-year-old insurance clerk, I was waiting in El Cabala for a Swedish girl. For a second I glimpsed something about poetry which seemed profoundly important; then the 'thing' had gone; it's stayed in front of my nose ever since, unattainable like a point in time, the gleam I follow. I saw poetry clear in its act of uniting thought and feeling in immediacy. The stress is the smallest unit in this artistic formation. I believe poetry allows me to glimpse a pre-linguistic mind-state. Philosophy can't trap that belief without deconstructing it; that's why I speak simply about childhood feelings and avoid the language of literary theory. Art gives us confidence that poetic melody shapes emotions and thinking into the one rhythm, a repeatable vivid present; and it feels as if in that alone lie true knowing, true freedom, and true beginning of memory. Imagined poet and imagined reader meet there, in the poem, without the witchcraft of domination.

Witchcraft and torture attack the victim between minute moments of self-consciousness, between the tiny islands; they get through into unprotected immediacy where mind is constantly reborn and they taint its continuity. This can occur with a stab of fear or gradually, as in witchcraft murder: while memories form there is always unconscious immediacy between them, and another immediacy in which they are present, as memories, to the mind. Stevenson has a South Sea story, 'The Isle of Voices', about a warlock who transports himself and his son-in-law by magic mat from Molokai to the beach of a far-off island. There the two of them are, for the inhabitants, just disembodied voices (though it turns out that the spurts of the wizards' magic fires can be seen by the natives). The shells they pick up become, once home again, silver dollars.

As I pass in a wink from one vivid memory to another I enter newly autonomous unities in mind. Husserl says memory has a closed nature based on the unity of the temporal duration of the original impression which founds the memory. In my own picturing, memory is a temporal island whose centre pulsates with origination and whose boundaries seem secure just until we explore them. What are shells within one island become silver dollars in another; and in the unconscious treasure island of our whole self they become gold doubloons.

These passages divide between childhood and 30 years later. To summarize intervening years: offices, hotels, National Service, journalism including two years in Paris for AFP, mature student in England, lecturer. Family warmth, family deaths. Always poetry. A common sort of life so far. But, during my second time in Paris, separated from all I valued, I lost much sense of the deeper self, which speaks my voice of conscience. Rich harbours of memory became blocked off too and I had to rediscover access to them.

Leaving home island

You don't step out of union but leave home land,
a car door snaps shut at the ferry port;
and it's easy to cross-Channel if gunfire is withheld;
for then the ship runs every night and ceaselessly;
its iron sides heave overhead
knapsacks of students jostle together on docksides
and Port Authority lights illumine girls
you will look at in the saloon, later.
Some word half in sound or memory: the sea could author it,
tongues' yellow slick on harbour mouth waves.

There, in the past, boulders struck dully by a Scottish loch
here, the ferry hull knocking, a bell buoy idling;
there, a dinghy's tarpaulin hauled over a driveway
here, tide across in the bay scrapes down sand;
there, a hissing tap in an echoing kitchen
here, the sea sucking its teeth;
much dear detail you regret having dragged along like chains;
here, the tide pulls stones along metal flanges of the dock;
there, chairs budged on wooden floors downstairs
or workmen dumped a plank into garage foundations
here, cleaners hump about within the lit ferry,
at the gangway's high summit a doorway opens on that light.

You wish to believe a word in your throat;
a word which yields and doesn't break
would moor the present to the past;
yet you must slip away to sea again
like the old-fashioned scoundrel, a pirate,
be a slip hand at escaping by sea swell
on a journey you morally permit yourself
since the fastening, yielding word
can't be spoken. The many sounds
of the populous sea arrive
from an island where voices continue to be.

It could be any moment in any adult life when a past island is left behind; a new one not yet reached. Unfortunately for them, poets often get their work out of such tenseness; they're washing about in a mid-sea, as if on Whitman's ferry, not within a parable concerning reincarnation, but on another real journey which is also one between the past of our life and the uncertainly forming future. 'The true paradise is the one that is lost' goes the old literary tag; and yet in loss arises hope of new perfection; so perhaps the true paradise is also that hope, and in the present we experience loss and hope as a real élan, the authentic ambiguity of birth of mind.

At the personal level, betrayal may be involved in the loss. That boy within a clifftop house near Shelley Park, Bournemouth, had dreamed of an idealized woman in white, Cariclia, weeping over her lover in the tide. In Heliodorus her loyalty survived all the rough adventures of this picaresque romance, replete with pirates and thieves. There may come a time in adult life when another person's idealism is betrayed irrevocably; and all the adult's past up to that moment closes off its shores and becomes the island we leave with much regret.

And it may not be merely personal. Halfway through my life, Britain changed to long-lasting Conservatism which, while I don't say it oppressed all poetry, oppressed my own. Nostalgia for a past world-role encouraged a chauvinism as narrow as that which gripped national life after the Second World War. For the sake of my own poetry, which seeks its patriotism in internationalism, it seemed essential to escape the closure of chauvinism. Returning to Paris, scene of my younger days as a journalist, leaving my country and so much that I value, I felt deep moral unease and a rage at necessity that lasted nearly six years of buffeted uncertainty and sea-change. Once a month I'd take the Sealink night ferries that ply the English Channel and each time the unease would become intensified.

My mind shuttling between Britain and France and between various personal loyalties, I lost the emotional purity of the boy in the sketchbook, dreaming of an island where Cariclia, dressed in white, received her lover's loyalty. My judgment, personal or political, was not trustworthy, as if I were trapped in the temporary alliances of a ferry boat.

The Ferry Pirate
(Variations)

When the brain's black with demonic crisis
and its inky sea peopled with lights
that prompt memory, loved souls
are borne out on the wake from high boatsides
and in that world of waters float lit rooms
wandering away to past sunsets. Swaying,
the terrain of darkness lost to you.

And always a lover ashamed to have suffered,
always marriages left inland,
always the sea carrying out black pram covers,
the wandering of unsteady thoughts;
then the
whispering at the captain's voice tube says:
'When I came early to my new love, Cariclia,
I found her kinsfolk weeping
for her old love and she far too faithful,
despite the sea changing either through time or fortune,
and I carried her away across the blackening waters.'
You won't find quite this in Heliodorus.

That sea is always fairly near
under the rails of night ferries
swaying with unsteady thoughts, blackening in crisis,
roughening with time or fortune, drawn on
by inkless nibs, as if the written surface
were integral with liquid rooms of memory
distorted in the currents undersea.

That sea is always unsteady with thoughts,
polluted by the pram covers carried out
into tracks of moonlight
borne towards lit rooms beyond the horizon
memories of a mother's kitchen
where the dead kinsfolk sit down to a table

distorted in a childhood's inky sketchbook,
washed in black, bound in black.

To have left a lover suffering far inland,
to have sensed the pram covers heaving away from
the moonlight track and faces sinking like flat-fish
under a sea peopled with receding lights
governed by smoky stars
and then to have seen
a modern Cariclia in the dress of Grecian white
a handbag strap as if of the quiver of arrows
walk down the scudding ferry deck
entering risks of piracy in a classic romance,
this, in another poem the cause of melancholy.

But here the sea is not integral with the writing
and keeps bearing the lights and memories away.
At moments of crisis,
the voyager sways from the rail towards her:
you won't quite find the classic mood in him or her.

In the French 'Hexagon's' capital, I would think about islands as symbolic not just of our self and selves, but also of nationhood, ideally a grander experience of self. Other, smaller island states became important for me. My 45th birthday party, I sat with some New Jewel leaders from Grenada outside at 'Le Maquis', a Montmartre restaurant. A year or two later, the Americans invaded Grenada following a week during which the New Jewel premier, Maurice Bishop, had been seized by a rival party faction during a public speech and assassinated along with supporters. US invasion propaganda had made civil war seem imminent. A few months after the American action, I toured the Caribbean with the journalist who'd organized my party, journeying on trucks into Haiti's arid mountains and scooting round 'liberated' Grenada on a motor bike. I sat down to a mongoose dinner in a Grenadian cottage restaurant outside St George's with, by chance at the same table, the Bishop associate who'd led the premier out to address the crowd the day he died and the brother – visiting from the US – of the New Jewel rival then on trial for masterminding Bishop's assassination. Conversation, about skin diving, was stiff but not unfriendly, for the island is no more populous than, say, Cambridge, England. Reagan's bullying victory, easily prepared for by economic destabilization, was a *realpolitik* success, welcomed by many on the island; but each failure of indigenous government and success on external power tarnishes politics.

'Who cares about little Grenada?' a British embassy economic adviser had asked me in Europe a year or two before the invasion. In larger scales of concern, the history of the universe say, who cares about Britain or the US either? How wide is your self island, your nationhood, or your humanity, and how open to expansion?

Expatriate, worried about British chauvinism, I would always like to be writing my '*Britannia mia*'. I'd have to be a Petrarch, a Leopardi to do so. How real a Britain do I imagine? A smaller island imagined in the vast unconscious self, which has accreted experience from more than just one country? It's solipsism to think that the external world, since imaged only in our own mind, is uniquely constructed by each individual.

Part of the whole, unconscious self certainly is 'my Britain'. Is it still smaller than myself? When I lived in my literal home island, at each moment the outer British world became part of the deep self-creation: my family life, my village, the near-town, distant friends, work and travels, and 'media-Britain'. Both outer and inner worlds were being built into the whole self; and this was a long-lasting real event in space-time. But the outer was also, in that space-time event, distinct from the self incorporating it; and also inner and outer were actively interpenetrating each other. This makes many Britains for me: one that is part of my whole self-island and is smaller than it; other Britains experienced either consciously or unconsciously as separate from me, or as something I belong to; then there's a Britain still penetrating my self in all present remembering and all new experience of it.

Much that lies dead in us is alive on an island of voices
whose cliffs are steep as ladders to the mind.

Round their heights shrapnel flying off
laughter blows a hurricane,
the sea moves with its mountains,
broken lights in those narrowing mountains of sea.

Clouds panic about the island in bitter rains
the waters twittering with chaos
a flock of gulls gusts into unreadable auguries
past black outcrops glistening with saliva of questions.

No oracle while the island lies at a distance;
there all your times and all your loved ones
can roam unique through rainy jungles, surprising meetings
in sunny clearings within a greater, unified memory.

Much lies dead in us. Will our hearts reach that island?
Will our hearts be appointed at the appointed hour?

But you stay shifting and remote
on the planks of your history, a stage
awash, an old ship sailing these fickle waterways,
of one love merely equated with another.

On each side of you the sea's draining face glitters
as if with fireflies under green-haired crests
or, alternately, he's suddenly bald or hair like weed,
the anonymous made antiquated and quasi-personal.

The voices in you become ridiculously classic: 'Oh to be
a dolphin fomenting rebellion against the shape-changer;
rather than be a falsity to each pair of eyelashes
curving in the swell of his waves.'

The dead voices of soul lament and are funny in lamenting
as if the seas should usurp the ancient oracle of earth.

'Oh to be, oh to be, oh to be in something other
than this migratory mood, constant ferrying
between one point of value and another.'
There has to be some place where voices and times meet

among these impoverished other islands of spirit
each with classic or modern scenes by the shore:
lovers seated alone on rocks of your spirit-world
watching torsos drifting in Poseidon-bearded foam.

However small the right island, to reach it, make of it
a wider politics of self, let prison-arrow swifts
head off for new dawns across the entirely relative,
this sea giving up uncared-for populations at its edge.

In France, I worked on prosody, visiting linguistic laboratories and putting electrodes on people's throats to record their readings of poetry. Once, because I was writing a fiction about a boxer named 'Tune', I recorded punches, accompanied by the vicious humming noises some boxers make, onto a spectrometer which showed a contour map of vocal frequencies in glossy photographs. The punching looked like a horrific version of the poems I had previously recorded, all the subtlety of vocal modulation and stress replaced by continuous, violent vowels and sharp blows. The punches hit exact rhythmic points when the violence, empty of thought or of all emotion except self-will and its triumphs, can be imposed on the victim with maximum force. To strike most exactly, the boxer trusts to the flow of his own fighting.

By trusting the continuity of their mind-acts, to which the easiest access is by feeling, poets also strike the beats of their rhythm, uniting in this movement emotion, sound and thought. I have called the beats centres-without-location of mental islands, moments when part of the poem's past and future is experienced as a beat and when great vividness lies in potential. It's not just paradises that we lose by being unable to make vividness conscious, because there are depressions and hells at these centres too. This is easier to grasp when we think not of small islands of consciousness such as beats in a rhythm but of larger forms, whole areas of life which seem a unity to us and which create a whole life's rhythm.

I held a respectable job in Paris but for a while lived in the miniature barn of a studio on Avenue Clichy that I've mentioned. Sort of, I loved it. But I had left in England a whole half of life, and yet had to live a new half. When emotional transition between two large areas of personality is extremely painful, psychosis and schizophrenia are a danger. I became only mildly Jekyll and Hyde (the nightmare Stevenson had in Bournemouth), the blindness between my past life and the present being incomplete, the forbidden personality, which was joyous, youthful but prone to folly, being only partly unacceptable. But, lacking comfortable continuity of feeling, the moral rhythm of my life was broken.

Autoscopie

The middle years in England pull and halt.
A younger man but still yourself
greets you off the Gare du Nord boat train,
as if the ferry had shuttled
between your 1970 Paris and now.
The you you left in France takes your bags,
as a son would take his father's.

At the cab line you have two journeys:
splitting into father and son who live differently:
one cab to the studio of the self-son
in a corridored block like a hotel,
prostitutes and illegals in a burnt-out building next door,
opposite, tric-trac tables, fights,
a police-fire-ambulance route whopping and whistling all night
on the Avenue de Clichy, centre of the unexpected,
the road constantly a roaring river.

The self-father lives quietly near the station,
typing at an old steam-driven computer,
this old, steam-driven commuter,
this old teamster driven by paternal anxiety,
in a mortgaged flat above the crystal *quartier*.
Indisputably *cadre*,
in British institutions where carpets
climb the walls in furry bear paper,
he enters steel-faced elevators
arrives in rooms where business people
present him with old Armagnac.

Restless in these disunities, the self-son
roams out at night with journalists
tries patois at the L'Epi d'Or
high on cheap Calva at the Bar de la Mairie,
brings someone too young for the father home.
As the girl sleeps with the self-son,
the disquiet father tends the foot of the bed.

At midnights or mid-days, exactly on the tick,
he remembers that morning's two glistening sides,
one side night-cold, one mid-day blazes
rise unimaginably in their instants,
past the darkened or golden rails of balconies
past the lordly inter-stellar or sunshine spaces
up to the wings and wheels of never-endingness;
if a one-self endures the many selves that endure.

Under moral tensions in Paris, my psoriasis, which mildly attacks my face and chest, became a little worse. When I called the sketch that of a 'beautiful boy' it's partly the boy's fresh, clear face I thought of. More recently, I read in the *New York Times* that, when people with multiple personality disorder switch from one personality to another, rashes, welts, and scars may disappear: handwriting, handedness, epilepsy, allergies, and colour blindness may appear or disappear or change. For doctors, it's the power of the mind over the body. In my own poetics, it hints at something else too. I have read something of the modern philosophy of space-time and of deconstructionist literary theory; but I tentatively believe that a pre-linguistic, unconscious 'self', a real creation in space and time, survives the conscious self's dissolution into ever new stages of itself.

The temporal home of this entity is immediacy. Much human behaviour, especially our profoundest moral sense – the simple wish to be 'good' in an undefined way – implies that, unreflectively, people do have this belief. I have no religion at all; I have only tentative belief that the good persists in time.

Multiple personality's strange features seem some evidence of this: there may be an almost autonomous space-time creation of a second or third personality and of a bodily state that accompanies each of them. Something that persists in time but, because of disorder, is imperfectly built into the form of the whole unconscious self like an inappropriate stanza in a poem. In psychosis, this particular area is held in unconscious immediacy until we switch into it. This is why switching is so swift. Then, perhaps, our body recognizes that another spatio-tempo region has been entered, and the skin responds to the recognition.

Immediacy is hidden from us by finite mind. The body, its visual perception, and the electro-chemistry of its brain are comparatively crude instruments. If a compass could think, would it believe in the perfect circle? With the two clumsy legs of its argumentative apparatus it would be at a loss to justify its belief except by drawing one as best it could.

The islands of voices

On Saturday, I told myself of the islands of voices
By today, Sunday, I had lost access.

What happens on the islands?
There are invisibles and the great one
yesterday was my own spirit, revisiting,
betraying my presence by fires that I lit;
they sprang up and died down on the beaches
like dust devils, beside my heel print
which filled with khaki liquid.

Without meaning to,
I've brought many islands to life
and left them there in the sunshine of my dead days.
Hotels, a tall white city in the bay,
or I'm back in Poole, sailing by
a mansion castellated from toilet rolls
guarding Brownsea's neat harbour.
Others are the islands in a child's minute attention,
idealized, tropical, forested,
ringed with sand, fringed with white, usual steel-blue.

Revisiting, I saw human forms slipping behind trees;
they could as well have been Pacific figures
on Stevenson's Isle of Voices,
I couldn't hear
if they were ever my companions.
Had I spoken they'd have listened, startled,
receiving the voice like a ball returned
round the corner, to children, by unseen hand.

These are my pasts, these islands
and I'm barred from them by mere turns of mood,
day to day. My own childhoods at play
in their forests, suddenly appeared to me, yesterday;
but shadows dappled the shorelines,
among the birches and elders;
it's hard to match transient feelings
with that precise shadow patterning,
my presence fizzing, flaring up on the beaches.

And today, Sunday, I have lost access.

Separating from England almost cleaved my unconscious identity in half, an irreparable harm I'd done. You wrote to me, Alice, when you were about to fly to Luxembourg where we were both to read at a poetry festival; and we planned for you to stay in Paris with me afterwards. Not the repair but the reconsolidation of my unconscious began then, followed by my present move to New York to be with you.

At rehearsals in the plush little Luxembourg theatre, I had a spot trained on an easel bearing some diagram-cartoons which I show as I read a sequence. The sequence starts in apparent humour but themes of death and politics gradually enter; there's a similar progression in the diagrams. For two days, Italian, French, Belgian, Luxembourgish, English and American poets had performed in a great variety of styles from hilarious music-zen to the chair-up-to-table serious. I knew that our French friend, Jacques, was about to read a sequence concerning the death of his wife and you one about the death of Ted; so I intended to emphasize the humorous side of my diagram-poems – I can read them in many ways. But the theatre's hand-held mikes faded immediately out of mouth-range and the stand-up model I chose rooted me to one place. Also, once onstage I found the diagrams unexpectedly out of reach under their separate spot; and the humorous performance depends upon moving about, pointing out their details. Instinctively, I put my lips near the mike and let my voice softly play with prosody – a purely technical question of stretching out syllables, minutely delaying consonants, altering pitch, timbre, vowel quality, and loudness; I felt nothing, being quite distracted by changing my plans. About halfway through, I noticed my unusual tension, and the audience-darkness was quite still. When I came into the foyer I was shaking, our friend Wendy had tears in her eyes and said, 'How do you manage to go so near that edge?' I wasn't consciously aware I had done so.

The gravity of a poem lies in its whole form, and the prosody alone, being part of that unity, is sufficient access to it without the performer having to feel anything. The whole form lies in the 'unconscious' of the poem; it is its ineffable nature, just as I have a nature developed in me by birth and upbringing. Even if, as I was, we're brought up in some middle-class, snobbish, racist suburb, once we touch more profoundly natural unconscious sides of ourselves all the cultural rubbish falls away and we recognize a deep kinship, an international kinship. We felt such a kinship that evening after you and Jacques had read. As Jacques said, 'It was verray intense.'

For Kind

Kindness acts idly or unnaturally,
leads you into fear. Act in kind.
Kindness makes you idle, worse, unnatural.
Don't be afraid of the darkness of kind;
for it's the birth darkness, vertical twist
of opening lips in the night: life that follows
belongs to you in kind. Don't be frightened
of darkness of origin: it is this darkness,
similar tints of our flesh in the night
of kind. The kind you are, with slim
mammalian chest and, walking to the bathroom,
hip-swag: how naturally your walk sways
in kind. You are humankind,
my kind, kind to me, born well and gentle.
We believe in kind:
birth, origin, descent, nature,
sex, upbringing, race, our natural property,
so many things we naturally have
and have no need to struggle for
merely out of kindness to each other, or,
worse, to struggle for unnaturally.

Where I'm writing on Manhattan's Lower East Side, the poets are gradually leaving as the rents rise and the number of panhandlers reminds me, Alice, of that Caribbean tour and of Haiti's poor. Papa Doc, the older Duvalier, made a horrific racist pantomime of the way Fascist dictators bewitch the centre of politics. A Haitian film-maker I know would imitate how Papa Doc had telephoned him in prison, the hypnotic monotone fit for Duvalier's famous black-clothed impersonation of Baron Samedi, the Voodoo god of cemeteries.

The son, Jean-Claude, was a sad-faced giant who inherited a 'noiriste' political structure set up by killing off the mulatto middle-class opposition. My journalist friend and I gate-crashed one of his presidential receptions at a white walled medical centre on baking slopes far out of Port-au-Prince. The president's wife, Michèle, the real power, outshone everyone with her buttercup yellow dress and gold shoes and made an Eva Peron-like speech to a flattering audience. The nasty Interior and Defence Minister moved among the champagne glasses and dangled a light automatic, while a battery of rifles protected the valley and the presidential anti-aircraft gun rumbled up on a flatbed.

My friend was investigating Press repression and food riots after one of Baby Doc's ineffectual gestures of reform. Prominent politicians would secretly brief us, low-voiced, looking nervously over their shoulders if in public places. One journalist had recently been beaten with rubber hoses and had the little finger of his writing hand broken. An opposition politician under house arrest said that all his Haitian visitors had been taken to the *caserne*. The police slipped out of a car as we walked downhill and just took our names.

The following day, we went out to see the Christian Democrat leader, who because he was a working-class opponent had been many times tortured by the Duvalierists, as had his daughter, Jocelyne. Their house, on a hillside, had a forest of stick-scaffolding at the front. The politician's son appeared from a gateway opposite and pointed to a property where the police kept watch on visitors. Jocelyne was at home but not her father and we had a chat. That was July 3; the day afterwards, my friend and I took off for the north; the political weekly *Le Petit Samedi Soir* came into our Cap Haitien hotel from Port-au-Prince. It said that on July 4 Jocelyne had been pistol-whipped near death by police and had then gone by car to the Catholic free radio station to report the brutality to the nation. I became extremely anxious in case our visit had caused the government assault.

Later, I learnt that the American Embassy, no doubt seeking to pressurize Duvalier to liberalize and to let the US Congress know they were doing so (and thus speed aid packages through Congress) invited several beleaguered dissidents to their July 4 celebrations. The Christian Democrat leader had stayed an hour, then slipped out the back door and joined the maquis. The regime's response was to raid the house we'd visited, seize copies of the party newspaper, and beat up Jocelyne.

Though as a foreign observer I was safe, it felt edgy to have official violence so near in a country no less notorious for it after the fall, not of Duvalierism, but at least of Jean-Claude himself. In the slums of Port-au-Prince, the worst I'd seen, or in the countryside it was hard to see how even an incorrupt government with massive aid could cure the poverty, deforestation, erosion, aridity, and lack of roads. One hot day before we left I saw two boys sheltering from the sun by holding a yellowed newspaper over their heads. I paid over a dollar and found it a rare issue of *Le Jour* for 1966, commemorating a visit from Leopold Senghor. Papa Doc had a romantic poem of his own in it, describing exile in his own country before he took power and installed his political solution with blackness and witchcraft at its centre.

On an old copy of Le Jour

Barred like a franked stamp, a gesture sent out,
brown US stamp, bit of blue, on a letter
to Greg about Grenada and Haiti.
Yet another failed revolution,
yet more torture and exploitation overlooked.
Walking along by Gem Spa, Lower East Side,
we're calm, walking across discards:
filter tip on the sidewalk, an ensemble
of beige top and white cotton trousers
at home by the laundry bag.
Which of these is squashed flat
and barred by a rubber sole?
The hasty flipping aside of the fag,
remembered hands sliding clothing down and up.
The tarmac boils up at the corner,
an unmoving but seeping shellac
crawling with lights like maggots.
And I think of reseeing Jean Cocteau's
Les Enfants terribles with you, Alice,
how in the adolescents' search for evil
they hoard an opium lump seeping like the tar,
something to smoke, to forget with. Calm,
walking down streets of bad headlines
as evening falls. Back on my desk
there's a browning *Le Jour* from Haiti, 1966,
when Leopold Senghor visited Duvalier, whose name
hid evil but Senghor was hot foot for negritude.
Below their double portrait, the appalling nerve
of Papa Doc's poem about his sufferings,
'The Tears of an Exile' (in his home island):
no wonder the white paper has browned
with this poem that civilization discards
where the villain is hero, under cloak,
limping along Port-au-Prince tarmac at midnight,
hearing beggars' cries; I imagine his feet
treading on the clothing of the poor.

Duvalierism and the New Jewel: the fake priest whose uniformity was imposed by murder, violence, and fear – a boxer's politics; and the men and women of the people, who believed too optimistically that they could unify national sentiment to accord with their own left-wing cause; despite US power; despite the ready disaffection of the poor when they realize their life expectations are threatened by shaky markets; and despite the presence of political prisoners on a small island. Complete unity destroys the state. Economics, statecraft, and citizen virtue form indissolubly one politics.

These last thoughts are classical Greek. As a younger poet, I would consult burlesque oracles – in rushing water, by the sea of the drowned, in breeze through the trees of my old playground Shelley Park, in bird flight, in caves. A bee flew into a cave. I had a waking dream of a waxen city constructed by the bees sacred to Demeter and to the underworld; the melting city was constantly reborn in each act of mind, the kindest city-state you could imagine, for all its citizens lived in readiness for utter change.

Then came those days in Paris, which I compared in my mind sometimes to the rule of Dionysus and Poseidon over the oracle, after the foundatory rule of Ge, the cave/earth goddess. These intervening years of corruption and change. Just before I left for New York, I went to Delphi at last.

By rising at six and going out of your hotel into a drizzly dark Spring, you can have the oracle site to yourself for two hours. I passed by the tourists' misted coaches and, on the little plateau's outskirts, as dawn lightened, crossed the road from the temple's perimeter walls; there by the Kastalian grotto where the plateau narrows into the mountains. From the precipice ledge, I watched luminous clouds at eye level swagging the valley roof. The rain cleared. Four nightingales were in the olive trees. I turned and, very pleased, noticed blue beehives like lunchboxes on the verge opposite; I lifted my head to see small brown eagles crossing Parnassus. This was before we met again in Luxembourg, Alice; at this concourse of oracular elements, even though I don't believe in oracles exactly, my temporary life began to melt like the Witch of the North.

The parable of good government

A spiritual Mayoress in perfect mind proposes
that all remembered cities be one city of wax.

The walls last for one act of her fine government
ever reborn in the matrix of her absolute goodwill.

Let them appear again, the streets of wax sarcophagi,
low walls of houses rising, honeycombing acres.

In the instant workmanship of this mind-moulding
within seconds you see town hall vistas

past cereous porticos of churches; and terraces
with doors crude still, gouged like pigeons' nostrils

into façades becoming vertical. Overhead, those
motorways will never be firm enough for vehicles.

For some moments you have a stretch of lifetime
to lean against slippery walls, peer into alleys

where brownish dusk drifts with purple-grained dust
in the smoky smell of the mind's making.

The deadened streets have no time to fill up with crowds
but you can find magnanimous hints of citizens

in graffiti carved into soft walls saying
'I want no vengeance and will forebear my envy'.

The city melts already, candle flames spurt
on battlements whose age is measured in moments.

Yet there's time to see not views but a view
of the whole of your life spent in cities.

Doves with waxy beaks settle round St Paul's rotundas
Parisian boulevards look encaustic against blue sky.

All holds trembling like a line from *The Merchant of Venice*
which passes the lips sweetly but stays in air:

    'Look how the floor of heaven
is thick inlaid with patens of bright gold.'

This parable written in New York, its present malleable
only through lower development taxes, ousting the poor.

I am only now regaining comfortable access to the more treacherous areas of the past. Tonight, restless, I rented an old British thriller movie, *The Curse of the Demon*, for my American step-sons' VCR.

Above my desk hangs a runic good luck charm, cast in the old ogham script by a friend. It alliterates throughout on the letter 'B', which stands also for 'bees'; and it was sent to me because of this and other of my obsessions; notably, there's a sacred child mentioned in the chant. I think of the word 'Kind' in my poetry linked not just with nature and fate but also with the German *Kind*. I regret loss of the rich Renaissance meanings of 'human nature', which included what we are in immediacy, regarded as precivilized, before we've time to think. It's a fictional state of mind but I believe in it in ways I can't explain.

Near immediacy, when the conscious mind hasn't quite emerged from the unconscious, I am unprotected from emotion which colours all I see. Once, before my elder daughter's birth, I almost broke down under the stress of such vividness and altered sensory perception. I suffered a radical attack from Poe's Imp of the Perverse: the thought that, while you've always been good there's nothing to stop you turning crazed and murderous at any moment. Perverse, because it ignores the overall tenor of our lives. The colour red became unbearably bright, I couldn't look at knives, and certain voices of friends sounded like circular saws nearing my ears. Also, I was interested and went to thriller movies to test my fears. Terrified at myself, I walked out of a German film with slab-like bodies and whippings, a film about a schizophrenic axe murderess, and *The Hands of Orlac*, the Mel Ferrer remake of Maurice Renard's story in which a pianist thinks a surgeon has grafted a strangler's hands on to his damaged wrists. Each walk-out came at a character's moment of personality change.

A film I nearly walked out of at that time was *The Curse of the Demon*, from the M. R. James story, 'The Casting of the Runes'. I found the moment when a bewitched man awoke from a catatonic trance hard to withstand. The film concerns a runic spell, which, if accepted willingly, makes the recipient liable to a personal and terminal visit from the demon at midnight on such and such a day. As a grandson of the manse, I have always had superstitious fears of being damned. The trick was to pass the curse back to the witch who created it, for it was hardly a good luck charm.

Garlic bread

Watching the movie, I fell for the bait
last night, sooting my mouth as I ate
charcoal edging on garlic bread,
witchcraft on that side,
the charred border of a runic charm dooming
a scientist hurtling towards midnight;
his hands grip the steering wheel
of an obsolete car to escape his fate,
single headlight flashing past tree trunks.

He and I crossed through a spell of night
ruled by *The Curse of the Demon*;
smoke huffing out from a point in the moonless sky,
or rapidly shrinking and vanishing,
mutilation that approaches and withdraws,
a man's staggered black silhouette in wartime branches
in hidden floodlights raying out round bushes.

He and I only invoked the curse casually;
we weren't born with it in our belly.
We simply glittered with personal effects
and treasured reputation.
Another was chosen
but a spell passed inadvertently to us:
we were spectator until we had victim.
Then we were the victim.

A bramble whip scratches white on a negative plate.
The night clears, though abruptly,
into absolute sunlight, a thirsty sky.
I can jump out of half my life
and leave a black destiny behind.
Oh, but that's not good either:
not if I'm on an unshaded island of self,
where centrally a well
has deep sides of straw.
This is the well of poison
so leaky it's always nearly dry
in hot light of self-regard;
its drib-drabs from the spout
instill in us non-virtue,
for we have invoked darkness to create light.

This evening I'm calmer and my head
knows aspects night, aspects day,
fishing, easy under trees overhanging a shore
crowded with silver birth and elder, lights and darks,
hardy shrubs enduring life of conflict.
The island self slips generously under the ocean
and becomes the general earth,
no Treasure Island
no latitude, longitude, spyglasses and all that stuff,

but oak leaves floating on dead water, knobkerries
of brown-black reflection in estuary oil,
tobacco stains in toothed wood,
my old teeth stained but my field of knowing fluid,
surfaces of moving words:
'It was just a movie, just the dark
passing over the blaze of selfishness,
poisoning the occult centre.'

The normal good wishing of my whole life protects me somewhat from the wrong I do and is all I know of salvation. Civic virtue begins in that. I return to Mona's sketchbook, angling it again in the streetlamps, looking at a preparatory drawing I remember her making for a watercolour of the Shelley Park of my childhood. Trees, undergrowth and grass bear the names of the colours she would paint them.

The sketch builds into a whole period of my life; the pencilled variegation forms into a whole that remains varied. So, the minor forms of myself are retained in the higher, greater forms of it, right up to the highest forms of all when my self becomes indistinguishable from the not-self; *still, even while it becomes a figment*, as Kierkegaard said about his dialectic, the lower forms persist in the higher. My deep, whole, healthy self that is constructed of all unconscious vividness built into it, that self remains as a real entity and space and time even in the space and time that envelops it. It is possible, despite the ancient logicians, for a thing both to be and not to be.

Camouflage

Sketched in caran d'ache, this lame partridge
spreads its camouflage into the whorled scrub:
you can't get away from it, drawing techniques
scribble across borders, and the pencil marbles
the grass and blotches birch trees with the same patterns
this windy April day in the nesting season, eggs
hidden in undergrowth. The sky tugs up in tufts and hollows
until the whole scene is perfect grassy earth
and among the green-brown strato-cumulus, overcast,
the shading hints at corrugated iron sheeting
mottled with moss; for you it roofs a collapsed
iron age ground dwelling, a fogou,
found once in a Cornish aristocrat's garden.

Or you might block in a hawk at the top of a nightwood;
out of unconscious rain of branches extends this one hook
to catch at a moment's meaning and it might tear
the red silk skein of evening; or again, with other shading,
a hooded crow, light-grey as summer cloud that rhymes
its colour masses on large-scale against June weather,
as the crow huddles on the high branch of a hedge; at its foot
three brothers group their mantles together, shadows
of the clouds variegating the meadow alongside them,
air and birds alive through light as the hawk is alive
because he is made of dusk that is almost trees.

It's the same with a black-headed gull camouflaged
for the white rills and gloomy gulphs of ocean.
He's standing on a rock. Once you sketch him
the rock dapples with sea-tones; mirroring this,
the bird looks ready to slip sideways and swing with waves;
the waters wing up and show white feathering;
cloud horizons swoop down with tornado beaks
and near at hand sip at the leaping up spray.
The crayon can't keep still, swinging with it,
for you know that behind all possible 'scapes
lie unions of waters, winds, earths, times.

If a past memory comes into the present and simultaneously the present is vivid, then the past shares in the immediacy; for a second or two I sense a potential to bring all the intervening life into the immediate as well. It was like this just now, as I painted our Manhattan apartment door blue and I reflected on what had been written so far. Often the poetry is like pages of my own private sketchbook: but if England, Paris, the Caribbean and New York could hold in mind, contemporary with the quivering flame of my blowtorch and would even stay awhile until the brush-strokes that follow, the poetry would make me a kind of salvation which would throw its light even on my brief excursions into politics. The self grown waxen, fully citizen, and properly 'kind'.

I just need some entrance, some way into the past from within the present; and I keep returning to the very beginning of my poetry, to Shelley Manor, which I always think of as the harmless building.

The Blow Torch

A blow torch passes over an old door, remounted,
and paint bubbles into paisley colours;
quilted oils button down snub on to pine;
the flame returns; life's light returns
to events happening in new bedrooms,
curling paint into friable charcoal coils.
How do we get to these newly-prepared places?
Did poetry bring us here, as we pretend,
that owl flying out of wooded night
into a trick theatre with salons of gauze,
the bird noiselessly circling a dark auditorium,
as scenes change with different lighting,
the bird still flighting there in present moments.

We should like to paint this door gold
with undercoat of black, but the boys say blue.
Wigged surfaces had melted in ripples.
Where the scraper has flaked off thick paint
blue polyurethane gleams in depressions
shaped like stagnant pools in saltings.
Some day lights up in a very distant past;
the wind ripples across marsh grass;
a shallow bogland, low and sour, a raging boy
playing tragedian in his head among billowing stages,
and then made tranquil through the variousness of gulls,
his eye following their flight
up to cliffs crowned with golden gorse
the dizzy blue.

That night, post-war, a quarter-mile from childhood,
listening to breezes rustling above dark walls
of a pinewood inhabited by owls,
the boy climbed past a sagging door
in the derelict Shelley family manor, Shelley Park,
and entered a theatre of art and varying times,
empty rooms constantly relit by flames that pass.

If art were a specialist human activity of purely aesthetic value it wouldn't matter to us. Poems and paintings are bound together in the way our whole lives are: that is the key to their spirituality. To make a curious phrase of it, we are spiritual because we have a life. If the life cohere round a conception of the good then a glimpse of our whole unconscious self is a glimpse of beauty's glamour. Almost literally, it has a face. The 'good' here will fit no conventional definition or morality and may look dual in the Blakeian mythology or have other more primitive, tribal form or be religious or be flawed and multi-formed. If it has the goodness appropriate to that flawed life, it will have glory in its whole form.

Just as a poem creates form by starting with the smallest occasions of it (in English verse, the stress), building through syllable, through musical verse unit and silence, up through cadence and stanza to the whole poem, so do our lives build a coherence from the smallest incorporations of outer world into inner self. If utter unity meant the disappearance of constituent elements, then Aristotle's political rule would hold: unity destroys the state, self, or poem. A poem would become a single vowel. Poems not only make their constituent elements coexist within form but refine the form itself into a beauty latent in the elements; and they allow us to glimpse the form in each performance of the poem and then make that glimpse repeatable. Therefore, a whole poem takes its place in the larger web of language and literature but always as itself; so all the islands of ourself expand out to the larger self and the larger self takes its place in the great, unconscious universe, but always as itself, and is a shining in that blackness. I'm not talking of after-lives; I have no idea about such matters. Unity of form disappears into ambiguous dark whenever we examine it analytically, but its heart is like the always beating heart of a poem: it is the precious origin of our lives' form, or of a true politics.

I have pictured myself as a young boy loitering at dusk in the grounds of Shelley Manor, Boscombe. When I pooh-poohed a stranger's story about Shelley's ghost haunting the park, I didn't know that the poet's heart had, during the mid-19th century, been preserved in the house by the daughter-in-law, Lady Shelley. The 'cor cordium'.

Despite this ignorance, the manor was for me, as I say, like the upper apartment in Hans Andersen's story, 'The Shadow'; that is, a place of personal magic. Andersen tells of a scholar who sees a beautiful woman emerge on to a balcony across the street. Behind her, light and music stream out from an inner room. He releases his shadow to follow the woman back into the house; and the shadow does so, except that it can't penetrate exactly to where the music comes from. On emerging from the rear of the house, the shadow becomes evil and dominates and betrays the scholar from then on, finally having him executed.

I have come since to think of ever-broader applications of this story: of the exact place where the music is, the inner music, of being the truly moral place, the hidden place, but also open generously to the world. The evil thing is to appropriate what is hidden and thereby win spiritual power: from the personal to international levels shadows dominate us, as if old man Duvalier were one of their darkest representatives in an unholy band of shadows. Though Shelley's heart was long ago buried, I now think of it permanently in the manor of childhood, the point at which poetry began for me and, coexisting with present times, begins, will begin.

'Cor Cordium'

Boy in Boscombe park, dead-hearted,
climbed into a decaying manor
loved by Stevenson, to awaken
his own talent, staging scenes within
a puppet theatre of future lives.
Walls' grey crumbled inward on him,
window fragments crystallized dust
in corners soured by tramps' faeces;
carpetless stairs rose to bolted doors.
Post-war still, time not moving yet.
Shelley's heart once in this mansion.
Remember now, my own ribcage.

Poet's heart, saved from sea-
corruption, from flames, would beat
in my oracle of the drowned.
Heart damply dead in its casket,
inside grey inner sanctum
of the lady manor. This a compendium
of all my homes, embodiment of adult
history of houses. Then silver box lid
lifts on mahogany surface,
velvet red, heart newly red.
Smashed window-hole, night outside
black as kitten fur, time pulsing.

In 1988, Manhattan's air burnt with
funerals. We recall Albert's "Nam".
I call back to Boscombe boy
that we are survived by deaths:
that such manors rise up vaster
than even I know, their rooms
fill with a world's peoples;
and they will disquiet him
with their constant pride and cruelty,
and thrill him in the house of poetry
with its mahogany and caskets:
the Shelleyan hearts enthusiastic.

THE
HARMLESS
BUILDING

For Tom

1

Kind Regards

For the moment the truth is hiding in obstreperous fiction. I can, however, say that a real mongol baby died and that his memory affects my life. In his mongolism I find an analogy for my own stupidity. He and I are united at that primitive level of thought where our ideas are fairly random, not ambitious, only half out of thought-chaos itself. How aptly mongolism is a symbol for the sweetness, 'stupidity' and near-harmlessness of a baby! Joined to an energetic and mature cleverness, such sweetness may become a force for good. Loving that real baby as I tried and still try to do, failing to love him as I failed – once crucially – and still fail to do, I have an index of how vanity mars my good intentions and of how, proudly shunning my own mental inadequacy, I so often cause harm.

This fiction may at times pose as clever, but you will bring the moral to it if you succeed in tracking my stupidity.

Above all, I should tell you that my life is nothing special, no more exciting than average; I possess neither a particularly original nor a distinguished intellect.

Attend to the half-resolved chaos behind my ideas, a chaos which I have sometimes guiltily disguised, as an exam student hides ignorance behind a learned reference or a sudden jump in his exposition. The project here will not be speed, poise, style, or the crossbow whizz of thought, though that may seem the project. Instead, I should love to keep a mongol baby alive in my mind, an outgoingness and kindness, a lack of coherence, an area of almost no-harm like a clearing in the middle of harm. In that babyish tea-brown light I should be dizzily at peace, content to reveal myself as pink-bodied and powerless, no longer concerned with dominating other people, but with a radiant mongol's smile on my face.

Unfortunately, to keep such babydom vivid in our adult lives is often beyond our powers. What I aspire to, the man called Uncle

Richard achieved. I shall nowhere give his real name. As far as I know, his teaching career never made him celebrated. He wrote a mathematics textbook or two, and old-fashioned imagist poetry; that's all. His intellectual calibre remained undeniable, most importantly because he never tried to hide his unintelligence. He let you sense that bland chaos always; even his sharpest thoughts opened the way towards it; and so he helped you to see what he truly said because the cleverness was only the half of it. I cannot hope to match that. Therefore, I repeat, search within my incoherence for the naïveté and rawness of my desires.

One more warning, the most serious: do not imagine that I know *any more* about Uruguay than the next person. I write at a time when that country is in the grip of cruel events. It would be unpardonable if an ill-informed fiction sought to have some factive meaning for Uruguayan affairs. Particularly, I do not refer to any real guerrilla movement or to any real elements of a 'current situation' there, however apparent a connection may seem. The reason Uruguay comes into this business at all is partly that we are all subject to the stream of news, and partly that a map of the country hung on the wall of Uncle Richard's lounge in that big house he called 'Blakeston' after Oswell Blakeston, God knows why. The map hung there because Uncle Richard's son-in-law, Frank, a journalist, had found himself a news agency job in Latin America after he left Rosine. With my preoccupations, I had a natural interest in their story, because Frank had left his wife after the birth of their mongol son. (But at the time he found other excuses for leaving.)

Donald Kipfer, an out-of-work journalist, once referred wryly to Frank as 'The Purple Land that England Lost', the projected title of a semi-autobiographical romance by W. H. Hudson, set in Uruguay. Donald's remark was ironic because he had taken Rosine and her baby to live with him after her marriage had failed and he could never be sure Rosine was happy with the arrangement. The couple inhabited four or five curiously-furnished rooms set apart in a museum building for the curator's use. The curator, a friend, chose to live in his own house, letting Donald have the flat free in return for his being responsible for night-time security. Donald is one of the nicest people to be left alive at the end of this narrative; so you may be sure he loved the little mongol boy dearly. It took Donald to christen the baby, 'Uncle Aubrey'. Nor was Uncle

Richard an uncle until Donald christened him so. Donald's highest ambition (like mine) will always be to combine the virtues of the two uncles: the harmless originality of the baby and the patterned wisdom of the old man. Probably he stole the letters so that their harmlessness would give him access to the wisdom of their addressee. But you never can tell.

In a town on the south coast of England, one late August afternoon, the twin objects of Donald's ambition were both asleep – the baby in a carrycot upstairs in a room of that Georgian museum building, and Uncle Richard in an armchair in his Victorian house only a mile or two away. Donald and Rosine had, negligently no doubt, abandoned that 'little monster', that 'James Cagney of babies', while they went to pay 'just a quick call' on Uncle Richard (all these phrases were Rosine's).

The two of them followed the postman down Parker Avenue that afternoon, waited until he had delivered to 'Blakeston' and walked up the drive. Beside the renovated front door of glass and new oak, the rusty doorbell pull hung in the past tense, though its sound always rang somewhere in the future. The ancient mechanism left the present moment, that 'baby moment' (one of my own phrases), unguessably suspended between pulling the lever and hearing the distant tinkle of the future tense. A very usual philosophical conundrum. When the longish white beard of uncle could be discerned through the door glass it represented the future coming towards them with the gait of an old man. No-one could have been more admirable than Uncle Richard, thought Donald as he waited in the sunshine, but from the old man the notion of the present was difficult to capture without his own spiritual endowment.

'I've some new music to play for you.'

Certain remarks open doors for us; the whole sequence of events jumps awkwardly; we cannot assimilate detail. The front doors being already opened, Uncle Richard's announcement about the music opened the door to his study into which he began to move with his *pantoufle* shuffle.

Something slippery certainly entered Donald's mind, for he spotted three newly-delivered letters lying on a table across the hallway, where uncle had placed them before answering the door. He took a sneaky look ahead: one of Richard's hands trailed behind him as the young couple slow-motion-walked at his heels in an epitome of their relationship with him. Rosine's red hair budged from that alignment as she glanced back at Donald who now glided across the hall, skimmed the three letters into his left hand and then stuffed them into a jacket pocket. Back to the study door in time to shut it carefully behind him: the door had its proper instant of closing which he ought not to miss.

Having already indicated that I don't know exactly why Donald did this, I don't find guessing any easier now that I'm about to describe what happened in the study while the old man played the piano. However:

Uncle Richard conducted a cheerful correspondence with anyone who wrote to him. Complete strangers would drop him a line, mention their problems. They must have treasured the answers because they kept on writing. He was locally famous in that line. No-one minded waiting for a reply, always sure that the eventual answer would represent part of his time, shared with them. Uncle Richard had so much time to spare that his minutes ought to have been rich and dense with time, like a baby's. But, his intellect being at the far end of the scale from a baby's, I suppose his minutes were really like those of a joyful crowd; that is, less dense rather than more because so much shared. Donald had a dossier of letters the old man had written to him but, in this sudden whim, wanted one or more written to uncle by someone else. 'Love between two people is expressed most perfectly in mutual admiration of a third party,' Donald had written once in a notebook. 'Love that stops short of this is just ingrown selfishness.' Further, so much did he admire Richard that he wished earnestly to be like him. By stealing a letter, Donald, though imperfect enough, could look from within his love for Richard towards another person's kindness or 'stupidity', see them through the uncle's eyes, and thus join in the perfection of the uncle's selflessness. Therefore to love the uncle himself more truly. That extensive correspondence into which good emotions were poured week after week aroused covetousness in Donald, an anxious poet of the emotions. He could just have asked for a look at some of the letters uncle received. 'But we have to own our relationships with other people, not borrow them,' Donald told Rosine later. And so he stole ten minutes of someone else's good will towards Richard, stealing, that is, a piece of a relationship. (Unfortunately, the whole episode turned into: 'The afternoon Uncle Richard died.') Eventually, Donald had three stolen letters hidden in a miniature wall cupboard near the lounge ceiling in his flat, where they remained stored as though in his brain – a fragment of non-cleverness stored there. Only one of the letters counted much for him; the other two were just mental grocery.

Donald and Rosine stared at uncle's back as he positioned himself, ornate in his red dressing gown, at a grand piano. His white hair is all we shall know of the old man's physical appearance. The sheet music of Liszt's Hungarian Fantasy waited on the piano rest as though it too chose its hour (which was true). Rosine remained in the middle of the room. For a second, an austere daughter who had knowledge of a theft was huge in her lioness role. She turned towards Donald with a conspiratorial smile. Not having the same need she could do that without losing integrity. The law about aiding and abetting is inapplicable here. Kept looking at Donald. He answered with an utter-rejection lip-pursing. Although he had been the thief, he momentarily felt it shameful to continue consorting with Rosine. But she stood sideways on and leant in towards the foreground a little, in the posture of Holman Hunt's *Scapegoat*; so they sat down together on a settee.

The piano music began. Books on white shelves round the room moved restlessly. Donald slit an envelope, pulled out the letter and, to seal the theft, began to read behind uncle's back. Rosine sat back and thought how tall she was. Her knowledge of the theft dominated Donald now and, as every western film can tell us, the more you dominate other people the taller you feel. Similarly for Donald, the upper part of his body, in which the stolen letter held steady at the centre, seemed elongated compared with uncle's back. Donald's legs, however, which had formerly loped across the hall, had ended up dominated by the slow progress of the old man across the study and were now quite short. Western films overlook that 'walking tall' (or 'walking short') doesn't necessarily affect all the body equally; it depends exactly what's going on.

Immediately I said Uncle Richard had a longish white beard you started knowing his beard before you knew him.

Music. I can tell you that his handwriting was light blue and faded. A man afraid of losing his goodness, which had been sorely tested in the 'sea episode'. Yet Donald could never regard him without thinking of the beautiful white underwear of an old man who had nothing to regret. Donald would tell other people: 'I know this man who spent hours in the water after escaping from a ship torpedoed off Singapore,' creating a fictitious heroism in Richard's life to justify him more extensively. This was what I have just called the 'sea episode' and it settles uneasily between fiction and reality: like the sea itself in some moods.

The books on uncle's study wall were stupendously unsurprising. How could he be who he was and read such ordinary books? It added merit. Bergson, de Gaulle, Maeterlinck, Kerouac, books on post-revolution Cuba. For the early 1970s, the bookshelves almost played Handel's Largo. He would have done engravings in the Thomas Bewick style.

Again, when Donald described him he falsified even that: 'Imagine an old man reading a mixture of Kerouac, revolution and Maeterlinck!'

Uncle Richard lived completely alone and I take it you do also.

In those days he had been eating practically nothing but beef extract. To eat only that you have to be of very managed will . . . When I think of the way in which Donald bolted his food . . . As uncle spread the extract on a slice of dry bread he created an analogy with rolling ink thinly across an engraving. He ate with great care, according to an archaic pattern.

'Blakeston' was too large a house, the room too sunny, the piano too large and shiny for its simple role at Uncle Richard's death. And to have the beach at such a short distance has become socially rather slimy in these days. Donald would have preferred uncle to have died in a slum before an old, upright piano, as long as he had kept himself adequately clean so that Donald's readiness for disgust did not spoil things.

I wouldn't call him a good piano player, I wouldn't call him a bad, I wouldn't call him a mediocre. I'm not going to mention all the pieces of music stored in his piano stool that afternoon as Donald sat beside Rosine and read the precious letter, daydreaming all the phrases until it was an outing of his own.

'I have had a most wonderful weekend at the Tacuarembo Hotel, what used to be Conway Manor under county education,' ran the letter.

The (whole) 'idea' of (?) a weekend . . . !

But the desired admiration for that third party could not be found within cynicism and Donald kept going. 'That American company has hardly altered it at all so far, I think you'd recognize most of it.'

Donald continued reading within the sound of Uncle Richard's music until he remembered an afternoon with Rosine and the baby when he had driven them 50 miles down the south coast into New Forest country. On the way out, pausing to buy food in a town near the forest, they had come across the old Conway Manor, already sold by the county education authorities but derelict and awaiting development. He had hopped over the locked gate and stolen some marigolds from the flower beds. Marigolds' bitter scent had always reminded him of the graveside. Lining Uncle Aubrey's carrycot with the flowers, he had whispered to the baby that the maniacally-perfect orange blooms had been kidnapped. Some distance from the manor, bracken in a summer hedgerow had been vivid green . . . Chords of sunshine gleamed on the smallest fragments of leaves, so that if you looked closely few points were a green recognizably that of the overall impression. Through gaps in the bracken he saw potato plants in a field behind, a far perspective of many rows of plants that curved down towards the sea cliffs. The longer he looked the more his eyes in an easy equation judged that the plants' green matched that of the bracken, even that they were the same plant species. He allowed that thought to dominate. He must have wanted that colour blindness, that loss of control. Any idea of detail fled and the will itself became dazzled, aimless, self-negated. An entirely different green, an entirely different life principle, had been confused because of colour rhyming. (He felt very close now to the unknown letter writer who had entered this memory of his own.) Through emotional mood, disparate perceptions had become assimilated: mood colours the lenses through which we see. As he walked back to the future Tacuarembo Hotel, the after-image of green travelled as a brown stain on the grey road covered anyway with real brown stains. Uncle Aubrey swung between them in his carrycot . . . 'We are always talking and thinking what Aubrey's reactions might be to life in general,' said the letter.

Uncle Richard stopped playing. It was in the middle of the Fantasy. The music graciously accepted a new ending, focusing so unexpectedly into a different time-scale that Rosine and Donald had hastily to reorder in their mind every note that had gone before. Quite changed now, uncle's hands rested, while he still sat upright. His eyes were closed just as before. All at once he toppled forwards to kiss the keys in homage to the magnificent ending. Donald couldn't find it in his heart to call uncle melodramatic for dying like that, though it had been an episode with dialogue (the letter), a definite musical accompaniment, sentimental, conventional, with strict attention to poetic justice and a happy ending. Instead, Donald closed the red dictionary and reverently placed it on the piano top by the beloved head. He did not go out hurriedly. Or make an emergency phone call. The curtain had fallen; there was no need to act precipitously any more. He sat gingerly on the edge of the stool beside the old man and placed his hands on top of uncle's hands. He thought of how Wilson, the fantastic athlete in the boy's comic, *Wizard*, had climbed Everest years before anyone else and had taken along Major Frank Duckworth. Duckworth narrated that, near the summit, his body was feeling frostbitten and he did not think he could go on. Wilson simply gripped him by the wrists and warmth surged back, apparently without the usual capillary pain. Now a magical coldness came off the backs of uncle's hands into the palms of the neophyte. Donald's thoughts grew as fresh as frozen food from a refrigerator. They were under control, very small and round, yet so tender, harbouring something like their original flavour.

From now on Uncle Richard was a pearlized shadow and his head was transparent enough to see inside it a duller music fall to the keys as tears. Perhaps it was the rest of the Fantasy playing out. Gratefully, Donald realized that his time, which might equally have come that instant, stretched ahead and the past could be reviewed as happiness. Beside Uncle Richard's moment of thanksgiving as he bowed his head in death, Donald lost his thankyous and reached back to a time of self-centred babyhood. At the death of cleverness stupidity cannot help but smile.

Before the Ricardian phase the lullaby experience.

As Uncle Richard continued to marry himself to the piano in such a virtuoso way, the fascia of the instrument, by the music rest, was seen to smile at him. Not: the funereal piano, having a lifetime function in killing off music, chose this smile as obituary for the uncle's 40 years as her master. On the contrary, the beaming smile came not from the piano that he had at last dignified by marriage; it was a principle sired within her, being born. What can an uncle sire but another uncle? That death had become the authentic Aubrey moment. So nearly original Rosine and Donald could catch the goodwill of the foolish baby in his Cheshire cat smile but saw little of the real shape of the mongol's face. The black lake of the piano fascia had a circular mottling, as though a trace of oil, round the smile.

'Within each system, however clumsy and unintelligent, there must be an essential mathematical diversity between its components.'

Rosine read aloud from a book she had found on the shelves.

'The only substances without this diversity are chemical and without reaction, indifferent to each other and to stranger-substances, a really closed world.'

Rosine had been speaking while Uncle Richard was dying. (The marvellous thing about her was that she struggled so weakly against her primary satisfactions.)

She joined Donald and they watched all that could be glimpsed of the baby regard the elder uncle's death. As I said, the baby and its smile were primary, more fundamental, of a higher spiritual order than this death. Of course, 'spiritual' is an impossible word, hoary with logos and so cranky. I mean by it that even thinking about the infant Uncle Aubrey made him deteriorate in the way a man once claimed in New York that a flowering plant reacted when he thought intently about burning it.

The mongol's burn-prone nose was apt to smudge with charcoal. There was no depinking his breathtaking eyes. His guardians never let picnic onions spoil the effect. Admittedly, it could be hard to tell if he wore the eyes a bit to one side, because the lids – those instant face-deadeners – half hid the inner corners. The interior of the iris ranked as a holy domain and Donald never entered without taking off his shoes. To be truthful, that ceremony always remained a bit kitsch and poorly-lit. Just the iris, then a walk through the oriental temple hall to a bronze statue at the back, with exactly the same smiling buddha on the throne that you saw when you looked at the baby's whole smiling body from the outside. Aubrey had the true blessedness allowed only to the really low in IQ, whose bodies are in their curious way immaculate. If the body becomes discoloured or creepy, coat with a blanket, call an ambulance, and think hard about something else so that you do not harm it any more. But if the skin needs shine checkers, the lips are buttered up and the neck greasy with heat, you can worship in the eye domain. When children are born with some handicap the anxieties and the rejoicing take on a different character.

'Uncle Aubrey's life started as a diminutive tough guy,' said

Rosine, looking at the piano fascia but also thinking of the baby in the museum flat.

'His life started as a diminutive tough guy whom every impersonator has immortalized with the phrase, "you dirty rat",' Donald completed.

Nobody could ever shave the lack of oxygen from the baby's cheeks. From birth on there was a continual bodily deterioration until his leg was found in a rail carriage. His body in a hut. Teeth. Laundry marks. 'Poor little devil – it's a lonely way to die.'

That was a death in the future. Uncle Aubrey knew reality for a moment, was later strangled, but at all times, through all changes, his mongolism, if present in spiritual or bodily form, would preside over any building Donald lived in, making it harmless. Uncle Aubrey was a guardian angel.

2

I've Never Been to Uruguay

Four days later they were, in Rosine's unpleasant phrase, 'warming up for Father's funeral' – which had to wait until Frank's return from Uruguay. One storey up in the museum building, through the Roman gallery full of display shelves, past a door marked 'Private', down a narrow, dingy room lined with broken stone carvings, then in the open door of the curator's flat, along a blue-carpeted corridor, inside Rosine's bedroom, Uncle Aubrey again slept in his carrycot. He too waited for his father's return to England and was, like most babies, punctual. The straw cot on the bedspread was called, however, a Moses cradle, arousing suspicion that he really awaited adoption by some foreigner. As though the love in his own home did not suffice and he had to go looking for more macabre destinies. The cot measured 3 ft long by 1¼ ft wide and an average of 1 ft deep, mounting to 1½ ft at the head end. You'd not think that offered much room to hide in. The cellular blankets were nicely humpy, the taffeta cot lining swelled inwards like bedroom curtains, but when you looked for the head or some visible sign of baby-flesh in the straw enclave, you perceived just a tawny world of shadows. Nevertheless, some presence dreamed there, something unintelligent breathed in gasps, the pillow was truly soaked by tears of dull, benign ancestry.

If I were the kinder man I should be, perhaps I could turn to the mongol baby as to a deity and ask him to fill my lips with praise for Frank, his real father. But with each tip-toed step towards the bedside my prayer falters as my liking for Donald increases; with each step away again my words for Frank become more and more waspish. Frank's face looked OK but his hindquarters left much to be desired.

From the moment he said: 'Fe, fi, fo, fum,'

and Donald called back to Rosine waiting down the dark passage that led to the museum's side entrance: 'Here's Frank,' and Frank said: 'It's all right. I'm harmless,'

and Rosine replied: 'Not to my knowledge,'

and gave him a kiss, though letting her arms train in the blue of her dress,

things began to go wrong.

'The point is, am I welcome?'

'Well, what do you think?' said Donald positively, who'd really been thinking of a negative answer like: 'No-one's now not.'

Frank brought a breath of the Uruguayan pampas to the side entrance: under the porch lamp he was so brown and far-away-looking.

'Who are you, one of the Creadores guerrillas?' asked Donald.

By this name, I suppose, Donald fictionalized the Tupamaros, Uruguay's Robin Hood urban guerrillas of the late 1960s and early 70s. Frank had furthered his career through radical-chic articles supporting these revolutionaries, many of whom at that time rotted in gaols. Donald had always protested that the effect of left-wing flamboyance had been to let vicious military governments seize power.

The visitor was just placing down a mottled blue, light-weight glass fibre with white piping. Just placing down his suitcase. Frank held in his other hand a brown fishing rod case in denim cloth. After his plane flight he smelt of sandwiches and was one of the badly-dressed men. The silky, grey suit crumpled differently from his torso which, behind all relaxation, was alert. Donald took the fishing rod case and they shook hands, both wanting it very much to be 15 minutes later.

'I caught a 5lb shad with that rod in the Montevideo estuary.'

The information was depressing.

'You've shaved your beard,' Donald said. 'You are a bit like Peter Finch playing Oscar Wilde, only younger. That is, like a fatter, early Stewart Granger with larger, lazier eyes. Only not so tall as either of them, more Oliver Reed height, if he really is smaller, it's difficult to tell, though not of course so dark. And much flabbier.'

Despite himself, Donald could not bar the way to a very clear picture which turned back the covers and climbed out of his remarks as though it had been sleeping there all along.

Frank didn't smile. He always did that some other time.

'You've shaved your beard,' said Rosine, as they turned to start upstairs.

'The gain is England's,' said Frank.

'Go on. He's all pink and lovely,' said Donald. Though he could have been speaking immediately afterwards, he was in fact speaking 10 minutes later, Frank having left his luggage at the door of the flat. There the three of them were at last, in Rosine's bedroom, the light not switched on for fear of waking the baby and the carrycot still on the bed, thank goodness.

It was so dark that when all three of them bent their heads towards the cot's interior they couldn't for the life of them see too much inside.

'Your son is a bundle of blankets,' Frank observed.

And that was when Donald, nettled that Frank hadn't for once in his life confessed authorship, replied: 'Go on. He's all pink and lovely.'

'Aren't we all?'

Donald fancied he caught a glimpse of the baby's smile in a long wall mirror. A pink suffusion making him happy.

Rosine noticed. 'You keep worrying away at mirrors,' she pointed out.

Donald stroked the balding patch at his temple.

'It's not as if you're still a working journalist, or then you'd have cause to worry about mirrors,' said Frank. He gave a heavy informative wink to the woman and bent again until his face browsed deep in the carrycot.

'You wink nicely, Frank, but I don't think you're to be trusted in that genre,' Donald replied, prophetically, as they were all standing in a very prophetic darkness.

'No. It's no good,' Frank joked, continuing his browsing. 'There's nothing there.'

Sunday in the museum flat was so quiet. They were suspended within the large mansion as in a miraculous egg formed in the infertile stomach of the dreaming building within the spiritualized body of the dreaming baby. I hope you can get that: the baby as presiding angel, the building within it, the building's stomach within the building, the egg within the stomach. All, all dreaming. Above, below, and on three sides of the flat even the museum's exhibits of the past did not on a Sunday exercise any influence on the present, which was an unguessable present housed in the eggshell's glutinous night.

The lounge was the only room in the whole building whose light was on.

As they entered, Donald quoted: 'I watch over myself and my thoughts like a night watchman in an immense factory, keeping watch alone.'

'I don't think I know that,' Frank confessed reluctantly, choosing an armchair with care.

'Well I'm not exactly sure,' said Donald, as usual avoiding an exact reference.

'So Uncle Richard's house passes to me,' Frank eventually said.

'Yes. It's an old will.'

'Ignoring that, do I get the place soon?'

'Not till after the preliminaries.'

'Whatever they may be.'

'Whatever they may be.'

'Whatever what may be?' asked Rosine, returning from the kitchen with a trayful of mugs. 'Provided one is bloody bold, one doesn't spill it.'

'The preliminaries. We were talking about the inheritance.'

'That reminds me,' said Rosine, immediately going out of the room.

Frank changed the subject again. 'I don't like this lounge when it's got all bits and pieces in it.' He looked belligerently at a collection of Chinese ivories on shelves far across the green carpeted sea.

'I call it the Chinese Baths Cafe,' said Donald, following his gaze. 'Paris, 1795. "The cafe was on the street level and by the number of its windows looked like a cage opened to all regards." It was where Babeuf and his fellow conspirators would meet and plot the world's first permanent revolution. They and the Khmer Rouge in Cambodia were the purest revolutionaries of all – far purer than your Creadores. Horrible. Horreeebul.'

'Don't quote at me. Don't impress me with the curator's possessions. And don't talk to me about revolution while, just for now, I'm a man with an inheritance.'

Rosine returned as though 'inheritance' was her cue once more. She'd only been for the biscuits.

'Won't you have to sell "Blakeston" to get any money from the will?' she asked, in a pulse of her UNTHINKING GOODWILL.

'It'd be a pity, that Victorian loneliness,' said Frank.

'It'd be a good thing,' Donald retorted, and then sidled into the background of his remark. Repetition of the name, Blakeston, had temporarily changed their time encounter and in tandem with that they had a quick shift of body sizes. Frank, huddling up in his chair but a bit larger now than Oliver Reed, leant over to Rosine. Her red hair had lengthened romantically, her face was pinched and smaller, her blue dress very long and flowing. Donald saw a piece of bread which, left on the breadboard since morning, had curled up at the edge, a page turned back, a letter turned in Donald's hands, a secret door near the lounge ceiling offered to open, but the offer was graciously declined. A thought sequence had begun that usually hunted about in Donald's mind until it reached a recess, near the ceiling of his brain, a recess stocked with secrets. The sequence stopped. Simplicity protected from the callous radical. 'At least that cubby hole is secure.'

He relaxed, and with that the museum building, which was in an intimate emotional relationship with him, provisionally accepted Frank. The tall traveller with the speed of the Creadores put aside his coffee and went to the door to get his cases. One more relaxation and the building would even expand generously for him, opening a dusky seascape under its eaves, dragging sand beneath their feet, the building becoming ineffable, fading into the clouds, the time encounter switching to tomorrow as by another turn of phrase. The building: a harmless, lived-in space presided over by the baby spirit of originality; therefore, whangy with the future, vulnerable to the least suggestion, a mere word from me that can flick the space into another day, an interior landscape flicking into an exterior one.

Frank returned with his luggage. His grey suit beautified the pasty-faced door to the colour of an insect bite.

' – of an insect bite,' Donald said. The fishing rod case fell from the doorway into Donald's arms. The lacing of the brown cloth came untied like a dressing gown and he could see the bamboo bone structure. In the abdomen, a hook dangled, trailing a piece of rusty ragworm.

'I want to get some shore fishing in while I'm here.'

'One of your intestines has corroded,' Donald replied, turning back the denim skin to show him the ragworm.

There's the phrase that works the time-switch. From Frank's arrival, bringing his fishing rod into the flat, the interior of the cloth case like a human body's organs, and then the ragworm leading our thoughts outside into a seascape.

They talked of brown estuary mud at sunset, comparing its gleaming patterns to endless stomach muscles stretching towards a tide-line. It was an insufficient idea of the body, because the sand-flesh spread seawards under the lip of the tide and then across the entire ocean floor; no-one could mentally equip that expanse with bodily organs. Inshore, the sand contained little real structure beneath the rippling muscles. Here or there you could dig up a piece of rotten ragworm, a remnant of the sub-oceanic intestinal system. In the spade-hole the worm fragment would come free from black streaks of the lost pattern. You could think of such a vast, flat body suffering, shuddering under clear sea water; but not suffering acutely, merely small fish darting, perturbing the refractions, crustaceans burrowing like an uncomfortable venereal disease. Frank and Donald sensed the tidal movement as a green sheet drawing back from shadowy flesh. The phrases changing time from night to dawn, the new day rapidly passing, the bedroom already gloomy with a new evening. The sun becoming a frump. They, in some other setting. Sand. Their ideas dimmed and they could no longer invest darkened sand with more bodily organs. They did not even know how their own bodies worked. As at all calm moments of obscurity, out came the idealized moon and stars. Not a hint of fear. An expanse of inky yawn. So the words make a night and a day pass. All Frank and Donald had left was ragged knowledge: isolated subterranean data, their bodies like a vast shore in moonlight. How many people can mentally equip a human body with its right organs, correctly arranged – let alone an estuary of sand with *its* under-surface organs and its sub-oceanic implications? Where does each ragworm and cockle have its home? How many people can detail just the passage of food through their own bodies? You see what I mean about the chaos underlying apparently clear statement? No wonder Peter Scott, who seems to know so much about seascapes, flings in a few birds when he paints his sepia estuaries. Sort of arrowy direction-finders.

Frank was as nervous as seaweed about conversations like that. They left the discussion in air, which partly means in the individual breath as potential stopped from reaching some approximate form; partly means the two breaths no longer mingled antagonistically; and partly means the sky was background and natural home for everything they had to say. You will observe that the words have moved them on to a seashore. A populous south coast resort renowned for its level beaches.

The three of them walked back across khaki sand and turned towards Uncle Richard's hut on the promenade. Sandy cliffs had taken the shadows in under their tufty hair, the beach huts looked like a butchers' shambles drawn out into a long line, and white promenade rails up on their little slope above the beach followed the parallels into obscurity. The night was drawing on as pompously as usual.

And, talking of pomposity, the shore fishermen, spaced out along the undercliff promenade as far as the eye could see, were in a mouthy relationship with the shoals of fish that they imagined as tonguing the ocean floor like prose-run-mad. From 50 rods tied to the white rails, the lines dropped seawards down identical idea pathways in the night air. Clothes-pegs gripped the rod-tips and silver bells wavered from them on wiry springs. Fiercely, the fishermen sent their hopes pulsing down those lines and far out into the sea, sinking their hopes down into the gulphs to become fish. At that distance, undersea idea-swarms of fish spread out round the hook. The fishermen each selected one mottled victim from the imagined swarm and by sheer will-power forced it to separate from its fellows and drift backwards towards the hook. At that moment the bell rang on the rod and the fishermen could reel in, masking excitement under phlegmatic countenance. Exaggerated self-importance gave their eyes the same pompous, far-away look that had characterized Frank's eyes when he had arrived at the museum entrance only a day before. The men's mouths moved in reverie far above crumpled newspapers at their feet where the ragworms writhed.

Now a lighthouse, on a fuzzy headland to the left, flashed over the purpling waters. Its beam was a quick indication of ragworms, fishermen, beach-huts, sea, or gulls; and it was clear that 'nestling at the foot of low cliffs' applied equally to all of them. Perching gulls, I mean. Huge rats that lived behind the beach-huts nestled together in a nastier version of the picturesque, however.

As the three walkers continued across the sand, Frank asked, for the first time that evening, 'Where's Aubrey?'

'Uncle is in his carrycot on the promenade by the hut,' Donald replied like a perfect butler.

'Should he be left on his own?' queried Frank, unwarily putting Uncle Aubrey into a syntax of danger.

'It's just for a minute while we come to fetch you,' Rosine said complicitly.

'Your fishing reel could be the mouthpiece of a walkie-talkie radio,' Donald remarked.

The rod-tip trembled ahead of Frank. Behind, the aluminium end of the cork base trailed a line of intention across the sand. The sun had already had its heart attack; the body-image that the shadowy sand could no longer retain retreated into the wind-roughened sea, the 'body of waters'. Rosine placed her wet footprints exactly on the line of the rod-spoor. A crab listlessly handled a stone to one side of their marching.

Frank stopped. He hoisted the fishing aerial and spoke into the mouthpiece: 'This is the Creadores calling the nearest patrol car. We have the ambassador and unless you free the 623 political prisoners he will be executed at 2300 hours local time on Sunday.'

Donald looked at his watch. It was 2100. Curious how there was so often a gap between what he said and Frank's reaction. It was not slowness. More a politically-timed assassination.

The crab lifted itself because it thought of something to say but collapsed back on to its love-object. Rosine caught up with them. Stony silence.

When they had climbed from the shore up slippery promenade steps to the beach-huts they found those modest sheds without intellectual soul. The huts were near that definition, 'indifferent to each other and to stranger-substances, a really closed world'. Unlike a house, a beach-hut could never switch on an upper light and have a sudden idea. The best you could do was to light a candle slowly and an ichthyolatrous flame crept upwards, about as warm as Bob Cratchit's knuckles. Donald went into Uncle Richard's hut alone. The fish-smell was overpowering. The deck chairs were rickety. He sat in one and leant his elbows on the rickety card table. The candle flame was rickety and probably the whole hut was rickety too; anyway a sea gale carried off most of it the following year.

Through the glass door Donald saw the colour-reduced figure of Frank bend down outside the hut as he laid four mackerel on the chilly promenade beside the carrycot in which Uncle Aubrey slept. Rosine and Frank began walking up and down under the promenade lamps, and were talking on guard duty, which was forbidden.

As the observer in the hut lowered his head to the card table his eyelids shuttered down; their night horizons brought their pink levels beyond, then warmly under, the eye.

Donald's favourite realm of inquiry: the eyelid swarm. How, out of the developing chaos of our lives' stories do the patterns emerge? A small-scale demonstration, factual, oh so much more empirical than the fishermen's idea-fish, moves there under the eyelid.

The dots of light that swarmed behind the closed lids (he called this 'the eyelid swarm') had many networks of tension that complicated the mysterious rhythms of self-firing neurons in the brain – a self-firing which, some suppose, causes the dots. But Donald did not choose to live within his own era's scientism all the time. So he concentrated on the eyelid swarm in a mostly-19th-century subjective idiom, full of Coleridgean usages such as 'Will' and 'Understanding'. (a) Minute, amber hyphens and slashes of light were pattern always immanent. Scars and blotches of light were also imposed by: (b) Residue from the retina's daytime energizing; (c) Influence from whatever light still struck the lid outside from the candle, the promenade lamps, the lighthouse; (d) Pressure of the lid on the eyeball, if subjected to a finger-tip's aggression obliterated the emerging pattern; (e) The ever-present background of combinational probability laws that were a more-modern hesitance of the swarm towards pattern, a swirling and sparking; and (f) The Will, now fear-haunted lest Rosine be magnetized away from him, could not leave all this incipient pattern uninterrupted for an instant but reestablished it into new images, fit for dreams.

His quarrel with Frank about Rosine usually became displaced into a bitter political debate: how does the smart-ass betray the proper, honourable emerging of pattern from chaos? So:

(a) He sat at the card table. The name of Uruguay came back to him. Great hordes of people, no sense of social system, a confused attempt to picture a terrain.

(b) He continued thinking feebly about Uruguay, the name of its capital, Montevideo, bits of information streaming forward from the 'daytime energizing', memories of a week's reading about the Creadores urban guerrillas, about the former 'Switzerland of Latin America', about a 'failed essay in democracy'.

(c) A sketchy article by Frank himself in today's newspaper took precedence over these memories because it was more recent and therefore its facts seemed harder. Brash, unstable patterns were imposed across what had been slow energizing. An economic crisis in the 1950s and 60s.

(d) A drink of beach-hut coffee carried farms, shining beaches and vicious cities down Donald's throat and it was, at that moment of swallowing, hard to maintain the mental patterns, which span into a sympathetic whirlpool.

(e) The despairing stipple of 'random' eye-lights returned, the likeness of hordes, a so-called South American pattern, a failure in world wool and meat markets, the emergence of the guerrillas, the hopelessness of governments, military harshness, torture.

(f) The Will searched the past and, as crudely as sword-strokes, scored shallow but vivid judgments across the stream of facts and half-facts. This, a 'political point of view', whether of right or left, which steals the vividness from the present.

Outside the hut, at about this time, one of the mackerel alongside Uncle Aubrey's carrycot disappeared. The fish had been lined up with the cot like exclamation marks on the promenade pavement; it was the one farthest from the cot that had gone. The theft was essentially mysterious. With it, a premonition of loss began life, though at first the premonition was just a fish-shaped body of air hovering above the wet print that the missing fish had left on the pavement. If it makes you feel more secure, ignore the premonition and blame for this theft the rats that lived behind the hut, where it leant against the cliff-face. Then you can revise that error in a minute or two, after assigning the blame has done you good. Donald had no such comfortable stratagem. The kindly world that he had been living in before Frank's arrival shuddered with cruelty. That is, he experienced the presentiment of harm as the fish was stolen but did not think the presentiment strong enough to act upon: and the body-reaction to those tensions is to shudder. After all, you could hardly have a pre-sentiment that the pre-sent moment itself was to be stolen, along with all its hope of benignity.

Rosine and Frank came in through the glass doors and stood on either side of the dark hut. Donald thought they looked very pleasant there, bordered by folded deckchairs, and in a temporary switch of mood felt quite willing for something to be going on between them again. She comprised such a large phenomenon. (A second mackerel was dragged away, and the premonition of loss hopped one space nearer the cot. Rosine and Frank appeared to be treading water at either end of a tawny pool, the candle light reaching up to their necks. Their heads were thus left above water. The bodies could be imagined as naked beneath and willowy in the ripples. Figuratively, Donald could see Rosine's pubic hair, despite that curious green dress decorated with a deeper green clover pattern. In pictures of Ophelia drowning Donald always saw the pubic hair too, despite the dresses and the river weeds. Rosine's patch of reddish please-yourself-really had a movement of its own, floating disconnected in the watery greens, browns and creams of the beach-hut interior. Rosine's fanny hair was nice. The pool was not so much an image, more a lie.

Nevertheless, they sat down under the ripples and in the dizziness Donald saw Frank was grinning. (The third mackerel was taken. The carrycot was not endangered by the hopalong premonition of loss; but still Donald did not trust his feelings.) On the wall of the beach-hut, as on the wall of a poorly-lit public lavatory, Donald was reading a story about Rosine: 'I was walking along at night by the seaside when I saw a light coming from a beach-hut. A beautifull girl (23) was standing in the doorway and calling me over. She had a beach towell over her shoulders and it covered her up. When I got near I saw she had taken off her swimming costume and was nude underneath. She had a lovely red hairy fanny and let me feel it. She saw I was getting hard and took down my trousers.'

'If we want power we shouldn't get lost trying for complete knowledge,' said Frank at another moment.

'A question is, knowing this, what sort of man *seeks* to be a president? To be willing for so much power with so much inadequacy . . .' Donald finished his reply with a locust gesture.

Frank continued with a narrative about his days in Uruguay. (The story didn't simply belong to another country; Rosine and Donald thought it belonged to another century, say ancient Rome. 'Didn't we, Rosine?' Her head nodded every second and a half. What sort of a clock is that?)

'. . . the crowd, as it raced round the building to stone the buses, froze into the pattern of a banana trying to circle an orange. This was a few years ago, my first visit. An hour later, they straggled over the streets, quite elated at having hampered the transport company. A pattern of groups formed, the shape created by individual wills but equivalent to a basic idea that the crowd possessed . . .' (For all Donald knew, the luminous discharges under his eyelids were continuing even while his eyes were open.

Then as he closed his eyes an act of will could not be prevented; patterns snaked among the points of light, filaments quickly burnt yellow; and to ash. The more the concentration the more dialectical change under the eyelid. Yet the sense of dots and patterns always. You could dream of a very young baby's eyelid patterns, so random and little willed, but you could never replace that randoming into your own eyes. Naturally, you can will your death but not your birth.) '. . . I suddenly decided to cross the road and speak to Jose Diaz. His conversation prompted one or two neighbours to repeat the same themes in different phrases   the   cost   oftransport, the sit-ins   at schools, the need to   consolidate workers in a general protest against   increased fares. It   was   true that speculators had helped the country's ruin.   I   ran with   the shadow of the crowd round my   feet. A glimpse of the students, like Romanswiththeirshields, immobile at   the top of   the   Aventine Hill   , right arms threatening to   hurl stones. As soon as I attended to the crowd movements I noticed the guerrilla tactics had begun, the forays of rapidly-dispersing groups.'

(The fourth mackerel had disappeared. The carrycot was now alone outside the hut. Its blankets stirred uneasily.)

'The crowd seems very unoriginal; it could have been Paris,' said Rosine.

'Yes. They were being stage-managed,' said Donald. 'Babeuf and his followers would do just the same back in 1795.'

'If in some way the crowd were not given a will it would be sucked into a whirlwind and would no longer act; it would be shapeless. Besides, you've forgotten the genuine issue of the bus fares,' said Frank sharply.

'Not a whirlwind,' Donald replied, thinking of the earlier dimple in his cup of coffee, or his throat swallet, of the madness of Antonin Artaud, and of the twister tornado in *The Wizard of Oz* which sets going such a sizeable proportion of the film's plot.

'A large crowd's originality is impossible to pin down, because the overall rhythm always seems unoriginal, a simplification. But it masks smaller pulses of creativity. The pulses must be present,' said Frank. 'A caucus can be original, or the invisible manoeuvres of three people in a crowd, two, one . . . one person's courage at a certain moment within a certain tensional network.'

Rosine suddenly froze. 'Where's Aubrey?' she said hoarsely.

'Any crowd is only a battalion in a sort of world crowd,' Frank finished.

'Outside with the mackerel, I suppose,' said Donald, but he had the same doubt.

Rosine jerked at the beach-hut door which swung brusquely open onto a carrion void from which gentleness had disappeared. The three of them saw that in the hut they had been living on a small stage: they had to step down. The sea flashed its teeth spasmodically in the blackness. A lunar wind came from the void where the mongoloid moon had vanished. The sense of loss they at last experienced was timeless. They realized that Uncle Aubrey's originality was most authentic when he could not be found. Again and again that stupid originality had surprised them and it surprised them now. Yet those who misappropriate it for reasons of power are deep-dyed criminals. On the pavement by the hut were four wet patches, two or three bits of straw.

Frank began to reconnoitre. Down the promenade to the right: blank. To the left: blank. The sand: desolately, obscurely blank. Behind the huts: rats. The sea: don't be ridiculous – the best clue to Uncle Aubrey's whereabouts you'd get from the sea's carelessness would be a low whistle of amazement coming across the wave-tops from the horizon.

As Frank came back, Donald's eyes strayed from fixity: he was erring badly that night.

'Even if I think Uncle Aubrey is better gone, I don't think it's better he's gone,' said Frank, who had come back with nothing in his arms. All three were tremendously sure that they would not find the baby.

Rosine said: 'But I'm not seeing very well. It can't be.' Her body could contain only part of the fear that tried to rise in her: the rest of the fear remained outside as promenade lamplight.

'I suppose we must really hunt about first,' said Donald.

They turned to begin what all felt was a hopeless search but a wild shout sounded from about half-way up the black cliffs. What they could see of the slopes waved shrubs and bushes at them, but that was too near at hand. A man's voice. Farther up. It might have been hailing them: 'Hey! You down there!' Or the shout may have been 'Abracadabra'. Either way, its effect was magical. The three friends stared upwards into the night and their eyes homed on a single lamp-post placed near the top of the cliff-path at an awkward turn. The distant circle of light created a magic vignette, a peep-show. A small group of men, impossible to say how many, perhaps a woman, hurried from nowhere into the lamp's misty haloes. They were carrying something up to the cliff-top.

That peep-show of movement passing through a single phase play-acted classical problems of how time passes through an instant. As the group of men crossed that phase a new time-relation sprang to life for the three watchers on the promenade, succeeding the timeless moment of loss. A desperate conviction seized the three of them that the men's burden was Uncle Aubrey. The cliff-face skull-duggery was not so far above them, perhaps 40 yards up the steep path. Together, Frank, Rosine and Donald sprinted towards the concrete gateway some 200 yards away that signalled the path's entrance. As they sped along the pavement, a huge fisherman wished them goodnight. It was the least he could do. Asphyxiated in the lunar wind, carrying the Creadores' message in whispers across the waters . . . 'we have the ambassador' . . ., a smaller fisherman called out, 'Mind how you go.' A woman in a red, woollen hat took in the flash of the lighthouse beam and rocked back and forward against the white promenade rails, working off her stomach wind, probably – and also feeling deprived each time the light passed her; so rocking in a deprival motion that was nicely apt for all concerned.

Frank skidded round into the path first, one hand steadying himself on the entrance pillars. Rosine was close behind and Donald at her side. The walls of the defile closed head-high on either side.

Who says 'sick with fear' should for the benefit of medicine stop to explain himself. But we have no time now. Running savagely uphill. Throats in addictive spasms of breathing. The cliff path smelt of seaweed and strangers. Clothing like startled crows. The baby was a pink mind-cloud close above their heads. They hurried up the steep path towards a more-distant mental vignette of men with a carrycot; but the vignette idea lodged very obstinately up the cliff beside the remembered lamp-post. They could not will that idea higher or lower, so sharp had its impression been. Unfortunately, the robbers had certainly passed on by now and left that misty cameo bereft of human significance. They were therefore chasing a phantom. The damp stone walls of the path obligingly slipped downhill beside them as they ran on an apparent treadmill. Their legs stalled at the thigh each time the foot struck the upward road. The slapping of their soles and the admiration of their breath intake applauded the kidnapping whether they liked it or not. Frank increased his lead, reached the lamp-post, went past it and disappeared round the fishy bend. At that second, the other two heard a car start somewhere on the top of the cliff. The engine revved hard; the car drove off. Frank's fault. He shouldn't have run through the magic vignette: by doing so he created another movement which passed through that single phase. Thus he triggered off a new relation of loss, but this loss was no longer timeless and therefore could end badly.

Rosine stumbled, righted herself against the path's side-wall, and began walking. She was badly winded, but gasped at Donald: 'That's them.'

She referred to the car and it was all the proof that Donald needed to persuade him Uncle Aubrey was being whisked away by his captors. He waited for her: for a second they gained breath, then continued upwards at a steady walk, reaching the top in time to see Frank racing across bumpy grass towards the nearest houses.

'Police,' said Donald unnecessarily. He hadn't brought the car.

For a change, she came to him. He held her loosely. The lighthouse beam swept by and the darkness across the sea below was briefly caused to have a lighter backcloth. Donald was bleached in the flash, out to dry, sprayed black, and then he quickly faded to his natural night colour again: he was squeezed back into shape like a meatball. His limbs felt slightly doughy in the wind. He sent out direction arrows from a central point in his chest to replot the internal body territory at all limits south of his gullet and more direction arrows from just behind his eyes to all parts of his head. Strangely, there was little difference in the time taken by each set of arrows to accomplish its mission, though clearly the head arrows had so much less distance to cover. The conclusion was inescapable: one of those arrows goes more cautiously whenever the internal space is more emotionally complex.

3

The Dividend

Uncle Richard's funeral was a moment in the overall series: twice the crime plus the one you first thought of. With the death of pattern, originality is whisked away.

No-one had responsibility for the funeral arrangements *in toto*, except for the body-conveying part, handled so nicely by the undertaker. 'My nice undertaker,' said Rosine in a kind of phrase Donald loathed. For the rest, anything might happen, though very little did. This explained the funeral's success. Mostly, it was a touch of the chatters, a touch of the astral, plenty of sunshine, some pretty gardening, and a long wall, covered with plaques, which led to the red brick of the crematorium 'chapel'. Frank had parked the car down the road, for cars of early arrivals cluttered the gravel driveway. The undertaker, a fair-haired young man with chuckles in his job that matched the blond hairs on his black suit, welcomed them at the building's entrance. The architecture was concrete Greek and its pillars snuffed out the sun between their fingers as the mourners went through tall, engraved-glass doors. Inside the chapel, the pews were packed.

. 'All the corresponders,' murmured Rosine, looking round the light oak seats where women in bright prints sat shoulder to shoulder with many kinds of men. To be clearer, many, many kinds of men.

'Aren't the seats an unfortunate match for the wood of the coffin?' Donald gossiped to the undertaker, thinking also of his blond hairs.

Rather than chuckle this time, the young man gave a grimace that was part of his repertoire. Donald didn't mind because doing that job by god you need a repertoire of some sort.

Unfortunately, though most crematoriums manage without tombstones, they still have the memorial plaques, books of remembrance, and gardens of this and that. The stonework inside the chapel is yellow ochre, the light from the cupola is ice-cream colour, the chiselled lettering on the wall plaques is staunchly Times Roman, and the Hammond organ's oak matches the pews, matches the coffin. I'll cut the description at this point, because all this decor places an intolerable burden on our emotions called into banal order at such a time. So, as you read this paragraph please think anything you like. Have a cup of coffee by you as you read. Behave as normally as your digestion allows. Only don't feel reverent on my account. We've all got organisms to heave along from one minute to the next. I look forward to the first burial in a cinema, with a plaque in the aisle that is illuminated from within when the house lights go down. Perhaps in several decades' time, when the world has been at least severely shaken, the ancient magic of description may revive. But for the moment there's nothing supernatural left in it. So if I happen to drop a few clues and, despite yourself, some pleasant scene emerges, that's just kindness on my part.

Or weakness.

No address. No music. No service. Just a short wait.

They looked up at the cupola and listened to the gaily coloured conversation around them. In front, by the wall, the brand-new coffin – well, they're all brand-new aren't they? – rested on stainless steel rollers. Food packing plants. Black-suited blondie lurked tactfully, another item in his repertoire, waiting to 'send Uncle rolling'.

Though I don't believe in reincarnation, it's pleasant to think of a painless identity that gradually becomes motionless in the body when it dies. Just a single direction arrow, broad and thick, sulking in the middle of the chest like a grumpy lungfish. Then in cremation there'd be a crazy moment when the arrow explodes into a transmigration of little arrows hurled into the air. They wing into the sky and fly south as autumn begins. If you do believe in reincarnation that would be a moment to believe very strongly.

Donald glanced at a very old man four rows away, who earlier that day had been digging his garden in Liars' Avenue. He was talking to a brownberry lad about nine years old beside him and for all Donald knew was stroking his thigh. No harm in that. The boy's mother was on the other side and you can't deny the elderly every bit of pleasure.

Pleasure was a key word. The 'ceremony' was pointless but

pleasurable. As though pen friends had met for the first time after years of corresponding. Donald hadn't the heart to give the signal to the undertaker which would end that companionship. Messages of love and mourning clung to the walls; under their aegis every other emotion was shielded. The angelic hand shielding the thigh; the boy a growing man. As for the mourners' age generally, that can best be stated as lonely. Think of various lonely ages and there you have it. Top hats, black veils and slow movements go mostly with mourners who have full social lives. Here the women's hats were selfless expressions of vanity, a concept I personally believe in. Previously, these people had been invisibly linked through their correspondence with Uncle Richard; now they were visibly linked by their conversation about him. The warm smell of their own living flesh was in their nostrils. You could not call it a sea of faces, but even that, as a negative statement, gives a fair impression.

This noise, this gaiety among the lonely, should have been maintained as long as its internal tension would allow. But, most annoyingly, Frank flicked his fingers at the undertaker. Blondie turned and whispered through a stone grille in the wall. The coffin started to slide along the rollers. Curtains parted. All conversation stopped. After Frank's signal (not the agreed one because Donald was to have nodded his head) the undertaker must have thought: 'The other man's too upset. His friend has murmured to him, "Had enough?" and he's nodded back, "Yes"; the cousin has flapped his hand at me. Seems to be all right then. Yes, I'll give the word to Dirk.'

It's hard to blame Frank for again pushing time forwards a little faster than natural. Consider his internal irritation of mind, mental reluctance to dally, concern with the aesthetics of speed. Blame him, though.

There was only one thing left to do in the chapel after the coffin passed through the wall. That was fondly to imagine the roar of the furnace, which was probably the coffin being dragged off its rollers and stacked to be dealt with later.

When all the people had gathered outside, it was even plainer from their gravelly footsteps that they didn't know each other. They stood in ones and scuffed the stones, or at the most scuffed them in groups of two and three people. Donald did the best he could, hurrying from one person to another, but the connection lines formed by his passage faded too quickly behind him. Rosine and

Frank stood to one side talking as gravely as they were able to 'their undertaker'. All Donald's hurry could not prevent these people from getting into their cars and the roaring sound as they drove off made him say, 'That's the second cremation Uncle's had today.'

'I hope it's the last,' said Rosine with very little prospect of being right.

When the cars had gone and the pedestrians were safely walking down the driveway, she added: 'You should take on his mailing list.'

'I wouldn't have the same time.'

They were tallish, the three of them and that undertaker, who refrained from sympathy. That restraint itself was a service worth £78.20.

'Do we get a dividend?' asked Rosine, as it was a co-operative society who were handling the funeral.

'We should have had music,' said Frank.

'All the music has already been played,' Donald said, referring to Uncle Richard's piano-playing activities at the time of his death.

'I think the next time we ought to have music,' joked Rosine.

'While it is always possible to alter an ending, even after it has ended, we should end with this ending for the moment. I name that an alternative definition of the word: teleology,' said Frank, who used such words as situational punctuation.

' – Or eschatology,' Rosine added even more inaccurately, like a wavering dash after an untidy colon. If she didn't take Frank's arm she made an anticipatory plan of doing so inside her head and aborted the plan into a small shoulder shrug that didn't escape Donald's eager eye.

'Did you notice something about Uncle Richard's funeral?' he asked as a diversion.

'No.'

'That's the thing about funerals; there's nothing to notice, unless you're some sub-species of Edgar Allan Poe; and he's extinct, isn't he?'

'You'd never guess it,' said that determined film fan, Rosine.

They were standing in the Garden of Memory but could hardly remember even why they'd gone there. Around them was a low, well-cut laurel hedge of a kind forever associated with croquet matches. On the other side was a school sports field. The Garden of Memory was fairly small, considering its function (even granted the small size of memory itself – in germ, that is). The soil was studded with paid-for rose trees. Beyond the hedge a school hockey match had started; the first of term probably.

'There should be more than three of us left,' Donald said desperately.

'There should be Uncle Aubrey left,' said Rosine. They hadn't heard anything about the baby from the police.

They sat down on a new wooden seat sporting a donor notice in brass, and looked at the neatly-weeded flower patches.

'Three's the number we started with.'

Just a sickly garden full of ash.

'They should have Human Baby Seed for this garden,' said Rosine.

'When you think of Uncle Richard what do you think of?' Donald asked.

Frank: 'I think of a Bewick engraving.' (Difficult to see how he could have plagiarized this remark.)

Rosine: 'I think of a hotel where all the guests are talking, even the lonely people.'

Donald: 'I think of things that are pacific, like quiet oceans, rolling piano chords, patterns of kind behaviour, ignorant of harm.'

'You can't make ignorance a virtue,' said Frank.

'Well, resolving of harm. I was reaffirming the virtue of kindness.'

'You shouldn't take Uncle Richard's death too hard,' Frank told him.

(Donald wasn't taking it at all hard!)

'Deary old me,' Donald commented, but it was an auto-criticism.

'You are so innocent,' Rosine said, fondly but treacherously.

After a moment he replied: 'That's not a bad thing to be.'

'You baby,' continued Rosine inexorably in a situational punctuation more natural to her.

'Yes. Patterned kindness. Or otherwise moments of near originality, moments or places in which there is no harm,' Donald replied impulsively. 'That's what I'd like to see: not careless revolution but a pink and lovely baby full of kindness sitting in the middle of Uruguay, in the very heart of political process: all the shrewdness and toughness extending outwards only from that.'

'Are you criticizing the Creadores?' asked Frank.

'Not exactly. I don't want to support hard-line governments. I don't want to toy with poverty. I don't even want to mention the

Creadores. And if by some accident of mental energy I do happen to mention them, or if in some conversation I get stuck with the subject, as I'm stuck with it now, I just end up embarrassed. What good's my kindness to anybody?'

'When will you ever step beyond it?"

'I am worried by the harm I already do.'

Rosine, who had been counting the wooden notices saying which rose tree belonged to which memory, said: 'I imagine harm as an astral body.'

Donald replied: 'Two people together produce an astral body that is as large and diffuse as how they feel about each other and what memories they share. Three people produce a larger body. A crowd produces a large, Grecian god that lies along the clouds. It might be harmful or not.'

'You and crowds,' said Frank. 'I'm more interested in what they do and in what people of brighter consciousness can make them do. Crowds vanish into history and historians mostly fake them up. To act effectively they don't have to issue a coherent manifesto, or leave some document behind.'

The sun was warm, the situation like that of three elderly people sunning themselves on a park seat; the emotional clash between them yawned and went to sleep. On the hockey field the sash team gained the ball.

'To produce an effect on people you don't even have to have a coherent meaning,' said Donald. It was suspiciously like a manifesto, that.

4

War Films in His Lungs

Two hands gripped his shoulders and a voice whispered at the base of his neck: 'Civilizations give birth to a spirit which rules over civilizations to come.'

Donald span round.

Rosine was in the kitchen. 'Did you call, Don?'

The voice had been that of the Magus Lagnel but he could not identify the hands. They were phantom.

That's what comes of trying to take up a few tobacco shreds of thought and weave them into a cigarette. It was improbable that the voice was, as you might say, right. All the same, the whisper was one of those 'why not?' comments, full of non-dialectic proto-Hegelianism. 'Why not?' extend it to personality, and declare that our qualities create a spirit which reigns over our children, over our own futures? Donald's knowledge of later philosophies did not alter the voice's compulsive hold over him and the hands had touched him too firmly. He smoked and worried. If you allow fear and malice to stockpile in your own body image you may create a very nasty spirit indeed.

The flat's door opened, and Frank, who had been fishing, burst in gaily and showed him a 2 lb sea-bass with as much pride as if it had been a 2 lb penis. 'Click,' he said, as Donald appeared so unwilling to work any shutter mechanism. Frank stumped off to Rosine, who said: 'Really, your waders, never mind, what is it?, oh you mean a little checker.'

They had a quick passing game with it, during which the kitchen door slammed shut.

'By the way,' Donald called out to the door, 'I'm giving up smoking. This'll be my last two.'

Eventually the door opened. Frank came out, took off his waders and anorak, and sat opposite him in underpants and stockinged feet.

'It's to confirm intellectual strength,' Donald said. 'Some late psychological repair. An acquisition of bravery.'

In the past, Donald had helped this man often enough with his newspaper assignments until their political differences had sharpened. Now as a change he decided to confide in him. He told Frank quite a lot that morning as they sat facing each other. But Frank only pretended to listen while the theme of occasional impotence kept weakly reflecting from the brick wall in front of them. That is, the flat's window was almost in touching distance of the slanting side wall of the main museum building. The glossy brick was sinuous with the last smoke. Perhaps he didn't make things dramatic enough. What appeared to hold Frank's sympathy most were the early morning cups of sweet tea, the wonderful intentions, the knowledge of two people helplessly diverging, sitting up in bed at night trying to be reasonable, the shared cigarette, the therapy of pornography. No need for Donald ever to abort his goodness because it was already infertile with humiliation and fear. Cigarette smoke rushed from his nostrils. Frank breathed the smoke in and then breathed it out as though it had been his all along. Not even to recognize your own cigarette smoke any more. With Rosine daily becoming less patient, and the baby gone, the museum flat itself was the only refuge Donald had left. The building wrapped him up so warmly as if still imbued with baby presence.

In the evening he went out alone to see his second war film that week. The director's cruelty of intention unsettled him. An airman, captured by the Germans, was allowed to see through a chink in his cell wall a neighbour being beaten with metal-tipped whips. When the airman himself was given electric shocks, the pain pulled his strapped body nearly upright, like sitting up in bed. At that Donald left the cinema.

By 3 A.M. his chest was winded with panic. He lay where Frank had already lain that night and tried not to roll down the mattress to Rosine.

Well, there you go, wanting to know how Frank got on with her while Donald was out. Given India, the possibility that stars are animals and that the outer surface of the universe is of polished wood, jealousy is a pretty flippant emotion and Donald had never wanted anything to do with it. Easily said. Still, he was more concerned about his chest right then.

His eyes open, searching the bedroom darkness for some reflection of his personality . . .

Frank's sympathy was in braille. To get anything out of it you had to agree to be blind to his facial expression. An undertaker's sympathy could not have been more worrying.

Now, you can't live on photographs of yourself. It's not as though you could give a man like Frank a 4 ft by 4 ft blow-up of your face and say here hold this I've some problems to discuss with you. Probably Frank would have shrivelled from frustrated ambition, sitting there holding the huge photo, trying to see round the edges. What that confidant really wanted to do was to swell to the stature of counsellor or judge or burglar and no matter who was telling him what.

Frank was getting too large. When he spoke a canary prattled from a mountainside.

Frank's domination placed a bedtime ache under Donald's ribs on the left-hand side. Under his pyjamas, at some deep level, the ache was an alternative identity to that part of his self-awareness which inhabited the chest. The proper chest-identity became merely a turbulence across the whole region, a whiffle-pink. The ache, much more precise and urgent, kept itself to itself, blinking at regular intervals and obviously wide awake. One of his images of cancer was of the frightened identity finding just such a precise hidey-hole for itself; an alternative growth centre which one day could become uncontrollable.

Some things Donald had to keep strictly in order. His image of certain vital organs, for example. He liked his lungs neatly parted down the middle by a piece of new rubber bronchial tubing, a heart which was not a gulper, not a fierce worker, an epigastrium laid out with as little fuss as a tidy transistor circuit, and a particularly small stomach – knitted up in tartan like souvenir bagpipes, if that's gayer for you.

Donald thought: 'Let doctors work out exactly how domination kills us. It's so essential to lie in bed and know there's nothing wrong within all that torso apparatus. Does wonders for your identity. If your insides are all right, there's nothing wrong with your politics: could he dare as far as that?

'You dominate me? As Epictetus said, there shall be a statue to you, as to the Goddess of Fever in Rome.

'Can anyone tell me why we don't have just one lung across the middle, the shape of a sailing dinghy's ballast bag? Nature's safety measure in case the lung becomes diseased? Safety, my arse! We couldn't manage a single site for our chest-identity. Binary is essential. The lungs-identity goes with our symmetrical make-up. No accident another identity sits in just behind the eyes. As far as chest-identity goes, the heart's a fake; ask anyone who is in love. It's the first of the really important organs to fail when we're having really lethal personality trouble.'

Twisting and turning beside Rosine, Donald felt the treachery of wrong air pressure between various enclosed body areas from anus to brain. He already knew the role that constipation, flatulence, starved lungs, short-windedness, heavy sighs, and gullet swallowing played in his hypochondria, depression, and cigarette addiction. Now his mind waited for the body signals which served that hypochondria: trapped air pockets that stabbed like cancer, or casual muscular aches that could be the heart's. He passively allowed anxiety about these signals to amass and rise like an air pressure either from the stomach sphincter up the oesophagus, or from the petrified lungs up the trachea. The two anxieties merged at the gullet's threshold, which was reinforced as an area of yearning. Yet the anxiety, still like an air pressure, rose quickly past his throat, up through imagined air channels inside his head until its pressure numbed the foot of the brain.

That night he didn't need mind over body in the sense of an idealizing mind elegantly resting on the pillows at the end of a horizontal stalk. Instead, he needed the mind collecting a counter-knowledge of health, again like an air pressure, that with steady will behind it would push the anxiety back downwards through the imagined air channel to the gullet. There, a second mental thrust is needed to split the harmful anxiety and force it down both trachea and oesophagus until each piece of worry is safely back in its site of origin, where it peters out. The pain goes, the alternative identity site is eliminated, and the flesh stays healthy. Then it's up and do battle for the honour of love and for the cause of goodness and patience in politics.

While he struggled to collect this counter-knowledge, his heart was unattended to and all at once inconveniently floated upwards, dividing into two hearts which rested one on each of his lungs. The lungs must therefore have looked like the wings of a peacock butterfly. From the brilliant schizophrenia patterns in his eyes, open or shut, and from the blurting film voices in his ears, he could guess the effort his brain was making.

We should be at least 60 before such hypochondriac thoughts assail us. His 30-year-old body was not ready for them, not complacent enough. He had strayed into these thoughts through a mixture of bumptiousness and fear. Consequently, despite the warning of only a few hours before, he inadvertently called up a new premonition of harm, which lightly rose from the image of his own body and left the bedroom.

Ever since that night he was to think of his chest's health as deteriorating, though he never smoked again.

5

Travel Warrant

If you suffer badly from premonitions wait until the date of the feared event is nearly due, then go on a voyage. That's my advice. It may be a premonition valid only for a very short time. Of course, it may have a travel warrant. Or it may be a stay-at-home-and-wait variety. When a premonition escapes from your chest the way Donald's had, it may combine both travel and lie-in-wait qualities, and that's the worst of all.

There's no problem with precise prophecies, such as 'You're going to break your leg.' You just say to yourself, 'What a darn nuisance,' and lay in the detective novels in readiness.

Donald's premonitions were always so vague. This time it was just as though one morning an anonymous telegram had arrived which read: 'FOR NEWS OF CHILD CATCH 2000 TRAIN TO NEW FOREST TUESDAY'.

Whether the telegram arrived or not, and the point is hardly important, his own body contained the knowledge: 'Stay at home . . . go for a trip . . . either way it's going to be FRIGHTFUL.' With some foreboding, he plumped for the train voyage.

The minute he decided to leave, the museum building came crowding round sorrowfully to wish goodbye.

As he walked through the museum its genial imbecility pushed at him: it wore the mottled smile of the inachieved, strangling in god-like episodes. Wasps zig-zagged powerlessly down the focus of his eyes, the road of rooms. A museum full of dead skin, imitation Koh-i-nohrs quite enough in lighter places, glint inside a historic make-up case, white shoulders of unlabelled birds, a remembered name, Mercedes McCambridge, the Italianate fountain incontinent with happiness, such cratefuls of splendour, little to recapture, he just passed through, a tray of gold.

Unintelligence tried to form words for its destiny of incomprehension. Aligned doorways called to him with sounds nearly like forgive. At night there, unpardoned, he had always looked helplessly for attendants and was borne through the middle of this bonaventure, foolish god, this building within the vast buddha-presence of the dreaming baby: its the dogfish-coloured hearts, the whiff of formaldehyde; its the goodwill like his in the showglass. He would travel from there still in the service of the mongol, some creature others keep in an attic, but which in the museum had all the harmlessness it needed.

He paused in the Roman gallery before going through to the flat. The curator had said: 'You can sleep in the far room past these shelves. I've transferred my furniture. We have made arrangements with a security guard service. You need only agree to a small amount of responsibility, just at night-time. The museum visitors need not concern you. It'll be fine for you and Rosine.'

For 10 months the security guards had behaved as if he were the fearful president of a rebellious country, suspended in wing of a white Georgian palace. His life was very safe in the insurance policy, where he was specified by name, back-referred to in case anyone had forgotten, put on his honour, allowed many freedoms and generally used as a skeleton for a very cold sum of money that because of him became almost mammalian.

When he entered the flat it was nearly tea-time. Rosine took up a shopping bag of green plastic net and held it against her dress, absentmindedly seeing if it would match. Her dress was red. Her wig was fawn. Her stockings were red to match the dress. So were her shoes. And her face was temporarily red from bending down. She was wearing this dazzling white blouse! It was so white! Donald thought it would burst! That was what he noticed mainly as she left the room!

Frank and he looked at each other irresolutely until Donald foamed and creamed and rolled sideways as part of the white wake of Rosine. Frank shrugged like a tug-boat and swung away to his room. He was soon typing something for one of the weeklies.

Should Donald leave him the curator's flat and Rosine? It would be two hostages. Well, at least he could lend him his interest in both, as far as the hostages would allow. And his Neville Chamberlain umbrella, despite the rain, which I should mention had lightly begun. Donald could nip off round the corner of the building while Frank was still fumbling with the ratchet mechanism up the handle.

By the time Rosine got back, the fugitive would already be on the train; with luck, if that's what you call it.

The cowardice in this solution made it at best a partial escape and Donald Kipfer did not get clear of the triangular relationship with his whole person intact. The triangle, you could say, had one of its sides missing but there were still dots to show where it had been.

6

Dorothy

To avoid fear, Donald had hurried to the rail station. He was unaware that fear was presently out of reach and in the clouds; its path was being tracked by frightened met men who called it Hurricane Dorothy. The rain-dampened crowd on the station platform had the stony sadness that hints at how happy the bearers are normally. Even the big engine, which should have come in with greater complaint, stole in very glad really and the buffet car jumped up and down excitedly.

At the head of the train, the other passengers gave way as diminutive Donald Kipfer parted them like an actor finding his way through the curtain, or like a housewife, having finished her washing and hung it up to dry, pushing her way through damp towels and into the door of the discarded rail carriage she uses as a home. The open-plan front carriage was full. Two mothers, each with one child, sat on every bench seat, except one that had providentially been left for our Donald. He sat there feeling quite improper without a baby to hold, a dress to smooth down, knitting in a paper bag to place on the table in front of him. His penis curled up in his lap and went to sleep like a dormouse. Not wanted on voyage, he mused, but was later that night to be proved wrong. With all those babies, the sense of home-life strengthened. Donald looked crossly at the pairs of mothers. We'll see who remains mistress of the domicile throughout this tragedy-wreaking night.

Behind and before him, the children hung off their mothers' knees, their collars held as by coat-hooks. One child leaned back against the side wall and stretched his arms outwards, laughing, advert for rio bravo with john wayne, and dying a little because happiness and advertising are so alike in ambiguity and in all situations something should bespeak the death-dealer. Just then, the cheek of it, a Frenchman came along the platform to sell watches. As Donald leant out of the window, the salesman held a smart time-pacer to his ear and its definite tick made the stainless steel mounting precious. The watch looked fine; instead of a second-hand, a miniature Father Time nodded backwards and forwards, which was charming. Too quickly, the Frenchman muttered something about customs evasion, evasively stroked his dark moustache, and slipped sideways with Donald's money, not handing over the change. The grass skidded backwards. The carriage went past three small girls and wind raised their tiny skirts in successive farewells. Donald could not stop. There was the rail carriage to clean, caught up in the developing hurricane.

He did some dusting, took a vacuum cleaner to the filthy strip of carpet that ran down the middle of the lurching home onwards. The mothers looked bored. They swayed their knees in rhythm with the hurricane journey and hugged their unwanted children as though they were the last things on earth. One or two women glanced up to say: 'Bereave me.'

Nothing easier.

The sideways nudges in the onwards motion were small moments of fear like gusts of wind buffeting the carriage sides left and right; Donald knew them, however, as a wayward potential of the wheels that made him think of the phrase, 'not necessarily so'.

Returning to his seat, he listened again to the watch. It had stopped already. Father Time, caught on a back stroke, looked aghast. Equally disturbing was the train's lack of location. He had as much idea of where he was as a baby in its pram. (They were to pass through several genuine English towns with names like Lyndhurst, but no-one was able to believe in them. Instead, the landscape, speeding by in darkness, shrank from recognition.)

Donald rested cold fingertips on the moribund green tabletop. He was brooding on Rosine's view of Frank's doctrines about Uruguay as they affected his own doctrines of babydom and seeing all this in the light of regret at Uncle Richard's death. Should he play in finger language one of those little melodies of Liszt which he liked so much? He let his heart loose at that; it stayed a cowardly centrepiece.

From time to time, one of the mothers took a protesting child to the lavatory and that was a minor backwards and forwards within the onward race, a race going nowhere like an instant trapped between two ticks. The heart seemed to have gone out of the major journey already and its pulse became likely to falter at any minute.

How did Donald measure the pulse of the journey? Well, the carriage windows were black but oscilloscope displays of passing light flashed across at regular intervals. In their role as electro-cardiograph screens, the windows promised a catastrophe.

He punched the empty seat beside him and found comfort in the answering wave of dust. It witnessed that the seat's faded grey pattern had served for many years – many years, many ghostly seconds, it didn't matter which; horse-hair, grey bone spiking through.

The dust's welcome smell did not last. The passengers brought too much rain in with them. 'Tonight the smell of fear is rainy in the subverted smoker.'

An hour passed like this and the journey's pulse was growing increasingly crisis prone. The windows shook in their frames and lights burst across their screens.

From his jacket pocket he took a blue notebook and began to jot down some ideas: 'Broken glass was among the grey railway stones. Broken glass was the brightest principle among grey chippings. Broken glass was grimy among the stones. It was too dark to see where the shattered window glass had gone. Most of the windows still had their glass. The jagged windows and draughty corridors. Broken glass was the brightest principle in the dark corridors but in compartments some of the glass had become vermillioned.'

As Tuesday night drew on there was no storm and the steady rain had eased. The weather bureau reported that Dorothy had slowed down and would not arrive until 10 o'clock. Still nothing happened and a dead calm descended. 'It's very impressive; nothing is moving,' said one of the mothers, as the countryside hurtled past.

'Guard your child well.'

People thought that the train was in the safe eye of the hurricane and were not worried when a quarter of an hour later a slight wind and considerable rain began. Visibility dropped badly.

'I thought it was the storm's second phase and that it would soon be over,' a survivor said. 'We settled down in our seats, reassured.'

They had all been fearing wind, but it was the derailment that swept everything in its path. Many people, surprised in their sleep by the torrential accident, could do nothing to save themselves.

The rain obscured the future. It slowly dawned on the engine driver that lights, apparently of a near-stationary train in front, were a very serious addition to knowledge. Maybe counterfeit angels were abroad that night and gentled him with prospects of becoming a saviour: 'Believe us, liar.' He may have had great hopes of saving at least his own reputation and heaved quite cheerfully on the brake lever. Perhaps he rammed the train in front. These details were never clear. At all events, the front train somehow sped into the mist (supposing there really *was* another train). The carriage wheels which had been going Uruguay, Uruguay, did a quick Phnom Penh, Red Khmer, then went silent, while down the line the sepulchres screamed and Donald's hand was at his heart, that resting-place for blood. They were slowing fearfully quickly. The train rode its hellish skid. Round the passengers the carriage walls timeless heaved, swayed gradually over to one side, while the passengers were crushed against each other and thought, 'Ooooooer'. With admirable poise, Donald's carriage heaved across the other way and came upright for 10 miraculous seconds. Unreal seconds. A loud clank may have been Marley's ghost dismounting; or possible panic-stricken real angels had disconnected the carriage from the unfortunate carriages behind to minimize the tragedy. Still the unsafe future yawned ahead and Donald, who was forced across his table with its edge ramming his stomach, yawned back at the future in astonishment. Suddenly, he was thrown backwards in his seat and safety gathered round him like a wet blanket, like his own mac falling from the overhead rack.

No-one in his carriage really needed to feel frightened yet about the prolonged and deafening noise that burst out behind. That was not in the same time sequence.

Everyone got out, never minding the bad weather that met them, more concerned that the whole rear of the train had reprehensibly failed in its direction. Donald soon realized that his journey had simply crocked its elbow. He could dimly see the tragedy like a hill in his past. The two central carriages had remarkably telescoped, a time-juncture; they had torn each other's metal aside in eagerness to come together and had reared up in excitement. The engine, quite unharmed, remained coupled on to the front carriage and was panting like a dog no longer interested in the night's orgy. Donald's famous locust gesture came upon him again, cracking his joints, which exuded darkness as the carriages cocked up and uttered that portentous wailing.

The wreckage nested in twisted lines and hurled-up sleepers and was not-a-sculpture. Donald's larynx failed and his lungs went baggy. The smashed carriages curled off the line and cut off his retreat. He thought stupidly: 'You place nine full pea pods end to end, tips downturned, and trample savagely on the last seven pods.' (If you're going to try that, set up a previously-damaged train of pods on a model rail embankment (papier maché?), whose sides slope down to what may be fields. Telescope the two centre pods together as described.) Huge pods; the green darkens; metal idea-rhymes with accident; becomes grimy, beaded with water drops, the towering sides. The night was natural size, but the train wreckage was the grandeur of nature; inside it, was the infinite universe and innumerable worlds: the baby moment.

At last, the colourless idea of rescue rushed from the train's side, fell down the grassy bankside, barged carelessly against a telegraph pole, smashed flat a flimsy wooden fence, and stumbled in blind faith across field ruts until an abandoned Nissen hut, until an abandoned Nissen hut.

Back on the embankment, rescue work was at first local, as survivors knelt by trapped bodies, flicked cigarette lighters, and meaninglessly fiddled with collar openings; or poured milk over slack mouths, smoothed down hair, had another go at bending back metal. Every so often a helper said, 'For God's sake.'

It makes me weep enough just to read this phrase from *The Railway Children*: 'You'll come to a bad end, you nasty little limb, you.'

A signalman within his box only a half-mile away hurriedly lifted a telephone, dialled wrongly, and dialled again.

Donald's eye visited the length of the train, intruding into every mournful wound. A bruised face resting on a slanting floor. Two eyes, yes, two eyes, full of too much leisure. The train was a living, galvanic thing but all its light was puny. A match flame passed from window to window of a damaged carriage. The jagged windows and draughty corridors. Down in the darkness one louder cry flashed like a torchbeam.

So far, Donald had been pretty ineffectual. (Do you blame him, you, the one who tramped on the train with your heel?) Yet he could not understand why his hands were bleeding unless that was from trying to bend metal. The phrase he said every so often was, 'Now he is having convulsions,' but he was not definitely referring to one of the injured: equally probably, he was thinking of an Olympian power convulsed in the doing of harm.

With two clicks, a set of points changed on the other side of the rear carriages.

The first police car headlights swept down a farm road below them and the vehicle parked by the Nissen hut. At 100 yards distance, across meadowland and behind silhouetted trees, farmhouse lights were already on. Donald could now see that one carriage had toppled halfway down the slope.

A policeman hastily climbed the embankment and asked along the line until he found the elderly farmer from the house, who was helping to drag the injured down carriage steps. The farmer stumbled downhill to prepare his disused hut for the doctors.

Eventually, the professionals arrived – admittedly with magnificent speed but in the nature of things late for work. Ambulances, fire engines, police cars, along with villagers' and doctors' cars, even one Rolls-Royce, clustered round the hut, in which storm lanterns were flickering.

A special crash-rescue train thundered into view, stopped at the rear of the wreckage, and switched on three searchlights.

Donald's first impression: it was the line's baptism. A parson muttering soothingly. Babies crying as usual, unable to believe their fortunes.

When the white glare, which in most respects reduced the accident to more manageable proportions, rested on the heads and limbs of the injured it enlarged the notion of pain uncontrollably. Most of the carriages were discreet enough to shrug off publicity altogether, holding great wheels and bogeys towards the searchlights. Only the two carriages which had fallen down the embankment (the earlier number of one was an error) bulged out their contents in an unmannerly way. The other coaches were hermetic: that is, devoted to eloquence (cries), foreign trade (cups of tea), thieves (those pretending to be more hurt than they were), and messengers of God (the blessed St John, the saintly doctors).

Down in the menagerie of the Nissen hut, the doctors in what they liked to call their 'field hospital' were caught up in the general hermetic mood and dressed each injury by closing it from the outside. One of them cauterized Uncle Aubrey's little leg and then realized what a fool he had been. He had cauterized the wrong end! The foot part was perfectly all right; it was just that he had no body to join the cauterized thigh to. Donald (and you can imagine how upset he was to recognize that leg in such hands) would not have respected the man's profession if he had laughed.

Within about three hours, there was hardly any more human chaos, just suffering, which may be worse than chaos, but try telling the average householder that. Rescue workers at the train still had bothers with one or two regrettable people, but nicely managed to avoid any suggestion of 'Look! We're getting cranes and winches; what more d'you want?'

The badly-injured had been taken to hospital: most of the dead and the slightly-hurt remained. Each care was laid in bandages down the hut's length. Many movements were directly caused by pain. Quite precious items, such as syringe needles and bandages, had been thrown to one side, without concern for the labour that went into their making.

To hang around uselessly in the hut was just to store up painful memories. (To leave was to fail to resolve the event emotionally, so that Donald would awake at nights long afterwards with loud cries fading in his ears. This piece of wisdom, however, dodged round him like a too-busy nurse with other patients to worry about.)

The last Donald looked, and he looked longingly, the messengers of God swung their stethoscopes from their ears, listening in to the heavenly ether under the heavenly, vaulted roof. They patrolled between long lines of feet. Sometimes they hurried, broke into a run even. What with the white coats, the storm lanterns and dust from old straw, a spiritualist haze arose and hovered over corpses and injured alike until astral bodies stood up on every side. Donald has often drawn that hut since, at spare moments, on lavatory paper or old envelopes. Relatives waited by the heads of dead passengers and were willing enough to have become horses if they could have dragged the human bodies to some different future.

A sudden premonition. One of Donald's specials. 'There is going to be a bad rail accident.' He rushed outside; climbing towards the overturned carriages he remembered that the premonition was too late.

At the top, he again noticed that his hands were bleeding. Now he recalled that for an hour after the crash he had been wrestling at the same carriage. It was impossible to get inside because the waggon was lying with its doors underneath and on top. It lay just on the past section of the train's crocked elbow, which hinged past and future. Through a roof rent, where one of the ventilators had been, he saw the interior was full of dead solicitors, not all thrown against walls, roof or floors; some were still trapped in their seats. A hand lazily completed a crossword clue, but in most cases the pen had strayed off the newspaper.

A horse whinnied from fields on the other side of the embankment. The whinny was in very bad taste.

Donald hunched and breathed steam: he had no diesel fuel in him. The world had not turned. The journey had just deflected.

One day a poem would come out of this. Something about people who survive. Changed. Perhaps none of the train accident would come into the poem; perhaps the less written about trains the more completely the accident would be included. That was a moral for the future. Just now, with so many passengers hurt it was hard to turn your back entirely on that (though Donald managed to do so).

Luckily, the train driver was unharmed and strolled down the line towards him. The driver, a tall Scotsman, walked with Donald alongside the tragedy's heart. They exchanged a joke and the driver offered Donald a damp cigarette. 'No thank you.' The Scotsman kept winking. 'I said, "No thank you."' Stretcher parties set off like silver fish from the Nissen hut. Not a vestige of the accident's former being remained but that one, miserable dream of silver fish. The searchlights, rain, straggling groups of helpers, the British Railway uniform of this companion, the damaged metal – these said nothing about a derailment or even a hurricane, but combined into photographs called 'War-time'.

Donald said how much he admired the coat of one of the gangers, dark wool with shiny leather shoulders. Then he said to the driver didn't he think he'd get into trouble? That brought on another spate of winking and the Scotsman pulled out a silver hip flask full of greenish liquid which Donald willingly sipped.

The searchlights bleached the driver white and Donald remembered how that makes you look older than you really are. The man's eyes were stern; his lips had no hint of a smile although he so much lacked seriousness. Donald felt drawn to him, as he did to many people he disliked.

The driver reached in his pocket and took out a flat, leather box. He handed it over and nodded encouragingly.

Donald thought it might be full of fishing maggots and opened it very carefully. Inside was a crimsony ribbon and a medal. The safety pin was intrinsically the most interesting part.

'The George Medal. Oh really?'

'I was awarded that as an auxiliary fireman during the war,' the driver said, to all intents, but not purposes, modestly.

He continued: 'It was an ammunition dump and a large, wooden shed caught fire during a raid. The stupid biddies had put a shell or two in the place for temporary storage – only done it that afternoon. Well, I didn't think much of what I did. I just stood in the shed with the fire all round me, passing out shells, which were quite warm.' He added: 'They were quite warm, you know.'

Donald mumbled: 'Oh yes. I remember reading about that at the time, I think.'

The driver pulled out a wallet, gleaming with use. 'I've got a cutting here from the old *Sunday Graphic*. I don't think they print that any more, do they?'

Here was a chance to display special journalistic knowledge. 'No, they don't,' Donald replied firmly.

Even in the brilliant light he could see the cutting was badly greyed. He pretended to read, but the print was so dominated by the light that it became afraid. That domination made the letters shrink and become impossibly small to read. Similarly, the driver's past heroism shrank before his eyes, because it was dominated by the present-day accident. He continued pretending to study the article, paying attention to the unreadable creases. The man's name was McFarlane. In his casual responsibility for tonight's crash McFarlane was huge. In his past heroism he was small. Donald's size was in the middle, perhaps.

'I think that must have been the report I read,' he said, compounding his previous lame comment into a multiple fracture of his body.

'But will all this save you from a British Railways inquiry?' he asked. 'I'm told they're very thorough.'

'Let me tell you, man, I'd welcome an inquiry,' said the Scotsman. 'I've got nothing to hide. In any case, they tell me only 20 people have really died; not like the old days. Do they have separate inquests on each death? Do you happen to know? Well, I'll attend any inquest. Each and every inquest.'

And he winked again, though Donald was beginning to wish he wouldn't.

The train obstinately rose up like a hill in Korea; it was going to be another day before they got that straightened out. A flash view of the accident returned: maggoty children's bodies hanging off walls as from coat-hooks; no maggots wriggling any more (must have been why he had that momentary fear of the leather box).

'They have only one inquest,' he explained. The information was superfluous to the driver.

'Where did you get that watch?' the Scotsman snapped.

Donald had revealed the new watch in brushing wet hair from his eyes. He was too ashamed to tell about his gullible purchase from the salesman. So he muttered something about buying it the other day.

'Not in a shop you didn't,' said McFarlane with a short laugh. 'I know those watches; they're hot as arseholes. You either bought it off one of my men, French was he?, or you've some pretty funny friends, my lad.'

Donald, in his own semantic trap, said: 'We all know one or two, don't we?'

It was unclear whether the driver believed him or not, but he patted Donald on the shoulder and said: 'You're with the right-wingers now, my lad: spirit of private enterprise incorporated and don't ask too many questions. Mebbe we can find a thing or two for you to do.'

They had walked some distance ahead of the wreckage. Donald could not help looking back. 'The rain's making everything sad,' he remarked, looking at the glistening carriages, rails the colour of damp ash.

'Sad, is it?' said McFarlane and chuckled. 'It takes more than a drop of rain to make me sad. Still, I like a man who's honest,' he added, transparently lying.

With those words, the engine driver created a picture frame of dishonesty in which he set a movie portrait of a bewildered Donald trying to be as honest as he could under the circumstances.

'Never mind. There's plenty more where that came from.'

'Children?'

'Poof, lad. Watches. Keep control of time and you keep control of people's lives.'

The Scotsman pointed ahead into the obscurity. 'Here's our train.' A pinpoint of moving light did its best to live up to the introduction.

This engine driver had enthusiasm for a new journey despite what he had done to the old one. It was clear the silver hip flask was at least one clue to his state of mind. That was what had released the night of *his* premonition. As for Donald's, who can feel angry with a premonition called Dorothy?

'However, Dorothy might only be the premonition's temporary alias,' said Donald to McFarlane. The engine driver didn't seem as good as Frank at picking up that kind of textual nuance.

Out of the night came the rear of a new train, one engine and a carriage only. Workmen brought up portable lights and white, circular buttocks were promptly cast either side of the carriage's crinkly, hanging-off bit which, it's no secret, is like a horse's rectum when it's shitting. Carriage connection trunking masquerading as the end of things, a very common kind of intellectual fraud. The engine of Donald's train was somehow hitched on to the back carriage of the newcomer. This new lead train was thus a mirror copy of the crash train behind, which still towed its own front carriage. McFarlane climbed back into his own engine. Ahead, the shadowy driver of the second engine stepped down on to the track, looked along the line, and re-entered his engine. McFarlane stuck out his head and gestured back at Donald to climb in the rear of this hybrid monster which was evidently ready to go. He stepped up into his original carriage home; but, alone there, without the children, he could not find the empty waste of seats homely. The new journey started as though the derailment was just a brief incident, on the whole rather a relief.

If only McFarlane had been the devil himself instead of a small-time right-winger, how much safer Donald would have felt. At least he would have known for sure where he was going. True, in one sense McFarlane was about to take him where the Scotsman wanted at the speed he wanted to go. But there was another engine driver in front of McFarlane and the speed and direction imposed on Donald were also imposed on the war-time hero. Life is very like that; somewhere, ahead of the fiercest person you know is another engine pulling you and the person who masters you.

No doubt all the events of the accident had duration but, despite occasional indications of hours passing, the time-scale can no longer be properly represented. The travelling, the crash, meeting the Scotsman, now this new travelling, merged into a single, swollen digit of time, or at least time imagined as a digit. In the interior of that digit a trajectory arced between the subjective half of reality and its objective half. Within this swollen instant the sense of value arises. Don't let power-seekers dominate your instants. Uncle Aubrey: the God of this moment. His spiritual participation in the derailment, via the *material* of his leg, contributed to the split reality. Donald remained inside that uncle's goodness. You have to imagine again a giant baby formed of blue gas, continually pulsing with harmless originality, and, within that, a wooden platform where Donald perched like a passive love-bird. He was surrounded by such originality that memory was very weak. To remember something we have to parcel out our mental time, to dominate the events until they are small and we can attend to their emerging pattern. Memory is part of the triad: memory, intuition, expectation. Compare: past, present, future. Throughout this journey sequence, Donald lived in an almost-present, intimidated by the engine drivers but safe inside the stupid body of Uncle Aubrey, where he refused to give up that birth/berth just for the sake of cementing reality back together.

Though the journey's duration was lacking, the fictitious relation of it, on this paper, carries its own textual time-scales. The description is as surely domination of your mental time as if you had been forced to accept a new calendar, studded for the right-wingers with memorial days of wars and for left-wingers with brumaires, thermidors and fructidors. This domination is locked in a struggle for time; but Donald's pacifism was a struggle to live in the truly original present. All the same, Uncle Aubrey, having once been born, was only almost-originality and had lived in a chain of almosts. Otherwise even a version of him could not be offered. The truly original has no shape, a page that's blank or with random letters and no time-scale. If what I wrote was original the only 'times' left by it would be the times it took to write and to read – the latter being 'your' time left unscathed by the passive text. However, you would not be able to confirm that such a page was original, nor when you had finished reading. You would have to live in the present to read it properly, in which case it would for-ever be being written and you simultaneously would be reading. I have a suspicion it would consist of a single vowel, the choice of which being impossible to make.

7

A Couple of Little Ones

Donald walked to the end of the open-plan carriage. The first step he took was drunk, the second was dizzy, the third was deceptive, the fourth was wrong-hearted, the fifth was drunk, the sixth was dizzy, the seventh deceptive, the eighth wrong-hearted, and so on down the aisle. He opened the shiny end door, turned, and looked down the nicely-hoovered carpet to the end of the carriage. Empty. Solipsism. It's hard to find a corner where the soul in solipsism can feed. He needed the lavatory. They were going through Black Diamond Express stations to hell: Drunkardsville, Confusion Junction, Deceiversville, Liar's Avenue.

The half-open lavatory door was biscuit colour freaked with wireworms. The sign said 'Engaged', but Donald partnered the door in the invitation waltz until he was inside. At a guess, he'd have said from the state of the floor that something had left the lavatory rather hurriedly at the time of the crash, though you never can tell what a box round the ears will do to a room. Still, there had to be some reason why the lavatory felt so vacuous. Something's departure had sucked all sorts of non-reality into that tiny space. He had walked into a hiding-place. But what had left so hurriedly?

Children. They're all the same – as independent as can be. When they've got a body upset it's a different story. They soon come running to you for a kiss and a cuddle. Then you need something as gentle as you are to get rid of the discomfort in their tummies.

Nobody told Donald about the children's departure except a doll lying on the floor.

She looked like a 24-year-old woman, quite brainy, beautifully dressed and well brought up. She was about 10 inches high. For the moment at least. Her eyes were closed. Asleep, her face was peaceful. He moved one of her arms until it pointed straight ahead and raised her until she looked at him in downright shock and dismay. Her name was Eva del Coso. Privately educated in Montevideo and Venice.

When he directed her blue eyes towards the window the iris did not change. He buried his face in her green, velvet dress which smelt of the Pongderosa, moved his lips down the sheer nylon stockings painted on her plastic legs and kissed the shiny, black shoes, one of which came off in his mouth. Her underthings were frankly not very fetching, some scrappy piece of rayon stuck round her crotch with gum. Beside the miniature wash basin of a British Railways lavatory she looked even more miniature.

He understood why she looked so small, intimidated by such official-looking furniture. After a while, the sense of being intimidated began to grow in Donald too. He pulled down his trousers and pants, sat on the lavatory, and began stroking his penis to constitute Eva in his epigastrium.

Certain optical illusions:

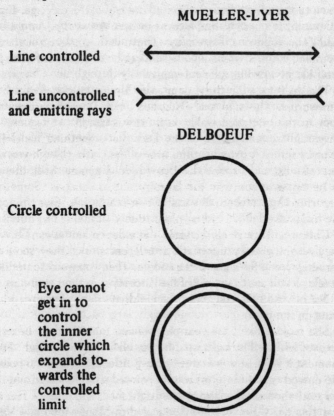

MUELLER-LYER

Line controlled

Line uncontrolled
and emitting rays

DELBOEUF

Circle controlled

Eye cannot
get in to
control
the inner
circle which
expands to-
wards the
controlled
limit

Penis and vagina expand and contract according to analogous illusions of our control over them; and we are back in the Western film subtleties of how domination affects notions of body-size. So the penis, sensed as out of control and yearning to ejaculate, dominates the mind, and feels and is large; the case of the orgasm-seeking vagina is rather more complicated for the woman, but holds to the same laws of desire exceeding mental control, with consequent sensations of increased size and openness. The gate-muscle to the vagina then lifts. Probably to the man the vagina would feel larger or smaller round his prick according to the fluctuations of domination that pass between the couple during intercourse, but he rarely has time to reflect on this within the larger variations of overall body-size wrought by the emotional exchange. (Nevertheless, the stronger the thrust, the smaller the apparent orifice and the more it is objectified.)

During the masochistic phase of his masturbation, Donald lived within the following knowledge: controlled by the doll's steady gaze, his body seemed small compared with its 'real' size. By empathy, he saw himself contemptuously through her eyes. But he could also seek subjectively and, this time, plotting the internal territory from those 'places' of identity inside himself, he found the inner space out of control, the brain area large, hot and expanding. He sent out commands to various limbs but, except for the frenetic control exercised over his one, active hand, the other commands were minute and weak and he could feel them slopping about in the over-size limbs.

During the sadistic phase of the masturbation he lived in the following knowledge: bestially controlling the doll, he sensed her body as a small and hard object. Because he dominated her, his brain also seemed subjectively small and under control ('mean-minded'); his inner space was also controlled and neat. His limbs seemed small and powerful (until his hand began again). Meanwhile, his external body had a colossus sensation because he was aware by empathy how dominatingly large it must appear to the doll.

The myth of the homunculus, he told himself in this sadistic phase, is a wish to dominate; to constitute the homunculus inside ourselves, say in the stomach area, where he can both be controlled and yet be ourselves. Having children.

He imagined the foetus of Uncle Aubrey inside the doll's womb.

Eva tried her hardest and, as her pregnancy advanced, a mirror image of the doll simultaneously swelled inside Donald. She eventually became a generalization of his own particular case and spread outwards incorporeally from him as an aura. His penis had rays leading outwards from the tip. When relief had come he tidily folded the rays at the end of the penis back along it like fountain pen clips and temporarily stowed the optical illusion back in his pants. It was still marvellous during the repetition and Donald Kipfer, severely indigestive, reduced himself to ecstasy before the dishevelled scientist, Eva del Coso. He looked at his chancy watch, which was going again, and he realized his own experience of time fluctuated wildly according to how large he felt in relation to his surroundings. It also varied according to a comparison of body heat with that of the room. If the watch was at last telling some correct time or other, he couldn't read that kind of semaphore, but, given the Frenchman who had sold it, any 'correctness' was unlikely.

He went back to the carriage. One of the mothers had left behind a pack of cheese sandwiches. For that second or two, gobbling them up, he felt pretty darned smart, and whistled to keep that particular pecker up. All the same, internal changes were already doing their best to destroy confidence.

For an hour or two, the train stopped in a siding and he slept. When he awoke, they were travelling slowly. Anxiety and sexual frustration were confused both in his gorge and at the cardia orifice leading from oesophagus to stomach, where an unease had built up both because of the sandwiches and the masturbation.

The almost-present moment stopped. He found some steps to the side of that moment and jumped from there on to a station platform in a familiar seaside town at dawn.

As the sun was unusually bright and fitful for that hour, it may have been running one of its temperatures. He felt loathsome now too, even though a sunny day invites us to enter its warmth and light. Our eyes normally send out something of ourselves, a puff of air through the iris, that expands momentously to live in the sunny surroundings. We end up joyful in a landscape that regards us, like a mirror or a true-love, partly with our own look. But this time spare adrenalin from that little sexual farce in the lavatory had stimulated Mueller's muscle and Donald felt his eyeball was protruding slightly. The puff of air would, on the contrary, have needed a contracted, lively eyeball to fire it forwards into the warmth. Lacking that, the puff was as undecided as Daisy-Daisy and unable to nip out to the waiting lover-landscape. Behind his iris life became glum. It wasn't so much different out front when the sun went behind a cloud.

Next, you'll be thinking the platform was deserted. Two pasty-faced girls, each with frizzy brown hair, came out of the hallway in the middle of the main station building and passed by Donald along the platform. Both wore dark sweaters and they walked sharply in step. From behind, their skirts, one beige and the other light blue, worked beautifully together. These skirts had brainy bulging at the top and a mature alternation of thigh-light that said to him, 'We are mistresses of your attempts.' He had the dusty green metal of the carriage at one side to remind him all was not well. And were those the tattered remains of Hurricane Dorothy fluttering round the end of the station building as though someone just out of sight were waving an old duster? Perhaps it was just Air itself waving hallo.

He almost ceased to exist. His breath dropped to minimum level as he watched the girls walk away from him: in his chest the flag of residence died down. His stomach tightened up. In the throat, the gorge muscles yearned inwards because the distortions of breathing were not enough and adrenalin from the masturbation had interfered with saliva production. When he had wolfed the sandwiches he had bought temporary relief dearly. Food mouthfuls larger than usual had countered the throat's addictive yearning by swelling the gorge, coating themselves with saliva, and pushing back the tired muscles. Then the food plug descended, hardly chewed, ramming a wad of air beneath it. The stomach sphincter gave way. Sandwich and excess air entered the stomach together. That deceived organ, because so unnaturally swollen and because the hardly-chewed food needed more than normal breaking down, exuded excess acid from its folds.

The voodoo death is in all of us who are dominated. All who snub and have contempt for us curse our stomach, lungs and heart.

Donald took a 6B pencil from his jacket pocket and wrote this slogan on the wall of the stationmaster's office. The sun momentarily came out and blinded the office windows with whitened net. When the window darkened he could see inside the room the narrow face of the stationmaster. He was on the telephone and looked startled when Donald shook his fist at him for good measure.

Then, like the sunshine, Donald relented and tried unsuccessfully to communicate with the official by telepathy.

. . . Maybe some other time Donald could have done much to help that man; but it would be intolerably wrong to suppose the stationmaster wouldn't have been able to help him too. So many people, whether mean or grand of soul, had told Donald during his journalist days how to school racing pigeons to reach their peak, what sort of anthracite to buy, what their dog has in its heart, the best way to sharpen a pencil with their pocket knives, what they saw on sentry duty in West Germany, how their daughter does her hair usually, what's on the menu at the ABC, the way they teach deaf mutes in a certain London suburb, how to measure up for a nice coffee table, what plants do when you play music to them, or how to win a harmonica championship. He had drunk this information in greedily. In return, he had sometimes told them what was wrong with the fierce, doctrinaire right wing and with totalitarian theories of left-wing revolution, whether flamboyant urban guerrillas in Uruguay paving the way for right-wing oppression or the *sui generis* cruelties of purist, Babéufian, permanent revolution. 'Forget Uruguay a moment. Look at the Khmer Rouge in Cambodia,' he'd say. And his erstwhile informants, bewildered at the very introduction of such subject matter, would look at him as if he were a social idiot.

8

Contrary Courtesy

The air turned blue with swearing. A clotted piece of matter left Donald's mind and went creeping out through the station hallway: it was a figure bent low, wearing a white raincoat, and it ran by a cemetery wall sheltering from bullets. The cliché figure of the journalist, hero(ine) and social pariah. Lies swelled his lungs with pictures. Courtesy was now his forte. Walked very tall and straight.

'Beige, that's my favourite colour.'

The small size of the beige skirt, now that her friend's skirt, the light blue, had decamped.

'You don't have to leave. You could stay right here. There's everything we need.' She completely added that.

'But your friend . . .'

They entered a double etiquette where it was natural to be moved deeply by whatever was to hand.

She smiled so openly it would have been discourteous (not) to respond. She had badly curved shinbones. Impatiently, her skirt nudged and her hips fell over to one side, settling over awkward legs like a dollop of icecream lodged in a biased way on a double-barrelled cornet. Only the cornet wasn't straight. Each leg was more like a penknife with one blade open. A dark green sweater, an open, friendly face, brown hair.

'You've met my daughter,' said McFarlane, coming up to them. 'This is Rosine.'

'That's not possible. She can't be called Rosine.'

'No; she's not called Rosine. Her name is Rosemary.'

'Hallo, Mary.'

She did not reply until at the very far end of the platform the second engine driver, the one who had led Donald and McFarlane there, climbed down from his train and went straight out a side gate opposite his engine. Following his own daughter, presumably. Blue skirt? Colour of the political right. Colour that led them there after the leftist convulsion of the derailment? Could the beige, apparent colour of sameness between human beings, be just a deception, a complicity with blue? It was not significant that Mary delayed her reply until then but it was rhythmic.

'I'm reading your second chapter.' 'Did I show you my newspaper clipping?' 'What second chapter?' 'I've got nothing to hide.' 'Where are you staying?' 'I don't want anything too dear. It's just to put someone in a false direction.' 'How do you like my train?' 'Did you have a good journey?' 'Sometimes you get a complete blank.'

In that blank came sepia lines, hints of windows; two engine drivers climbing once again down from their trains; a copy of Buonarotti's history of Babeuf's conspiracy in Donald's pocket; fearful anticipations of the hurricane that was in fact past; close to Mary who was exactly half attractive to him; himself feeling like two men for one place. In his heart he said goodbye for the moment to the time-scales of revolutionary catastrophe. In the emerging pattern, in that will, Donald's train crash poem was born. Though he actually wrote it just the other day, in horrified response to the war-history of Cambodia under the Khmer Rouge. And you'll forgive him that there aren't any trains in it. Just an iron river. Still, here it is:

'Why don't you come and stay at our place?'

BABEUF ENTERS THE CAMBODIAN WAR

The cage is an acrid travelling show and its prisoners
storm the wires of their acid history.

Bestial fears, reluctance, ignorance vaporize and the whole day
energizes, chicken wire gnawed by teeth, the tongues galvanic.

Men are becoming imagos star points snake
towards chain links already writhing with ideas.

A cage displaying men like beasts
jolts on its axles and dismantles.

The imperfect princes step from disgrace
and take first place in a country of puppet sovereignty.

A crowd waves from the borders. More true to themselves
than any, the hair-trigger men; dangerously original;

But their steps are sprung with assumptions, their borrowings all
     the more vehement;
their second best freezes and is classic.

All that meet them congratulate them,
one kisses their eyes, another their necks, their hands.

Breathless praise before the phrases of the gun,
the pent-up air; potential's bullet is static, until

it at last bursts from the day's throat
and a song starts down

a river stretching at least 100 miles. Our identity is
in that direction but some wavering in voice-tone

implicates us in corridors that stripe peaceful waters.
The river melody falls into an alibi, the café.

The absurd song:
'While the people, gorged with hate, eat iron like an ostrich.'

An uninterrupted orchestra of scouts, sentries,
police spies, foot and horse patrols; loneliness

is out of place in the Café of the Chinese Baths,
known statesmen at the tables, so little breath free

to sing with, under our hearts wedges of air;
and indigestion should have stopped now that ours begins.

Infinitesimal hate pumps past the stomach sphincter,
the mucus membrane goes taut.

The café is really the same inset,
walls syrupy with acid.

/The café was on the street level and by the number of its
    windows
looked like a cage open to all regards/

then former prisoners move past on the river
and ideal progress begins there, travelling slowly.

Patrician statesmen jump into speeches and drive at salary speed
    along the bankside,
but we have joy in the long drift that defies border conspiracies.

The café singer's voice flows away from the band,
the people, gorged with hate, eat iron like an ostrich.

Our identity opens entirely to that side, the song floating slowly
at least 100 miles, the crowd moving down the flood.

'You don't need to think all that,' said Mary.

No-one could explain to her that when a poem is started it arises
from all that has been thought to that point but suddenly skids
quite sideways, on no railway lines at all, and lands up in some
territory that could not have been expected. Even so, in that
oblique way, it creates new plot in our existing lives, not as
substitute for the old plot but as a weird amalgamation. The old
plot still had much in it to contribute but now it became striated
with deception.

The new amalgamation had a temporary title: 'If by dishonesty
we could love someone more, by truth we should love them less.'

'It's worth a try, though,' said Mary, nearly as expert as Frank in
nuance matters. They sat close to each other in the taxi and Donald
took pleasure in looking at her lap, skirt-over-knees, beiged-over
fawn. Donald's *two* favourite colours. Better even than red which,
at moments, can be too manic.

Outside McFarlane's semi-detached house, Donald could think
of nothing to say because there was nothing to say; that was his
endemic condition with McFarlane for ever afterwards. In the early
morning light, the road of similarly-mean houses gave up no
language content at all, except possibly, 'Don't expect anything
original,' and that's hardly the language to encourage a guest.

He helped McFarlane in with a large, brown trunk and they entered a dark hall, not two paces wide, with stairs going up on the right and two rooms on the left. For the first time Donald encountered the house's oppressive smell. It reminded him of carpets into which small boys' urine had soaked, of 1945 cooking, railway smoke, damp, and – he was to discover – every Thursday an additional smell of *steak au poivre* with a whiff of *Moulin à Vent*.

'Straight to bed for all of us,' said the girl with the frizzy hair, showing aptitude for sleeping according to the needs of the situation. It was straight to bed for Mary and Donald the following morning as well, though that was the first time together.

Before that incident, however, there was a decent interval for breakfast, eaten in the back parlour which overlooked a tiny garden surrounded by a high wall. The wall had in its middle a gate so small it could only be called secret.

McFarlane had discarded his uniform and wore a smart blue shirt, old grey worsted trousers plumped out by his stomach, and brown leather slippers. He sat at table with his back to the French windows and studied the *Daily Express*. As Donald sat down and as Mary put the breakfast cereal packet down on the plastic tablecloth the Scotsman jabbed a finger at an inside page of his paper.

'Take these young fellows now,' he said. His guest had no way of learning which story was indicated. 'Go for things that really give power – money, explosives, arms. Left-wing, right-wing, who cares?' Jab, jab. 'You must get the freedom to impose your viewpoint. Government. Worrrrld historical! Now, I'm going to get you a job at the Tacuarembo Hotel, the manager's a friend. I can tell you the names of 20 of my helpers and I haven't a good word to say for any of them. Have a drop of this wine.'

'Not at breakfast, thanks.'

'The more things we accept from other people the more use we are to them. I hope you'll take what's offered. That's how we live in this house. It doesn't do to try to stay too clear of offers. You become dangerous. Don't want dangerous people around, thank you.'

'I'm afraid I can't follow all your non-sequiturs,' said Donald with an entertaining smile.

'Non what?'

'Sometimes I become almost permanently indigested,' Donald added.

'Exactly,' Mary commented with ready but curious sympathy.

'Mary knows what she wants. Perhaps you'll meet Jerry at the hotel.'

'This is good muesli,' said Donald.

McFarlane frowned. 'Mary knows where to buy. She's one of my best buyers, nice and sharp.' He rolled the rrr to whet the word to a good edge.

His guest was thinking of Mary: 'And she's a bit provincial for my taste. Still all fannies smell the same, as they say.' However, with modern hygiene, to say nothing of feminism, that joke has dated badly and most provincial towns can boast a good Boots, or Woolworths, or even corner chemist; so in fact Mary's fanny smelt of deodorant and, a little while afterwards, of discontent.

'Time you two were going,' said McFarlane, rising and forcing them to stand. He ushered them out of the parlour, closed the door and turned the key in the lock.

'Perhaps he wants to finish my breakfast, or is he a believer in secrecy in government too?' Donald joked to Mary, who looked very bland.

He went ahead of her down the dingy little hall and confidently opened the only other ground-level door. The front room was a shambles: no carpet, no covers on the chairs, a settee on end leaning against the wall, bits of straw about, a large pile of magazines, two panes of glass.

'There's practically nowhere to go but upstairs,' said Donald.

She did not bother to look as if that was news to her.

In the almost-immaculate red tiled surround of Mary's bedroom carpet, one tile had sunk and was darker.

On the almost-immaculate swept-blue of the carpet, a white footprint.

Within that footprint, nothing but cleanliness.

Donald could not have coped with more than the dravidian lack of love-play resource that obliged Mary to live entirely in his behaviour when she was with him. Helplessly islanded in the love of dishonesty, the flat expectation lipping the shore . . .

. . . But sometimes when he returned to Mary's house at dawn after a night's work at the hotel she would hurry out to meet him. She'd be wearing her grey cloak and looking like some aged hag, and she'd put her arm round the small arrival as though he were a little boy and McFarlane were the child-murderer, Gilles de Retz, and she would tell Donald how her father could make him rich. They both knew that meant just some more watches to sell in the pubs or something like that, but they enjoyed the lies as the only possible form of currency between them. There was no reason to treat that currency as debased. That afternoon, following a morning spent in childhood, he'd work at a matching game, measuring his forearm against hers, shin-bone against shin-bone, thigh against thigh, nose against nose, hand against hand. When the sizes were exactly equal again and he was really adult, she really about 28 years old, he'd say, 'What do you want for your birthday?' and she'd say, 'Wait till you've sold the watches.' He'd begin measuring all over again, starting with her aged toes. That was rather like lifting up her dress, ducking his head underneath and coming up to find they were both wearing it. Not making love inside. Just measuring.

With lies and with measuring he restored a medieval courtesy between them.

He asked her how she endured the torments.

She said by love.

He asked her by what fire she could get rid of his love.

She said by the same fire that made her afraid of his love.

He asked why she feared him since she loved him.

She asked why he loved her since he feared her father.

He asked if her love began in her will.

She said it was in his will that she found her love of watches.

He asked if she could swallow and at that moment remain in love.

She said there was the love of the shared cigarette.

He said that was the failure of thoracic love, a love much harder to perfect than love through the stomach or the intellect.

She asked where was the light of the truth of his love.

He said in a luminous notebook. And returned the question.

She said on the stroke of each hour, marked in luminous figures.

He asked if she loved Jerry more than him.

She said she did, much more, but that added to how good this was.

He said truth mixed with flattery gave him his highest pleasures.

She said the lies and the rubies. The indices and the deceit.

He said he would show her some previous statements about thoracic love. He laid his grubby blue notebook on the pink quilt and opened the book at this page:

'Rats in a polluted atmosphere take alcohol in preference to pure or to sugared water.'
'Cigarette smokers drink more tea and coffee and consume more sugar than non-smokers, three separate inquiries have found.'
'Experiments on rabbits show that tea dissolves greases in the blood and helps to cure arterial lesions.'

She asked how his love of her was expressed in his love of food.

He said he loved her while eating beef, game birds, and drinking sleepy wine, or milk, but not while eating lamb, chicken, pork, or drinking strong tea.

She idly turned over the pages of his notebook and came to his poem about Frank and Rosine:

FRANK'S MISTRESS

He smelt of sandwiches and was one of the badly-dressed men.

'I cannot support your idea of dying of hunger.
Bring me roast beef garnished with chicken.
Prepare my bath. And before I bathe
You are going to find me a cuttlebone and a lettuce leaf.
H'm it's a marvellous sandwich.
I'm going to possess you and first I need various services.
Bring me a saddle of lamb dressed with turkeys.'

It reminded Mary of Jerry. 'One day I thought to close my eyes for a good night's sleep but Jerry closed them for me, for a week,' she said with a trace of a smile.

Mary didn't go on to ask Donald for any biographical details, though she was quite interested in the theoretical basis of his text. Charmed by that courtesy, he paid devotion to her lumpish thighs with their cramps and lumps.

His suspicion remained, for her father had made himself a scholar in that classical subject, the semi-detached house. He was the world authority on the ten he owned and a consultant on several others. Donald could not help feeling suspicious because the subject has considerable political overtones. The Scotsman had no need to drive nationalized rail engines for a living, especially with a public inquiry pending against him. He might be the very breath of private upward mobility with all its shenanigans. What was his secretive contact system? Who were the two railway employees who visited him on Mondays? What took place in the locked parlour room on Thursdays with half a dozen cabbalistic mutters, cartel whispers, and 30p worth of joss? What was in the large, brown trunk carried down each time for the parlour rituals? What role did the likeable Jerry, alternative lover of Mary and now his co-worker at the hotel, play in all this?

'Jerry, my arse,' said McFarlane one day.

The following day he said it again, just before he slipped into the back parlour.

Perhaps McFarlane was not aware of it but, apart from the expression's commonplace value as contempt, he was using a very beautiful image. Jerry's swarthy face belonged with the notion of arsehole, seen as a brown, rubbed crater straggling black hairs. It belonged as surely as certain middle-aged women, wearing long, white silk dresses belong with light, blue doors picked out in gold. Or some young men with rumpled Indian clothes and long black hair of Indian braves belong with a pair of navy blue sportswear underpants, drying on a radiator. Or Mary as a young schoolgirl, with eyelashes that are too pale, fragile brown hair and a frightened composure, belongs with a modest birthday watch that she removes from her wrist and places on her brown skirt to show her friend as they sit in the school hall for prayers.

McFarlane's arse was only one of these secret places where Jerry might be involved in the kind of crime that was possibly likeable (such as buggering stupid dairy shorthorn cows, strangling parrots), but could not be condoned.

'Jerry?'

Loose-jaw, sweet-tooth, brag-throat, habit-swigger, air-buoy, minion.

All over Europe the same myrmidons; now is not the best time to approach them, let them approach you, whistle at ferocity and whistle hard. As Jerry entered town they were the friendliest streets he had ever seen. He told Donald. Everyone about to smile. Let's really describe him. His finger-nail began in a thin, chalky edge spreading up nicotine slopes to a silken line of daylight before roseate snowscapes, a wide plateau falling to far darkness where the pain was. The two of them ate in a café on their way in to work: the sound of a road drill, of birds, a train. In the café people complained, said it's lovely, ate like the Doppler effect. The sulphurous crusts rose to tobacco-stained beards, dried milk was ready in the tumblers, crass-shit, shaking the door. You're a desperate character. Leave the handle down. The meal was full of swart tinctures. Then the white halves fell limply apart. Each spilt the hard yolk, whose texture is always so surprisingly pure but smears so easily. A yellow you only meet in paintboxes. The egg white held dark skull traces in its innocent hollow. We are innocent before these facts; don't blame others even when they blame themselves. Our far-reaching mistakes are often made with a clean heart that the environment makes dusky without our knowing. We have to help each other with continual poetry if we are to trace the first innocence of motive. We can still try to remind our neighbour of those unseeable colours, the blindness closed in the shell, the present-night, then the fresh cooking, the hens laughing in the coops, and we can still ask don't blame us, even when we blame ourselves. Blame is a carcinogen. Expertly, the café chef cracked 30 eggs, two at a time, into a huge saucepan and the air above the fat trembled. It was prophetic. The trembling of an alibi; a song on the juke box; the artiste a red-haired girl. As they left the café the country had changed. Easy enough, they just patterned the surroundings to the same needs. At the Tacuarembo Hotel Jerry, ex-welterweight champion, hung his grey tweed jacket in a wardrobe which was slim and of faded plywood. The management also had given him a bed, and he once more checked it out. You couldn't call it a room, just the enclosed end of a corridor. He kicked a flattened dog-end out the door. Who was on tonight? Don. Margaret was deaf and spoke in whispers. Neon lights went out in the hotel office as he came into the still room. He surveyed the other two despairingly, lit a cigarette and sooted lungs gave its smoke a subversive welcome. Secretly, he took his pulse. Alone, kind, the three of them lacked vehemence. Over cheap trays their utter silence coped with their situations. 'Did I post that letter to Rosine?' Donald's thoughts:

What I had to say was in the envelope: I blame
the mail train for the difference in story.
As a flock of lies drifts over town
for all I start knowing I give all I know.

9

Fun with Food

When the new man came in, the stillroom workers were more bored than ever, though he came in nice and dumpily. He was a once-very-fit-50-year-old from Dublin, with whitened eyes. Mostly a tramp in a filthy brown suit and only slightly a dishwasher in an apron. Not the same as Margaret, who was almost wholly a dishwasher with only a trace of English nanny, 1915. Stan Laurel, that was it! The new man. One of the best descriptions so far! Only you have to notice how comparatively burly Stan Laurel looked in some of the early films and then use his older, thinner face. Or just think of the later films and borrow a bit of Olly. (Anyway, if you're looking for endearing 'characters' and a whiff of exotic material, the television boys do that best.) The new man's trouser turnups had eyelashes at the heels and Donald half suspected him of having shy heels.

To see how important an evening this was you have to have a taste for its details. You could play it like 'Spot the deliberate mistake'. Do you remember the game in an old radio programme? Not that there's a mistake, how could there be? But you could play it like that – 'How could there be an accuracy?' – and continue it from there.

The long stillroom sink had three basins in its stainless steel aplomb which would have been the colour of stainless steel, if that weren't always some other colour. The whole expanse of the sink top was an exercise in urban architecture. The Dishrack Concert Hall, the office suites of Stacked Plates Ltd, the Saucepan Television Centre; knives slid up to the parking lots. Donald picked up a stacked building bloc of plates and dried an office floor full of giggling secretaries in one plate layer, clutching the rest of the building to his chest, never let me go, and transferred the dried floor to a different building, owned by another company, where the secretaries on the dried floor looked at their notebooks in panicky disbelief, telling people phoning up from down below, 'Will you please repeat that and also your name, Sir?' and 'No, I certainly wasn't the girl you spoke to earlier.' Occasionally, the girls looked out of the window of the new building, delighted it had stopped raining.

The four of them worked in a long line, all facing a steamed-up window. Jerry looked at it with likeable eyes, the new man looked at it with white eyes, and Margaret looked at it with deaf eyes.

Apparently similarly, the old dishwashing machine behind had one whitened eye and one clear eye. A double-sided, stand-up tank, it had a churning pool of soapy water (whitened eye) into which the two-handle dishracks were put first. The clear eye was the rinse tank. There, the cleaned rack of dishes was transferred into water that looked as if it might cry at its own goodness.

This was a typical sequence: 8.30 P.M.: Jerry grabbed a wooden scraper and whisked unwanted food off plates that had come through the dining room/ballroom hatch. He put the empty plates into a waiting rack; 8.35 P.M.: a rack was ready; 8.36 P.M.: the new man lifted the rack standing in the rinse tank on to the sink draining board; 8.36½ P.M.: the new man lifted the rack standing in the soapy water into the next-door rinse compartment; 8.37 P.M.: Jerry swung the waiting rack of dirties into the soapy water, and, on the far side of the new man, Donald and Margaret in that order began to dry the dishes from the 8.36 P.M. finished load, as it may now be called. The new man meanwhile collected cutlery to begin washing it in the sink; 8.37½ P.M.: Jerry picked up the scraper again.

They acted in unison and made way for each other. Perhaps you would call this decorum beautiful. In fact, as a chain of signification it was downright ugly. For instance, what about all those work-efficiency delays? Jerry leaning on his hands against the sink top? The new man idling, yet Margaret and Donald drying non-stop. Also the new man with his whitened eyes had responsibility for the clear water while Jerry with his clear eyes was responsible for the soapy. Did you notice that? It jarred every time Donald saw those white eyes with so little sight-power hunt for the two handles poking up from the rinse water. And what about the sequence of one person, male, newish but accustomed to the work (Jerry), another person, male, unaccustomed to the work (the new man), another person, male, now accustomed to the work (Donald), and a fourth person, female, accustomed to the work. Isn't that clumsy?

Then you have the plates curving from person to person in an almost perfect trajectory but as for the knives, just splosh! The sequence of hands was all right: two, two, two, two. But the shirt sleeves: two rolled up (Jerry's); one rolled up and one slipping past the elbow (the new man's); one singlet vest (Donald's); two dress half sleeves. Also the distorted sequence of their belts, vestigial trouser belts and not-belts; or the clashing directions in which their bodies turned; or their shoes, plimsolls and sandals, or their mutual glances of respect, distaste or indifference.

They all resented it when the new man began telling jokes in an impenetrable Dublin accent. After all, Jerry knew plenty of jokes and he wasn't telling them. You're not being told any jokes now.

First, to sweeten Donald up, no doubt, the new man offered him a rolled cigarette and gave another to Jerry. When Donald pretended to smoke he noticed the fiery charring was descending the cigarette towards a second, charred and pointed cone of tobacco, partly hidden, the tip of a dog-end the new man had picked up from some gutter and incorporated there to jog the rhythm of Donald's smoking. (How fortunate he was only pretending and had really given the habit up.)

Second, a joke began. 'Therrr ws dhis yngg girll wrra brr period wurra wurra ment thole and drugh chemist's shop and brr sd t'man beheent th cntrrr please brr de th stp brr brrwurra bleedin'.

'An th mn beheent th cntrrr . . . wurra wurra brr brrrrrrr don't yh trrr phnnnnnnnnnnnntlra.'

Donald smiled and began to laugh softly.

Edgily, the man finished the joke with:

'Ntr burra mony isn't norr . . .

'burra.'

(Or it may have been 'norrburra'.)

Donald laughed self-consciously again and Jerry was so annoyed that Margaret instinctively kept on working at the sink, not daring to catch his eye. Her candy-striped dress, with its brown leather belt, packaged her wide arse like a present, before the long rainfalls to her ankles. Jerry looked as if he would strangle her. She didn't hear a thing, the poor old stick, she kept working so calmly. Donald felt like going up behind her, putting his hand round to grasp her breasts and kissing the nape of her neck, not for lust, for the mere fact that he loved her silence. Only he'd aim too high for the droopy taters or too low and seize her stomach fat with witch nipples all over it. The impulse remained good.

Believe it or not, that Irishman told eight more jokes that night. And with each he got more idle, having come to the end of the spasm of energy that had led him to take the job earlier that day. Donald thought Margaret would die covering for him.

'Ntrr burra mony isn't norr . . .

'burra.'

God! He was repeating his jokes now.

All would have held if Margaret hadn't whispered to Jerry: 'Ask him if he's ever been a boxing man.'

Jerry span round as the bell went, and shuffled out towards the Irish champion. 'Have you been in the ring, son?'

The new man wasn't at all surprised at the question. 'I was the wurra burra champion of the old country and I chprr Eric Burra all the way. Me manager . . .' He drifted off. The referee hopped out of the ring and went off down the centre aisle shrugging his shoulders.

It was too much for all of them. But we have entered vicious passages of this book where the weakest go to the wall. So the new man held one arm. Donald held the other. They bent Margaret gently over the sink and she protested, but not too strongly – only in pleasant whispers. Though it was against all justice. Jerry went off to the kitchen and Donald took the opportunity to admire the golden orb of the stillroom light, the plastic fascias, rags hurled into works of art along the surfaces. Jerry came back triumphantly, bearing a brassy kipper which near outshone the orb itself, and was rich from dozens of lands it had visited during its oceanic phase. Margaret's long dress was now definitely the English Nanny, 1915. The new man lifted the back of it and tucked the dress in carefully at the white collar, under her grey hair. Old cotton hung from her sturdy grey back. Major straps from a waist apparatus held up her woollen stockings. Her knee-length drawers, which were of the same crumpled white cotton as her vest, clung to the inside of chicken thighs, and were damp and pink in the buttock cleft. Jerry pulled back the waist elastic and, feigning not to look inside, dropped the kipper in her drawers. With a quick flurry they restored her dress to normal. She gave an 'Aren't you awful' look and went back to work, smiling uncertainly. The kipper may have still been there when she got home. She may have removed it when she went to the lavatory an hour later, or had it for breakfast, or it may still have been there three weeks later. (You get old: see what *you* have to take.)

When Margaret did go to the lavatory, Donald announced happily, 'Well, that's the lot anyway.' He became not a dishwasher but a hotel night porter who had just lent a hand there for the evening and was now off to relieve a man with a scar on his head, their well-loved daytime porter.

As Donald went down the corridor to the porter's desk in the foyer he looked back and Jerry's room door was ajar. Mary was inside talking nineteen to the dozen, if you know what that means. That night, Donald got muddled with all the chalk numbers on the soles of the shoes, so that after cleaning a great pile of footwear he replaced it by the wrong doors, on the principle the guests didn't know who he was, why should he know who they were? Mixing with the working-class right wing, he comforted himself, he had not lost all sense of human sameness.

The next day Jerry went to live in one of McFarlane's semi-detached houses. It could not have been because the hotel manager had discovered the kipper prank – in fact, Jerry had played exactly the same practical joke most nights he'd been there, only you weren't told that. In some way, the Irishman's revelation that he too was a former boxer had made Jerry retreat and McFarlane had been ready to provide refuge. Boxing. The ultimate capitalist sport. Perhaps Jerry had been appalled at the damage his sport had done to the Irishman. Or he was scared an old hand in the business might find him out in some lie; or some time in the past they'd known each other and a damning surgeon's report still lay in a cupboard drawer in Dublin.

Something else was bothering Donald – apart from why did the hotel not notice the kippers disappearing?

Intelligence. Why was Mary so intelligent? Was Jerry as unintelligent as he appeared? What was the nature of their bond? Donald was delighted with this new phrase and went around saying it.

And was McFarlane more intelligent than he appeared? Such possible gradations of intelligence above him!

Jerry in the stillroom two nights later:

As the dirty plates came through the hatchway from the dining room it was his job, it is now known, to scrape the food off the plates into the wastebin. That wasn't good enough for Jerry. He had to save money, him.

In came a hinged chicken leg, leaking gravy but lying nobly on its plate. The bone, a Zorro among leavings, had escaped from a flurry of cutlery on the waitresses' side of the hatchway. The sound of sword-play receded and the plate with the adventurous chicken joint slid across the draining board towards Jerry. At the top the thigh was flabby, its yellow skin drooping over loosened meat. At the bottom, the ankle joint was charred and cauterized. The chef, at least, had known top from bottom, which is more than can be said of some.

Hungrily, Jerry took hold of the charred ankle. The leg hung from his fingers, and, between the gasping meat of the thigh, lungs were panting with fear. This morsel of chicken feared its dissolution just as whole, live chickens, attached by the claws to a conveyor belt in a broiler chicken factory, stop flapping their wings and pant as they are taken slowly to the killing point.

Jerry would call it a free meal, but most people would agree it was fear that his mouth opened to. His lips closed over the thigh joint and sucked the meat clean off it. He broke the thighbone away and tried the same tactic, almost as successfully, with the shank. Treacherously, the meat slid down his throat. The cleaned bones were jettisoned and Jerry reached to the cluster of wine glasses waiting to be washed after the main rush was over. His hand darted in and out whipping up to his mouth traces of red or yellow wine left in the glasses.

A word about his clothes. They never altered: white shirt, open at a frayed collar, rolled up sleeves, cheap grey flannels which bunched up at the belt, socks striped horizontally, brown leather sandals.

A word about the dishwashing machine. On the rim of the first of its two tanks – the one where the dishes were actually washed – were two apparently-identical buttons set into the stainless steel. Beneath the grime, however, one button was red, the other green. At slacker times, Jerry would do what he was supposed to do always: switch the machine off each time the new man was to lift the washed rack into the rinsed tank. Then the water in the soapy tank would slowly whirl and settle. Chicken gravy had made the water flesh-coloured. The two handles of the rack would poke out, the rack itself being obscured, and everyone would smile at each other as the new man began groping for the handles.

Jerry was defiantly recounting his boxing career. He wiped gravy from his mouth, took a crumpled single cigarette from his trouser pocket and lit up, before resuming his litany of harming others.

'I won the north, and went for the southern. George Bridly was my manager. A great big man. Big as . . .'

He hunched his shoulders, shook his head to convey generalized meaning and switched off the machine.

The new man reached forward, found the handles, pulled the load of dishes out of the water, and rested the rack on the edge of the machine so that he could take a breather before plunging the dishes into the rinse.

No clearer warning could have been given to Jerry. The rack had suffered badly from all its time in flesh-coloured water. Slow precipitation of food had furred the iron framework until its colour resembled a kettle's creamy inside. The rack still did its work, giving the browning water skeleton and purpose, but who could be confident about the cleanliness of its work in the machine, where the rack was the innards of a body of water that had corrupted it.

'I knew a boxer once, boxer like you,' the new man interrupted, 'who ate a lorr . . .'

Like Jerry he didn't finish his sentence, though 'lorry' could hardly be the last word. Instead, he walloped the corrupted rack into the last clean rinse water which shook its surface at Jerry to emphasize, 'Be warned.' Be warned of what? Internal corruption?

Secretly, Jerry took his pulse.

10

Lullaby of Marigolds

In the bedroom our personality changes according to whether we start looking at ourselves in the mirror or stop. 'We only ever know a small part of what we think we know totally.' (Apply this to political hubris.) As we glance away from the mirror into the normal perspective, hard real objects rush up and halt abruptly at just the distance of the revised eye focus. One night off from the hotel, Donald undressed in his room safely enough, though it was a tight squeeze when he glanced away from the mirror and up dashed the real objects like chained dogs and snapped at him. Then, because he had something to say to his body, and because without mirrors we are virtually powerless to gesture significantly at our own bodies and have to stroke them to say what we mean, because of that, he turned again to the triptych of mirrors on the dressing table . . . He liked his body for its own sake, smoothing it downwards from Adam's apple. At the chancy stomach region fingers dig in to coax out all the windiness. If Rosine had been there she could have done that for him. A genital flick, of course, to remind himself and it of attachments. Yes, there could have been two of them in the mirror. Or he could have looked in the side mirror and she could have looked in the front. His gesture would have had one direction for him in the side glass, another for her in the front, and a third for their warm bodies out there in the room. His body was composed of three rams' heads on a totem pole: 1. his real face; 2. his shoulders and their long face-torso, with nipple eyes and a 'these sweets are a bit sour' navel mouth; 3. a dwarf genital face with a long nose. He sensed Rosine across the gap of his train journey, reaching out towards the real faces. If she had been there, could they have guaranteed it would always have been their real faces in the mirror? They could have watched their hands in the reflection, that lovely phrase 'handling each other'. The phantom hands that ominously play a piano. 'Do not know what love is until one day you'll call for help.' If they met again before a mirror they would relive old stories, seeing the child, Uncle Aubrey, again, and hearing Uncle Richard clearing his throat in the next room. But within this little circle of right-wing provincialism he was far from that genial emotional dynamic.

Sitting, he deposited on the bed first his genital face on the pillow of his limbs; then he allowed the torso face to sink backwards until at last his real face was upwards on the real pillows. Half ashamed and craven, his personality crept up like smoke and seeped into those three centres of personality.

To say simply that his watch was not yet going properly is to give it far too great a prominence. Rather say: 'I may mention our patient, like all patients with depersonalization, complains that he does not know how long it will be possible for time to continue.'

The room was nearly as dark as the imagined interior of his body; that is, a very thick brown, the colour of the dirty water in the hotel dishwashing machine. His shut eyelids showed pink but he knew that was just the entrance to a cave of greater darkness. In the tea-brown light he suffered from auto-sadistic vertigo in which no outsider performed on him, only a personal force. (At a British Railways inquiry a few days before, the same personal force had made him dizzy when giving false evidence about a silver hip flask.) He might at any moment die. Normally a sweet thought. But to die in McFarlane's house so that by the chain of ownership part of his death would be, to put it mildly, rented, that was disturbing. The fear of death began as a dark spot in the interior of his body and rolled along passageways of internal space, gathering to itself the reddish brown darkness as it went, becoming bigger and bigger, more and more solid, increasing pace, until his heart suddenly loomed up and the hard-packed clot smashed into it. His trachea convulsed at the instant fear of a death inches away from this present time, just to one side, keeping its parallel track. For a minute or two cancer in his breast seized its chance to multiply rapidly. His lungs kept going, mercifully, but with such ill grace that it was clear they had forgotten none of his many quarrels with them.

At 6 A.M. he switched on the radio. It was 19 June 1970. The Conservatives had won the election.

The door at the far end of the bedroom opened and a familiar head peeked in.

Two other railway employees followed McFarlane into Donald's bedroom. All three men had been on a night-long drunk. Their rail uniforms were not so much dowdy as dee-dah, dee-dah. They shunted towards the bed, wanting Donald's company as some conclusion to their night. In McFarlane's right hand was a brown paper carrier bag. He spread his hands like a folksy Epstein St Michael coming out of Marks and Spencers. He was that tall . . . but not of mythological provenance. The other two crunched down beside the patient right and left, and both gave him a lot of side. The red-haired man by Donald's right arm was Masterson and the bald one by his left, Sonny. Or it may have been Mr Son and Sonny Masters.

If the conversation was going to lurch badly at least Donald could make the start firm.

'It's six o'clock,' he said, the words authoritarian but slightly inaccurate.

'Mmmh . . .' (Which one said that?)

'The Conservatives have won the election,' he added. And here history was to bear him out.

Masterson nudged him, as though they all had a special phrase for the election. Donald had but he was buggered if it was the same as theirs.

'Mr Edward Heath has potential greatness,' said McFarlane.

'So has Mrs Margaret Thatcher,' said Masterson, betraying a surprising interest in education.

'We are for all that,' said McFarlane. 'Give 'em supply. Give 'em demand. Let chance fight it out.'

He added: 'We've got a little job for you.'

He glanced at his mates.

'ISN'T

'that

'rIGHT?'

'We've got plenty of time,' said Sonny. Donald looked at his bald head and wondered.

'Pass me that bedside lamp,' said Masterson.

'Uhh?'

'The bedside lamp.'

McFarlane's mouth had a fish rictus; in its darkness words chuckled like dice. A dice pot then.

Sonny said: 'I suppose you could tell us a great deal of poetry, eh?' (Mary had been indiscreet.)

However, in relation to the dice and perhaps to the probabilities of supply and demand and because Donald was really beginning to feel quite chummy, despite a lack of pyjamas, he decided to try one of his Chaucer quotes on them, always good for a laugh:

'Yyyf that a princah uuseth hazardree
In allah govairnaunce and policee
He is, as by commun opinininioun
Y-hold the lass in reputatitatioun.'

The effect was dramatic. Sonny pushed back on one bare shoulder and Masterson the other. Donald was a male principle uniting McFarlane's two friends and he grinned at the red-haired man to show he had tumbled their little sexual secret. In McFarlane's mouth the dice rolled to double six.

'Ah . . . let me see now, lad. You used to be a journalist, didn't you? That's how you get all these quotations, I suppose.'

'I only do Chaucer, Pardoner's Tale,' said the man in bed, trying to match the tone of the gathering.

'Get paid a lot in Fleet Street?' asked Sonny, giving Donald's bicep a little jerk.

'It WAS with one of the NATIONAL papers. No DOUBT you got on very well there,' said McFarlane as Masterson flicked the bedside lamp expertly on and off, shooting red filter all over his chief. 'PROBABLY you put away a little nest egg. A little one. Just a wee bit put by. Just a little bit of the old sock.'

'I'm afraid keeping money wasn't very much my line,' Donald replied. 'Anyway I was never really persistent enough to do much reporting. I did more subbing and a bit of criticism, if you know . . .'

He had an idea. 'Hey up,' he said. 'D'you want me to sell some more watches?'

'No; I don't want any more time wasted on that business,' snarled the Scotsman.

'What do you mean, wasting my time? You can't waste my time when I like doing something.'

'I was talking about MY time.'

A voice whispered in Donald's ear: 'We want you to write us an article. You're MEDIA. You make and break HEROES.'

Masterson explained: 'You know, Sonny and me are good friends of McFarlane here. No need to go into why: we just are. So it came to us that he was a friend of yours as well. I mean he's lent you this nice room here and I think you see quite a bit of Mary, don't you, quite a bit, maybe, and the watches . . . a little article, a sort of eyewitness account about heroism during a rail accident might come in very handy right now, what with the elections and all.'

'Seemed to me the inquiry went off very well, though I wasn't too confident about my evidence.'

'I hope you're understanding well,' said McFarlane. 'I hope you understand all the interests I represent.'

Here was a chance to use a speech Donald had prepared some years ago for quite different purposes but had never used because its tone was too literary. At 6.20 A.M., however, the tone had proved pretty haywire already.

So he said boldly: 'Even when writing we should be at our best. How many journalists with the daily experience of being dominated by an imagined readership can live by that? So many political and academic writers too, posing as history's spokesman to the reader's present-day. They read up information from various centuries, then burst into the present like time travellers who spit out news that no-one can understand. Even if you knew all their sources you'd never know why they chose certain phrases to quote and not others. I couldn't be like that at the inquiry, when I was covering for you and had all those things to say. I pretended a use of time but the panel stole my whole time perspective. It was almost breathless in the timeless room. I can't write any article. Look, it's only for a newspaper but it should still have "endowment of genius, judgment from experience and happiness of mind".'

McFarlane brought a flat leather box from his pocket. He signalled Donald to get up and Donald rose as the hands of his bedside attendants fell away from their principal ballerina who was making such a lovely naked debout, to use the technical phrase for standing still.

The George Medal again. McFarlane pulled out a gleaming wallet and said: 'I've got a cutting here from the old *Sunday Graphic*. I don't think they print that any more, do they?'

Donald read the report again, saying politely to change the sequence: 'I'm not sure if I've read this before or not.'

The main headline read: 'Five soldiers die as ammo blast rocks camp.' An old-fashioned second-deck headline ran: 'Fireman hero hands out shells from inferno's heart.' There was a badly-printed picture of what could have been young McFarlane, or anyone else come to that, wearing a fireman's helmet.

The main head was passable, set across 3 x 3 x 3 columns, but Donald didn't like 'inferno's heart' in the second deck. (He kept these criticisms to himself.) He also wondered, seeing these headlines for the second time, why McFarlane had said nothing about any explosion when he had mentioned this episode earlier, at the train crash.

Pondering that and reading the article again, Donald realized they were wanting him to be suspicious. Can a man with simple intentions want you to be suspicious of him?

'The ammo dump blazed all right,' he said eventually. 'There was an explosion.'

'Of course.'

'What caused it?'

'Who could tell us, laddie, what ACTUALLY caused an explosion – INSIDE it? Don't you go asking a chemistry-johnny. He'd just say the heat and draw you a lot of little formulas.'

'But you weren't the man who handed out the shells.'

'He died.'

'Then I don't understand how the paper got the story wrong.'

'Mary was just a baby but my wife was alive then. There was a married journalist she fancied.'

Donald sprang at McFarlane, who was very strong. The Scotsman wrenched away and gasped: 'Ne dooth unto an oold man noon harm now.'

The Pardoner's Tale. Donald was aghast. He turned round and saw Masterson's gun was pointing. British Railways uniforms versus scuddy buddy (the words came in panic from childhood levels). Donald was outdressed.

What was the rest of the quotation? 'Namoore then . . .' He could not remember. He was outquoted. In some way the Pardoner's Tale had become a criminal signal as surely as the whistling of the song, 'Mona Lisa', had been a resistance signal in a film starring, as far as he could remember, Joseph Cotten, or someone. It was, however, uncertain that McFarlane was cast correctly within his own quotation.

Donald's adversary gestured expansively at his fire cover. 'I'm a pathological murderer. I might murder you today,' McFarlane growled.

The pointing gun gave the naked body a double sensation: first, of being a small, black circle with a white target spot (or at least of wearing such a target on its chest); second, of being a whole body expanding nervously, of its vaporously becoming part of the atmosphere where it didn't have to care about appearances.

All at once, a heroine rescued Donald. She was entirely fictional and bodiless – the fact that occasionally she is here called a shadow education minister means nothing (rpt nothing) in terms of either any real shadow education minister(s) or any real, substantive education minister of any political party whatsoever. This cannot be emphasized too strongly. Only electorates are deeply to blame, *en masse*; everyone else is just doing their best. None (rpt none) of the nomenclature intends slight against anyone, whether professionally, personally, or in any other way. Now surely that covers it. In fact, this 'heroine' was nothing more than a bunch of women's clothing which Sonny grabbed out of McFarlane's paper bag and threw on the bed. Let's look therefore at this 'woman' who bravely hurled herself between Donald and an eager bullet. Her personality was a tweed suit and she knew sex as a pair of real silk stockings, a white slip and panties, quite new, an old suspender belt, and a tattered brassière stuffed with two navy blue socks. Her shoes, Donald was glad to note, were sensible. The wig was grey. Something old, something new.

Masterson gestured with his gun. 'Put them on,' said the barrel hoarsely, for the barrel mouth was an extension of the gunman's body.

Now, referring back to Donald's 'speech', the only good thing about the word, 'happiness', for present purposes is its meaning of successful aptness, fitness, or appropriateness. In that sense, it can sometimes describe how a mind has struggled to reach ease, after due time has been allowed it to accommodate to a situation. But happiness is in that meaning a terminal word and Donald feared his time for happiness might never arrive, because the situation was too implacable, or might worsen or keep changing so fast, and probably for the worse, that his brain would end up racing. Like watching a television programme with too many jump cuts.

The clothing on the other hand offered stability, a fixed role. Also, it gave him a deep hint of a fundamental sameness between men and women. So after that pause, he was only too 'happy' to 'put them on'. He dressed himself in the underwear and stockings very quickly so as to regain a little authority – in the way newscasts are usually read quickly. He put on the tweed skirt and jacket slowly – in the way newscasters have when they reach a sincere topic such as a natural catastrophe.

Because Donald was so willing, McFarlane bent forward and Donald kissed his hair; again, and he kissed his brow; again, and he kissed his smiling mouth.

'Remember they are my wife's clothes,' the Scotsman said. His wife was dead; none of them had forgotten that detail.

Arm in arm, the four men started drunkenly (Donald by assimilation of movement) downstairs, went out to the street and, as day dawned, walked down the road to the bus stop. Along came the early morning double-decker, absolutely empty, barring staff, and they bought tickets for a six-mile journey to the marshland which bordered the New Forest.

As the bus moved off it was, perhaps, slightly, 'ammo blast rocks camp' on the top deck and 'inferno's heart' down below where they sat. But they were hardly travelling within that story at all; so no wonder the analogy was weak. Things were much more confused than that. For example, all kinds of ancient silk had settled in Donald's lap under the tweed and for at least one out of 20 male readers there is no need to explain what sexual confusion that brings. Rather like doing a perfect drawing of male genitals on a piece of tracing paper then screwing it up. The rest of you, ask yourselves what sort of picture forms, three-dimensionally, in the crumpled paper. See, you can't imagine it. Any more than you could adequately answer earlier questions about the passage of food through your bodies without referring to books, and even then . . . Or than you could say now everything that happened yesterday. Or what the political situation really is in any country. The present moment crumples up time too much: we can't quite get to it. However, destiny sometimes seems to help us to skate over our ignorance by offering a reassuring hand (though the ice remains too thin). A very reassuring hand indeed had crumpled a ball of newspaper and stuffed it in between Donald's seat cushion and the back rest. It was a strip torn off the *Daily Telegraph*, dated 19 May 1970, and it didn't seem to worry Masterson sitting beside him that he took time out to read it. 'It is the essence of the Conservative approach to the problems of man in society that society is a living organism which has its being in three dimensions – the past, the present and the future. It follows that the capacity to change and to adapt oneself is the condition of its survival.' Thus far Lord So-and-So's intro took Donald – to ignore, and that unjustly, the rest of the article and the book in which similar thoughts were no doubt to appear. The main thing was, Donald liked the intro's confidence: it was infectious. Politically, the remarks were either obviously true or alternatively 'You don't need this, do you? Mind if I throw it out of the window?' Given India again, Tory politics are pretty flippant. And yet . . . Donald discovered at this moment that the great betrayer of ideals is situation. There was Donald, as left-wing as an amoeba, trying to remain cool in this infernal bus, coping as best he could cope with a change of sex, an executional environment and a surround of hostile BR employees. He was not quite sure whose was the execution anyway. The brassière and its woolly-sock falsies sucked two holes in his chest. For all he knew, his predicament was as desperate as Scott of the Antarctic's. (And look how marvellously Scott managed on a sense of British tradition and destiny.) Besides, Donald was in need of a bit of extra time, sneaked from a reassuring Tory view of past and future. All that drunken laughter in the bus for a future which might not include him . . . These mean bastards had only bought 10p each of the bus staff's time and that was all Donald could be sure of.

Country lanes had succeeded each other until eventually one hedge sank exhausted to the ground, and the awaited marshland gave a sort of 'must you?' look as the bus stopped with the mournful cry of the great bittern. Across the marsh, about 100 yards from them, the forest climbed halfway up a hill then stopped and waited. The bus left the party to it. If the driver had only known, that was the wise thing he did during the journey. Everything else he did was merely following routine.

Sensible shoes gurgled with the pleasure of doing a good job well, as they sucked across the marshland. They hardly needed to keep to the tufty grass, but splashed through troubles. Tweedy clothes bore Donald along indomitably. He was a good sort. While all that muddying was going on below, his thighs had never felt so clean and this was only partly attributable to the silk stockings. The others' British Railways shoes, on the contrary, were used to having a nationalized industry provide hard standing under them. They kept leaping from tuft to tuft and wobbling there, to say nothing of discomfited ankles and swaying bodies above. 'Fear It can kill . . . but it's the vital spark to make you give of your best,' the old *Daily Sketch* had once informed Donald. 'Can fear be controlled before it reaches panic levels? In the normal, healthy person the answer is Yes.' So just at the moment there was no need to feel like the person at the top of that fearful article apparently saying 'Aaaaaaagh!' The black uniforms on either side of him had their reasons for going 'ruff . . . ruff . . . ruff' and Masterson for breaking out in an unintelligible song that might have been a rail shanty, if they have those.

They reached the sharp incline to the forest, the tree roots still above their heads. A trail led up from the marshland. At its foot the trail was black mud, became burnished green, turned to damp earth, and finally to gravel.

It was one of those borders between water and land where the powers of our own darkness rush in on us. McFarlane took out his hip flask and dipped his lips to the dusky interior. It was almost full and the brandy crept on to his tongue as a net of flaming wires. Many-coloured sparks swarmed down his throat, the perfect discovery of fire in vapour the colour of greenish chrysolite that filled his brain with new arrogance. In that single gesture of malicious individuality he gave Donald adequate grounds for a civil action of tort. Around them, at the foot of the hill of alders, oaks, beeches and evergreens, patches of morning mist were lurking about, helping themselves to the sunshine that was destroying them. Donald whispered Jerry's name into the mist. '*Ne mangez pas d'air.*'

When you walk up a steep path it is as though your knees are climbing your stomach. By the time you reach the top there's certainly been a great change of body-image. At the beginning of the trail into the forest Donald looked back to the road. As they climbed higher, what must surely have been the hill itself, internalized in his stomach region as a car jack shoved underneath his fear each step, hoisting it towards his brain and also elongating his body.

The elongation was annulled when they came at the top to a dim alley of firs and beech. A murmur ran through the forest as they entered. Birds crowded to the boughs, bright bushes glowed through tawny masks. The mist crept among those hollow glades, those brakes, thickets, interwoven branches, moistened herbage, those almost-brown-in-the-shady-tracks. 'You will find him in the shed over there, lying on marigolds.' The mist was also among the brushwood and breathed through a patch of berry-bearing plants just under a hollow sycamore.

A holly bush gave way. A forest clearing opened out to them and called out: 'Welcome, welcome! Mind the mist and stream on your way over.' The black stream, taking one leaf per minute through the parted humus and fir needles, was fuming.

Sun among the branches, tilly whim light, mist full of pantomime fairies, then why, why, why did they ignore the orphans?

Always, always look in the darkest thickets for the boundlings, a curious myth in which babies are rescued from their light covering of troubles if found in time.

Instead, on our way across streams all of us keep saying nothing coming is going to upset us. Our bodies will be at peace.

Yet the streams cannot even cope adequately with the falling of leaves.

On the other side of the water they set off confidently through the areas of harm to a quite inconsequential place.

It was a forest clearing, an area of no-harm at the misty centre of harm.

The talk was of alchemy and conservation, the politics of gold and of tradition. But under bushes flesh was discolouring, gold wire cut into the flesh of the boundlings, leaves choked up their mouths.

They are dim-wits. 'Look at the gold wire. Look at all we've done for them.'

A pantomime feeling that their parents must have been rich or famous.

The wealthy background Rosine never had that Donald could not help sensing in her.

As he sensed it in the poorest drunks (their legendary 'brilliant' futures when young men) and in tramps (their 'secret fortunes').

In the voice of McFarlane the orphans were entirely forgotten as he balanced on the sloping bank of the stream and blurted out threats of destruction.

A drunk of such fine arrogance, conjuring the harm that upped and downed in the clouds, invoking the daytime demon of munitions deliveries, treacherous smoke drifting through the woodland, a hot sun bearing on fuses, the rightness of war-mongering, the magical heat properties of superstition and domination.

Such sureness about people, a cut above everyone he talked to, doling out heavenly snubs.

At last he spoke of the massacre of the innocents, with the sun and moon descending to bathe in their blood.

He spoke in kingfisher glimpses, streaks breasted with ardent gold.

The celestial beasts, double snake-bites in the forest, parodies of baby-sleep.

No political, no alchemical arguments are left to try on such a mighty thinker, whose brutality changes every conversation into the terms of his own brilliance.

So this hero was meeting not an opponent but mirror images of himself with whom he wrestled.

A caterwaul of fixed opinions filled the whole forest with its ugly noise, drowning the sound of blood turning purple in infant veins.

Remembering the colours of gold and purple Donald was comforted by the 'prodigality of nature'. At any rate he had survived to this present moment leading towards the clearing.

Wearing that wig and calling himself a shadow education minister again. All his ideas without finance, powerless.

A huge grip on flies, though some escaped and buzzed out of his fingers.

The forlorn hope rose that past, present and future would still mean something as a relationship ensemble, even in clearings where there is no harm.

As he nodded complicitly at each of the Scotsman's cruelties, his assent was unfortunately part of his so-called 'real' belief, which he had hoped he was just betraying but was in fact displaying.

McFarlane's face bent over a stream of alcohol decorated with other people's troubles. The silver hip flask was unattended on a rock beside him.

Before anyone could wrestle for his eloquence, which was a testimony on damp parchment inside the flask, sleep seized them as quickly as storm vapours envelop a mountain forest.

The clearing filled with heavy cloud.

Action died on the lip, a falling-back under canopies of mist and darkness, McFarlane's voice even more incoherent and out there in the clouds, the grumbling of an enemy.

In the darkness spasms and slow pulses of light.

Sluggish beams glanced off rocks, a stream, a wooden hut, beech trees.

Clouds of garlic, smoke and brandy parted momentarily, green chrysolite vapour fleeting in the trees; and there the drunken giant stood once more, light streaming off him, his clothes fabulously well-cut, heart an ornamented hunter watch ticking its own, irregular time.

Across the clearing the trees shook.

Another shadow education minister broke through the beeches.
She was arrayed in the morning sun.
It was 7.30 A.M. and a sober time.
In that mirroring of Donald
the figure's nostrils steamed
and scrolls of birth ornamented the forest.

The new shadow education minister was Mary, dressed identically to Donald, though hardly of the same political persuasion. The most ridiculous moment was when she embraced him and all the 'men' cheered. In gun law, he thought bitterly, cheering is the easiest thing in the world.

He said: 'Marigolds. Then we are not far from a memorial garden.'

Mary put a finger to her lips and replied: 'Don't disappoint me, dear.'

Minded, funded like that, she must be in his lungs already. The word 'dear', in his chest, a CS gas canister burning a small cancerous scar into his lungs and making his breath acrid.

More riot gas kept back the mob of trees and the party continued up the slope to a small, wooden hut, which stood on the crest between two beeches. Bushes scratched at the flimsy wooden door like dogs pleading to go in.

The door swung open with a bang. At that moment the hut filled with reality. A baby, dressed in a pastel blue stretch suit and black cardigan, lay asleep on a low mound of marigolds that covered the floor of the hut. The baby lay away from them, facing the interior of the hut, one leg unnaturally straight out and pointing towards them. The other leg was curled up to his (blue for a boy) stomach. All told, he was the shape of a leg of ham. His shoulders were so relaxed that Donald knew very well what 'sleep' meant, what that stiff leg meant.

No premonition reaches happy conclusions until our eyes are blinded with the truth.

The baby lay like the word, 'dear', which only seconds before Donald had found such an unforgivable gift.

'Dear,' said Donald and bent towards him.

The body did not at first answer Donald's hands, until he pulled more strongly. The black cardigan stirred willingly but not the body underneath. Weighing so little, the baby could not resist for long. The upper body twisted at the waist and then the whole body rolled over into view, the face dallying but tagging on.

Uncle Aubrey – if that was he, for Donald had never seen him so close before – had been strangled with thin, gold wire.

This forest, so good at orphaning children, had bereaved two parents.

The wispy hair (was that Stan Laurel *again*? No, James Cagney) looked charming, and the mother-dressed neatness of his body was free of dislocation, holes or depersonalization. The face was an unwelcome map, or pattern, full of meaning. The capillaries, desperate for oxygen, had frozen into a crimson-brown network of fixed routes that would have revealed their stability at once had Donald been less dizzy. Mucus had drained down from the baby's nose because he had naturally been crying – surely you would not blame him for that? – and the mucus had dried on top of his swollen upper lip. So two fragile mucus-teeth had formed on the outside of his lip. He had no more time to offer, as once he had offered it in the stretch of a baby's pacific seconds. His real teeth, which had only partly emerged in the slow months of his life, would not now complete their set.

FACE (Uncle Aubrey's) to FACE (Donald's).

In the face-to-face situation the area of meaning is established moment by moment in gradual barter.

How does the barter work if one of the faces has broken out in a final map, not embarrassed, pleased or fearful, but just geographic? When it's you that's the live one of the pair, some of your friends might imagine such a moment as unpleasant for you. In fact, unless you are very unusual, a smirk comes to your lips. The smirk comes from the centre in you that dreams idly of a serious accident happening to your wife or at first finds it funny when a mother turns on her child (but secondly is discomfited when a blow lands heavily). The death of any child makes the future at first seem so unencumbered that it would be churlish to destiny not to feel at least an instant's happiness before the hurt begins, the notion of 'destiny' being in any case a product of some very dubious emotions. And, far from unimportant, this moment of joy is the most crucial failure of your goodness, whether the joy comes at the sight of death or creeps into consciousness several days later. The flaw in goodness is also a wound in your image of your body. Nothing was owed any more to this baby in the hut, who gave every appearance of being ill but was healthier than Donald's ultimate selfishness, as he stood there swallowing down the real meaning of this encounter.

Its meaning in terms of himself. Since the baby's face had become utterly phony.

When you have the highest need to shed your ego you'll shrink from the death in the mirror.

To the vanity born in Donald at the death of Uncle Richard he now opposed this admirable quality of unintelligence, displayed selflessly in Uncle Aubrey's life and perfected in the stupid discolouration of his dead body. The perfection of a man's last piano chord opposed to the strangled cry of originality.

The baby angel said: 'We love you, Intelligence: look into your heart.'

The quotation revealed the wound in Donald; but even then he had only a glimpse of red far beneath the fatty tissues of conscience.

The three men grasped his arms and shoved him forwards on to the heap of flowers. He had a fleeting: 'Oh Lord, not the kipper gag again' and then the door closed, leaving him in the dark, face down beside the baby corpse. The marigold cuttings gave out the dank smell of strangers.

This end-comprising-the-beginning was an ideal setting in which to rediscover the emotion of love. A fierce bar of sunlight in the dark.

At first, love came to Donald like the fear of the death beside him and of his own death. Next, like guilt for having a premonition of death and being able to do nothing about it. So the hammer-headed pterodactyls took tea with the bishops; inside the head of man was a mass of black-magic grimoires. Then love came like a knowledge of the difference between himself and the baby: the virtuous, unintelligent, willing, short-lasting, powerless, truthful, minor, chuckling, crinkle-eyed, original, stumbling, vulnerable, contrary, agreeable, sovereign baby and the moral, intelligent, reluctant, durable, powerful, lying, major, boastful, watchful, conventional, strident, armoured, complaisant, agreeing, vassal adult. And the love reconciled these differences but feared death still because it trumped the differences with its dog-eared ace of spades. Next the fear of death became naturally assimilated and, instead, that initial moment of joy as the hut opened took over. The joy was robbed of the sighs and tears which had surrounded it with guilt and glowed as a fierce electric bar of self-love mounted on the hut wall. The heat burned through the fatty tissues, searing unbearably as it searched inwards to cauterize the wound. The pain was insupportable. Such love would destroy thought. Donald could neither rest nor sleep while the joy remained so punishing, forcing him to love a self that had been demoniacally joyful at the baby's death. After hours of contemplation, the joy was not seen as demonic but as a basic energy, the amoral beginning of the subjective-objective interplay that brings the sense of reality. You have to love this cruel energy for that and say goodbye to weariness and the luxury of mental illness.

Now love came like the knowledge of sameness: a middle-aged woman with permed brown hair meeting an old man in a beret outside a window; the knowledge that Uncle Aubrey's life and Donald's were interchangeable; that there was much Donald could accomplish that the mongol's unintelligence could never have attempted but that this included nothing important. That there was a love between Rosine and him that could compensate for this child that he had cradled for a long time inside this hut. He looked for that goodness in the philosophy of loving. In the interior of his chest, some calm place among the eddying; among streams of busy cars, a calm river.

Eventually, the future stood before him minus one leg.

In the cemetery it is bad form to question the terms of the legacy. But it doesn't really matter whether you wait decorously for the moment in the solicitor's office, make a journey to another town and wait for the solicitor's letter, spend the whole sum right away, or place the money in a deposit account and dip into it several years later. The question remains: 'Does there ever come a time when you may without fault use the money?' Either the money no longer belongs to the dead man, in which case it is everyone's, or it does belong to him and is not yours. Sneakily, you invoke the impossible concept of posthumous gift; a gift made for a dead future over which the legator has only this theoretical right. Uncle Aubrey's legacy to Donald was unintelligent goodwill. Could he use it despite his moment of joy at the baby's death? What right had he to take that goodwill for his own?

Only one right: to use it well.

He so liked morals; and what a marvellous kind of mental health is available to us if we can only purify our energy and clear our stomachs and chests of misery and guilt.

Uncle Aubrey pleasantly lay there as Donald scribbled the following resolutions into his blue notebook:

To be a good man as a matter of mental health.

To stop: searching for friends, merit-rating people, panicking.

To re-create our happiness.

To slim.

He realized that McFarlane had erred in pushing him into the hut because he had given him a gift of time, the same gift Donald had thought it forlorn to hope for on the bus. He could not win him over through fear.

He kicked the door down. Apart from a certain lack of personnel, the outside scene had hardly changed at mid-day.

In the sunlight, he looked down into the hut and saw that Uncle Aubrey's face was a patchwork of politics. The mottling was now recognizable as a map of Uruguay. One of the burst capillaries reaching up the side of his face represented the River Uruguay, separating Brazil and Uruguay and forming with the Parana the Rio de la Plato. The coast followed his chin-line. His cheeks had their heights, their place names like Mercedes, Tacuarembo, their forests, rail connections and coastal plains.

11

Playwrights Three

'The main worry,' said Rosine, 'is Uncle Aubrey's dynasty.'

'He was infertile. His dynasty had already reverted to me,' Donald replied.

'That means,' she said, 'it's still your responsibility.'

They were in the museum flat and Frank was dozy-doing the porcelain figures on the shelves while Donald told them about his ADVENTURES.

He had one of his quick intuitions that were always wrong: 'Don't you see? A frame-up. Mary, looking like me, laying a trail to the hut containing the baby. The bus crew in McFarlane's pay. The murder of a baby laid at my door, or rather me laid at the murder's door. I suppose I was expected to walk away with the baby instead of replacing it. And all for the sake of a newspaper article,' he finished bitterly.

'Oh, stop thinking about yourself,' said Rosine sharply, tossing back her long red hair like an impatient filly. 'I don't believe that for a moment. You have probably missed the whole point or translated something quite mysterious into something banal. Even if you were right it would be no better than saying the point of going to the cinema is to watch some meagre little story.'

'It's certainly true we've our whole lives to live,' said Frank sententiously, turning his Peter Finch/Oliver Reed profile.

Rosine glared angrily at him, but put his remark to use all the same: 'And we've dynasties to sort out,' she said, sticking a radio antenna into the closed nutshell of Frank's tautology.

'So I don't need to worry about alibis any more?' Donald said, brightening.

No-one, of course, thought it worth while adding anything to *that*: so there was silence, broken at last by Frank.

'Why don't you write a play about the death of Uncle Aubrey: change it from a right-wing into a left-wing dynamic?'

'Why don't you write a play about the Creadores?' Donald countered grumpily.

'Why don't you and Rosine collaborate in writing your play?' Frank added, not just to include all three of them but to ensure that Donald's would be finished.

'You shouldn't try to profit out of poor Uncle Aubrey's death,' Rosine warned piteously.

'It wouldn't be a question of profit: we should merely live for a while inside the news of his death,' said Frank professionally.

That was beautiful. It made Donald see Uncle Aubrey again as a museum building or as a gaseous baby figure, giant, with all three of them this time riding on a platform in his middle.

'When you say "live inside Uncle Aubrey . . ."'

'Inside the news . . .'

'Well, inside the news, how would the play be performed?'

'What we could do,' said Rosine slowly, changing from her filly's look to her mare's look, 'is form a touring company to present both plays.'

'Great, great, great, great. That's a fantastic idea. I know a terrific Latin American actor, who knows about the real revolution,' enthused Frank.

'We have our own company, we'd have control over such things as bad taste,' said Rosine, still bothering about inessentials.

'I don't know,' said Frank. 'You'd be using professional actors and we'd only be amateurs. Perhaps they'd have the whip hand.'

'But we've got a cast already,' Donald observed.

'It isn't . . . er . . .' guessed Rosine.

'Yes. Everybody can play their own parts. Mary can play Mary. I think you'd like her Rosine, once you'd got over your jealousy, but you'd have to watch her – she's a bit tricky. The new man at the hotel can play the new man. Jerry can play Jerry. The British Railways men and all that. I'm sure they'd be delighted. There's only one thing . . .

'I won't have McFarlane in it. For one thing he's such a bore, gets drunk, wants to be a hero, he'd want articles written, he'd hog the stage. I'm fed up with his being Scots all over the place, he wouldn't allow the change of politics, and there's no need to limit our play to the time-scale of events finishing up with the hut in the woods. We can give it any kind of sequel. And Frank wouldn't get on with McFarlane.'

Frank did his eyebrow-raising trick.

'You're such an intellectual snob, Frank, for all your left-wing; oh yes you are. McFarlane is just the sort who'd annoy you, quoting Chaucer when things get awkward. No, I say we give McFarlane another name and get a professional actor, your Latin American if you like: he could be in both plays, yours and ours.'

So that was settled.

Rosine said in hers and Donald's play they could do Uncle Richard and Uncle Aubrey partly by stage illusions and, when they had to appear more solidly, the professional actor could double Richard and McFarlane and Rosine's other baby (whom I have deliberately not mentioned so far) could play a flesh-and-blood Uncle Aubrey.

'Trust you to write in a part for your baby,' Donald said with a gentle smile. 'Unfortunately, I think we're past the stage of wanting a real baby for Uncle Aubrey. You'd better park our child with my mother.'

'What I like about this set up is that we'd have a perfectly-balanced cast to do my Creadores play as well,' said Frank. 'I don't see that either play needs professionals, except for my man for McFarlane and my own male lead. But we could do some other good doubling, what with three women, two attractive, and that deaf Margaret creature. I think mine would be semi-musical comedy – oh very Free Theatre,' he said hastily.

With that remark the spirit of the late 1960s gave a tired sigh and held itself in readiness for another outing. 'Don't forget to see if you can plunder anything from conceptual art,' Donald said resignedly.

Rosine raised one of her practical difficulties: 'Where would we perform the plays? I mean, who would have us?'

'You're the drama critic,' said Frank.

'Shit,' Donald retorted, but it was true. He had been a stand-in critic for several months on one of the nationals.

'I think it might be easy enough,' he added later. 'I can find us enough contacts, maybe a bit small town rep sometimes but I should think we'll get by.'

'Then if it's a real success we could tour American universities,' said Rosine, swopping into one of her wildly optimistic moods.

Nobody said 'Steady on' because to tell the truth they both thought 'Why not?'

'We'll need some money to start with,' Donald reminded them.

'Blakeston,' said Rosine immediately. 'You don't need it, Frank.'

Frank said nothing, which was encouraging.

Rosine added: 'I have one stipulation. It still seems to me we'd be having a lovely time touring round and there's Uncle Richard and Uncle Aubrey dead. I vote that if we do make any profits above normal living expenses they go to Mencap.'

'That's very middle-class of you,' snarled Frank, whose idea of charity was to contribute to arms purchases by revolutionaries in countries he'd never visited.

The profits question was, however, settled to Rosine's satisfaction.

'Rosine had a stipulation; now I've got one,' Donald said. 'If she and I are to collaborate on our play it seems only natural to me that we sleep together. There is really no distinction between the writing of literature and any other part of life,' he added, to give the strategy philosophical lift.

'I'll have Mary,' said Frank, after a very long pause.

'She's all right.'

'Suits me,' said Rosine, with a sort of boys-together matiness.

So that was settled.

'I have a final stipulation,' said Rosine.

'Oh yes?' Donald murmured apprehensively.

'Our play has to have a moral.'

'Plays with morals are nice,' he readily agreed.

All along, the job of the collaborators was easier than that of the solo maestro.

You pull the chain in the shower, the water spreads its unctuous hand over your hair and that little voice from the heavens descended hisses out of the sprinkler: 'Know thyself.' You climb out of the shower and dry yourself and, sooner or later, most of the play's draft is quite dry in your hands. Along comes Rosine, peels a few damp sheets from your back, retypes them, chivvies them up, adds scenes, and you've got a play, probably very much like 'The Death of Uncle Aubrey'. Probably very much like 'The Plot so Far'.

Frank's dubious methods: sighs, days of ill temper, of 'inspiration', 'free' writing sessions, all those tiresome 'stimulative' techniques. He had a lot of good ideas. Which may explain why altogether Donald didn't like his play one bit. Well, he liked one or two bits among all that . . . that . . . what do you call it when a comparatively wealthy westerner plays about with the desperations of the poor? Ah yes, wowlfaring. The authentic Creadores songs were fine but Frank most liked a song by Sylvain Marechal that he sneaked out of Donald's Buonarotti book on the Babeuf conspiracy and translated into a form as traditional as a bit of a 4 by 2 rifle barrel cleaning rag:

The people's rights are out to lease
Death from hunger and disease
       Grief in the slums
The rich behave with cruel grace
Present the poor a smiling face
       Baring their gums

The new men swell like bees with honey
Seize the hive and seize the money
       Rich yet drones
But you, my toiling fellow man
Eat like an ostrich if you can
       Iron and stones

Oh profiteers, our flames will burn
The plans to make your dollars earn
       Spare us your tears
Without you, we shall know again
Equality and with its reign
       Honey-rich years

Though prison may be waiting for us
Let us be of the Creadores
       Bend to the task
The poor will learn my song by heart
One day they too will play their part
       That's all I ask

Here was where they should have seen the last of Frank. But no. He just hung around. The song remained a museum piece, when it should have written him into a hovel: and there he'd be, saying hallo to Mrs Jenkins whose husband has left her with all those children, and visiting the old dear with the aged budgie. Instead, he went round singing, 'Let us be of the Creadores', as if they were the Ovaltinies.

'Whatever you or I think of any guerrilla movement, neither of us has the slightest opinion that could be of use to Uruguay,' Donald told Frank. 'Just because we've read a book or two or handled the odd news dispatch, or paid a flying visit, or even spent a year there, like you. The whole theme is superficial to our lives and present purposes and yet you're treating it as a luxury to which you have a right.'

This argument took place in the vestibular centre at the base of Donald's brain, near where ear liquid swirled. The argument sent him completely off balance. Within the ear liquid Frank pirouetted on an island called Uruguay. It was bye-bye to land connections with Brazil, to third-degree methods of interrogation, to Frank's corny ideas for audience participation. Then sickness and vertigo returned and he'd hear Frank again, explaining how members of the audience prompted by their kidnapped actors, were going to try to ransom them with the 'authorities' on stage. Donald muttered: 'That sounds horrible.'

'It sounds horrible but it works,' claimed Frank.

'So does my arse,' said .... Rosine.

'I thought you said this was going to be a musical comedy,' she added.

'So it is. The actors can sing their "I'm alone and kidnapped in this shed" numbers from all over the theatre. The cast can sing back threats. Members of the audience can tune with oldies like "True Love".'

'"For you and I have a guardian angel,"' Donald quoted appreciatively.

Rosine remained on the attack. 'What a hackneyed mess. And you've borrowed the shed from the Aubrey play. It's going to look really odd.'

'The shed's needed for kidnapping. Anyway, what do you think is the minimum test of originality?' asked Frank nastily.

'That's a ridiculous question,' said Rosine with considerable philosophical exactness.

'Look baby, you just don't know. You know? That's just riding me up. As for you, Don, you may think yourself some godawful drama critic, but you wait and see which play the audiences prefer.'

By fortunate coincidence they both replied, 'Hum-ti-hum.'

As I say, their own play was very much like the story so far but with some additions, sort of 'Knocking at the Gate in Macbeth' scenes.

Rosine wrote a good scene for herself. They had two Uncle Aubreys in the cast: the dead one and a phantom-light apparition, mostly hands and face. Rosine's scene, which was supposed to star her alone on stage with the dead Aubrey lying on a piano top, kept straying into another reality. As most of her ideas and many of her phrases came from *Les Mains d'Orlac* by Maurice Renard, that wasn't surprising. Still, it didn't matter: Donald realized why she felt close to that book which he liked even better than Lowry's *Under the Volcano* where he'd once seen it mentioned – and the way she stole from it was nice.

'I'd appreciate your scene even more if you read it to me in the park,' he said. Eric Morecambe gave a quick leer from the television screen and vanished.

12

Correction: Playwrights Four

In the park, late-abed seagulls circled overhead, calling 'Jacques Lacan, Jacques Lacan', without giving further details. Rosine and Donald entered an iron gateway on the far side of which they would be together for a moment. Beside them was a black pond, whose fountain had died down for the night, and ripples were graylings across the submerged nozzle. Under the shadow of damp trees the primary opposition of obscure and clear, the veteran couple of *yin* and *yang*, had been vanquished by evening. A little owl hooted imputations of harmfulness from a tall oak. An aggressive reaction fell into series. Gravel paths stretched away from the two humans and crept round gloomy foliage. With brutal explosion, a blackbird darted from a bush, flew straight down a path to their left and, banking off to one side, disappeared into an old-fashioned cold war. In secondary opposition, a branch of the same bush was overcrowded with roosting starlings and its tired limb lowered to the ground, where they all courteously alighted. Donald and Rosine walked a few yards in the melody of walking and came to a blue mist lying in the hollows. Their thoughts were horizontal – – – – They were playing the game of those who hide themselves, the long-ago, the daligone, the ostrichry, her white scarf and long, black coat, lost arm lost in lost arm, the *pris au piège*, the nonsense park, cold superstition breathing across wet grass. Chains between low posts went 'yup, yup, yup, yup' along the side of the path and led to a halting point. An empty pair of boy's grey flannel shorts ran away across the grass about two feet above ground. 'They're not mine,' Donald remarked. They were at the cross-roads where they had left their dreams. The park ghost in the wood thought it about fucking time to start; a concrete heron fell into the pond mud.

Rosine said: 'The world's most frugal meal, heron shank.'

Behind them came the sound of a car engine idling. They turned. A black saloon had drawn up outside the railings. Three men, two in British Railways uniforms, came out of the shadows and got into the car. They must have been waiting by the railings when Donald and Rosine walked into the park.

'I thought there were only going to be two railmen,' Rosine said.

'Frank's brought up his professional actor friend for McFarlane's part already – the Latin American.'

'Already I feel it's not personal any more.'

He was about to tell her of his plans to re-create their happiness when she gripped his arm. 'Look,' she whispered: 'the hut.'

From the pond, a stream led into the park wood. On the other side of the stream, among some ornamental bushes, stood a good-enough replica of the hut in the forest.

They crossed over the water. Rosine opened the door and found the famous child they loved. The baby was only an amputated pair of hands. They were wet with perspiration; she cuddled them in her breasts. The hands had been cruelly tested: hundreds of cuts had left a network of purplish-red scars.

ROSINE: 'The child's left hand first: fractures of the wrist and metacarpus, of the first and second finger joints, rupture of the extensor and flexor muscles, severing of the supinator muscles, contusion of the ball of the thumb, crushing of the short abductor, lumbrical, and interosseous muscles, veinous ruptures, multiple ecchymosis blotchings.'

To be resurrected beginning with the hands . . . there was in the dead child's ego something new . . . fear, aberration, boasting, that the state of his hands did not justify.

Those hands. So heavy and lumpish, a single crease across the palm like an ape's. But dispensers of joy, glory, abundance. The child had loved Rosine and Donald, but not so much as he had loved his hands: twin gods, demanding and infertile. These simple scar patterns awakened their most intense realities.

ROSINE: 'With one finger, a single, timid finger, he picked out the theme of Liszt's Fantasy, the last work he had performed . . . the Hungarian motif recalled the spirit of the masterpiece . . . Harmonies sang in distant sonority . . . light breezes in the sacred wood.'

The two uncles came very close to her spirit. Somehow, in their real lives, their own play had begun.

Eight P.M. Despite her thick coat, she shivered. It was the low point of her spirits. Anxiety tortured her epigastrium. The supernatural was in some way indigestible to her. Rosine held fast, brave girl. But in the shadows the enemy held fast also.

Still affected by past conversations, worried about the future, she felt herself light as if her flesh's density had really diminished. Mysterious eyelids, not her own, closed over her eyes. She saw the ineffable eyelid pattern of some other person: a sort of companionship in her nightmare.

A grand piano on a road.

ROSINE: *'Un piano à queue sur un estrade.'*

When they remembered the child, a thin beam from a weak torch battery flitted about a wrecked train carriage. The strangers' bodies smelt maggoty. That incense estranged them from themselves. The soul of arrested speed worked on them. Back in the park, the slowness of a Catholic service took over. Rosine tried to constitute in herself a self full of sang-froid.

Under the trees Donald whispered comfort: 'If we had closed the play on the hut scene, it would have been like a book with portraits of the two uncles on facing pages. The book closes and falls back and there's nothing left.'

'Put this in,' said Rosine impulsively. 'The light of evening falling on a book. As our activities speed across ice our bodies change. Long distance. Rosine and Donald skate towards each other from opposite sides of a frozen lake; as they draw near their hands are searching for each other.'

'I can't put that in anywhere,' Donald said with a grimace. 'We shan't be playing at the Westover Ice Rink, you know.'

'Doesn't matter,' she said carelessly. 'Just a sudden picture I caught.' She no longer breathed. Or more exactly her breathing was short-winded, superficial, and halting; she felt an alarming pain in the heart region and a weight on her stomach. The child – represented by hands – was safely back in the hut.

Rosine stroked the live purple of her lips with a gold fingernail. In her wide eyes was the same blaze Donald had noticed in the pupils of the child the day he was stolen. It was not the light of knowledge but some reflected light of another's kindness. Donald was innocent because her eyes were also. For a moment, her picture entered his own mental landscape.

They knew all sorts of people were hating them, refashioning their faces into ugly shapes. The sky was dark grey and the sun winter-bleak across unexpected ice. Rosine was a dusky ninepin.

Beautiful skating . . . the speed men . . . their arms swinging low. An escape from hurtful feeling across the cold . . .

Donald traced her eye surface with his finger and thought it was like cupping a breast. He kissed the darkness behind whose hymen a light shone for her. He kissed the rim of the iris, kissed the stupid white surrounding the central cloud and her eyelid flickered over the smart. A sense of her eye patterns, a knowledge of that firing behind the lid, entered his eyes. Together, their lids closed. The child became a friendly god, crawling towards them across the ice, showing them it would be all right. Deformed by the thoughts of others, Donald's body was yet at peace, which was a very high compliment to her.

They held each other tightly and broke gladly, without awkwardness.

Then she said: 'What's the moral going to be?'

'Well,' he replied, as an old piece of newspaper crept along the path to eavesdrop, 'I've written that already.'

NOT IN ANOTHER PHOTO

Your photo in a newspaper. The hotel
fire. No. That's a mistake on
the uneasily-stirring vehicle
of day. The paper,
bearing a dead woman's photo
slides over cracks to
lie half in evening. Our child
is safe with us, meanwhile
a burnt female body
soaks in your chest where
children have already drowned. Warm
nightwinds arrive. We hurry our son
out to the car. Your charred body
sits away from me in the corner.
You look as dead as a queen, not
in another photo, I mean a real
queen, waving. The seat between us moves.
This journey will express the

jerkiness of fear, not its passion, to
drive through cold flames, light passing
across your face. The hotels
of conversation are all on fire
under the wheels.

'That doesn't sound much like a moral,' Rosine said. 'It sounds
more like another piece of plot, mixed with bits of some other
story. Don't you think it puts us all at risk, what with your
superstitions about poetry's ability to foresee – that fire in there,
for instance?'

'Oh, you mean a moral like "When the pig's snout be among the
ivy tod, guide yourself through the trees,"' he said.

She nodded enthusiastically: 'Yes. That's almost it. But too
proverbial.'

'I'll have to think about it.'

For the moment, however, the poem would have to do.

Frank's saloon car must have had others to collect because it
was arriving as the two of them got back to the museum just
beating all the crowd to the side entrance. Rosine and Donald
stepped inside the door, turned, and he broke into pure broderie
anglaise:

'Hallo Mary, nice to see you: how's the watch trade? Masterson,
come in; you haven't met Rosine – that was a great show you put
on in my bedroom. Now, Jerry, no rape scenes please: have you
met Frank? Come in everybody. Sonny, take Margaret's arm, will
you?'

Sliding sideways, surging forwards, concentrating inwards,
exploding outwards again, they entered.

Frank took Donald on one side. A cigarette from a low level
appeared in Frank's lips as white innocence issuing blue beatitude.
He said quietly: 'His name is Joel de Sotas. He's damn good and
politically 100 per cent.'

The meaningless last phrase became a smoke ring and floated
upwards as a halo above the South American actor, whose back was
still turned to Donald. Long black hair fell over the collar of a khaki
overcoat. Very basically, Donald didn't believe in haloes; and they
were diabolical coming from a tainted personality like Frank's.
Mary clasped her hands, shut her eyes, and prepared not for
worship of de Sotas, as feared, but for speech: 'Let's see who we all

are.' The suggestion was, typically for her, provincial and stupid; but, also typically, was sly, pretending to be ignorant of knowledge that she patently possessed in the main, and for all these things was existentially challenging.

The South American turned and Donald caught a glimpse of a bronzed face.

Joel looked at the new man from the hotel and saw a poor man, looked at Margaret and saw she was deaf. He was not filled with compassion but with interest anyway. Frank looked at Joel and awoke late, but was in time to see a Latin American turning. Rosine looked at Joel and seemed to be waiting entirely for Donald. He looked at Joel and in some strange way. Joel looked at Rosine with ancestral darkness, and if she did not at moment have an orgasm she knew that come 'Music at Midnight' and the last cocoa she'd be at the brink. Joel looked at Donald at last and the engines of Donald's life stopped turning.

'Man overboard,' said Frank.

'We're one short,' said Mary.

'Full steam ahead is the phrase, I believe,' said Joel in a perfect English accent.

Behind them creamed a steady wake. Joel was supposed to have supplanted only McFarlane but unaccountably tossed Donald out of the cast list too as if kindness was the most unwanted principle of all.

Rosine brought out whisky, gin and mulled wine. They all counted each other. They were nine.

'Perhaps we'll prefer it that way,' said Rosine, paying little heed to a hut door banging angrily down in the park – Donald presumably having gone off in a huff and shut himself in with the hands they loved so much. A luminous star, like the silent soul of a roman candle firework, rose above the hut roof. Rosine was so momentarily dazzled by Joel that this departure was only a graze with but a slight smart of reality in it. Yet only an hour previously she had recited the wounds of the hands. She has no responsibility for apparent fickleness: you have to consider narrative sway and its influence on her, as strange a phenomenon as solar wind.

'We may need a few more people but that can wait until after the journey,' said Joel, while they all wondered 'What journey?' Asleep or awake, Joel was out of prison. The pallor of his face when he was in earnest. The coldness of his body.

That evening, under Rosine's expert tutelage, they all got awkwardly and unhappily drunk. Rosine slept with Joel, Frank with Mary, Jerry went out looking for his and arrived back at 6 A.M. with nothing to say but with a keen look on his face. The new man was shoved into bed with Margaret, and the two British Railmen pleased themselves. Above the hut in the park a dwarf star watched Rosine with a dense frown. Without love and heavy with honour, the star.

Joel first entered Rosine as they leaned against the bedroom wall. Their genitals were at the ground floor level of two large buildings connected by this short passageway. Liberality, beauty and pleasure were rooms on that level. For ten seconds the fire of confidence raced along the passageway, through an open door and into a lounge. Having got there, the ragged flame flared up snakelike and darted its flickering tongue forward. Fortunately, the lounge was almost empty and dripping with damp; the flaming snake in a despairing gesture stalled in mid-air and fell into a pool of liquid where it remained as a coloured streak of oil for a full five minutes. Then the brightness drowned in its own milk.

Rosine told him that and the darkness replied:

'If you say you cannot love at this level . . . clear, pure, clean, truthful, subtle, simple, valiant, diligent, luminous, full of new thoughts and ancient memories . . .'

Her side of the building shrank inwards to a tall line: in the shadows the enemy was also a tall line, exactly matching her. A tall H connected by the penis.

Though he had spoken of Love she knew he meant Hate.

She half-remembered another man. By numerous veins the man came to her heart but it was not an exact knowledge, just a half-memory of something he had said.

'The height of love is praise for third parties,' she said.

'Beside you they are clay dolls.'

Though that was not good enough, she had to be content with it; they finished undressing and went to bed. The next morning Joel lifted his body from Rosine, not that he'd been there all night, and his long black hair slowly withdrew from either side of her face. She was still repenting – a very big word which is always worth playing about with because so many things you can do with it are true, or, at least, affecting.

Joel's knees and hands surrounded her like fairground knives.

No they didn't. Like paws. As his lean, 28-year-old body crouched over three-quarters of her length, his hair flopped down into black cocker spaniel ears on a golden labrador body. Rosine laughed bitterly, for she saw that while her own body had always been golden colour tinged with earth there was eight hours' more earth colour in it now, which, though a very minute fraction (and absolutely natural it should be added too) is pretty grisly when you actually see it. 'Don't grieve. Do grieve,' said Joel, changing it the instant he saw her eyes. That didn't exactly fill her with liking. He stood up. She was overwhelmed by a man for whom she felt no liking. Every second some hesitation in her face yielded to his look.

The former emotional ground floor of his body had shifted halfway up a skyscraper and a rolled-up pink duster was hanging out one of the windows. Joel drew up a pair of navy blue underpants to his middle, with the concentration of an architect having second thoughts.

'How old are you, Joel?'

'28.'

As, in various rooms of the flat, everyone else got dressed, a third play started to emerge. 'Oh God, not another,' groaned Frank, as he and Mary dressed with their backs to each other.

It would be close but wrong to call the new play an amalgam of the Creadores musical comedy which Frank had previously outlined and the Uncle Aubrey play: it was more a new spiritual body that arose among the nine of them and spread outwards, surrounding the whole group like an aura.

Frank and Mary had to sleep on sand-coloured foam mattresses in the lounge. Frank stuffed his 'provincial sexpot' so hard during the night he left a kakon inside her, still upping and downing the following morning. His language didn't help. For him also, the night was an opulent memory but not a particularly good one, like memories of a Gilbert and Sullivan evening or (to be fair to G. and S.) *Oklahoma!*

Mary finished dressing first and hurried off to the museum's staff lavatory, where she met Jerry coming out. They held a muttered conversation of which Rosine, passing by on her way to cook breakfast, just caught Jerry's words: 'You're to try to keep in with both Frank and Joel, Mary, McFarlane says . . .'

Meanwhile, Margaret lay back in bed, suckling a flabby hot water bottle on her stomach wastes, under a new cotton print nightgown. The new man put on his best clothes: vest, back corset, brown shirt, white overalls, and were you ever a housepainter, my love? The new man's eyes and Margaret's memory of the night were a discussion about how long the two of them would stay together. They asked mutely if there was something in each other at the present moment they could love: an interrogation by that triad: memory, intuition, expectation. 'She wurrnt murra to go on. But still.' Later, the new man smoked as he dressed facing the mirror. Between them the air was clear, but the glances exchanged via the mirror were cloudy with smoke. 'Your man is a cretin. You are nothing, nothing: you are already dead. Why don't I like him in this marvellous flat? I do, really.'

As for Sonny and Masterson, they woke up in the morning with all their pleasure before them and did not get up for breakfast.

Jerry and Mary breakfasted together alone in Rosine's room while Frank tactfully went out to buy the papers and some extra sea fishing hooks.

The question has already been asked: 'What was the nature of the bond between Mary and Jerry?' Only the questioner is no longer with us.

Every time Jerry sat at a meal in that flat he took the mouthful off the fork peaceably enough but swallowed it down with desperate gulps. Somewhere between intention and performance Mary and McFarlane were getting at him. Why else the nightly phone calls, the reports to Mary when he returned each morning from secret lodgings in a nearby Salvation Army hostel? His body was corroding in the steamy ambience of his corrupted purposes. Once more an opposing welter-weight champion was fouled and tottered about the Dublin ring, his gloves clamped to his eyes. Jerry's motives were all the time innocent, just wanting to win, not to harm anyone permanently.

The reason he couldn't help loving Mary was that she took care to blame him. Not explicitly. She just smoothed out their bed after breakfast, when Frank had left, broke the transparent plastic off a new box of underwear, pulled the white petticoat down over her serene face, and, as the garment settled on her sturdy figure, gave him a 'Really, Jerry!' glance that could have implied underlying meaning of either 'Was that the best you could do this morning?' or

'Don't get the idea you can ruin my eyesight, dear.' Then it was up with her panties, a brief scratch, and reach for the lovat skirt.

When she had done her hair, Mary took a beige skirt from her case, looked at it in disgust and stuffed it into the tiny wastepaper basket in Rosine's bedroom. Her lovat suit and lilac blouse showed off her neat figure. You can't help admiring yourself from time to time. She raised a hand to her head; maybe her hairstyle was a bit frizzy – still, you could almost call it afro – but little by little the provinces were shedding from her. She reached a hand under her skirt and pulled a cotton thread from her petticoat. One day she would dress like Rosine perhaps. No hurry though.

On the sixth day, Joel said of course they were rehearsing, just living there. Rosine said, 'Why don't we do some rehearsing in the park?' and Joel said 'No.'

Also on the sixth day, Frank said, 'Why don't we do some rehearsing in the park?' and Rosine said 'No.'

Try to remember that the new play is like a spiritual body that was beginning to spread outwards from them. Two of the glands in this body – the adrenal and neurohypophysis – were regulated by a direct nerve supply. The activity of the outer glands was controlled by humoral or hormonal agents carried in the blood stream. Or don't bother to remember this.

Or think of the emerging play as a giant figure, rather sexless, modelled in open wicker work, such as the Druids reputedly built and packed with prisoners, before setting the whole monument on fire.

Which of these you prefer to think of will depend (a) on your medical knowledge and (b) on whether when they explained magnetism to you and drew diagrams of oblong magnets with little N–S direction arrows inside, you could really get rid of those arrows in your mind-picture when the explanation became more complex.

Anyway, you can get away with just thinking again of a gaseous blue atmosphere, yet another giant, astral body, that spread upwards from the group. Unlike the Uncle Aubrey gaseous body, this play atmosphere was not guaranteed harmless. In fact, life in the flat became – evidently according to Joel's plans – more and more unbearable. It's what certain radicals mistakenly call a 'raising of consciousness' a 'sharpening of contradictions'. The new astral body was therefore a circuit of harm, though Joel had so far failed to eliminate one piece of innocence from it, an innocence hidden in a cubby-hole of the brain. Like an unsuspected tumour, that purity put moments of dizziness into the harm.

Allowing for this gradual emergence of the spiritual body, you must let Joel and the others lead their uncomfortable life (not without its momentary joys) for about two weeks. Then the flat's lounge can be rearranged in your mind so that, when all are assembled, the centre of dizziness can be identified without any detective work at all, just by ocular éclat.

It wasn't only Jerry's curiosity that first identified and then put this dizziness into effect. Some of the cause was his vanity, such as 'Go on, Jerry; you're taller than me'; some of it was his wish to make his next action a joke that would be quite sideways on to present events. He was just a discarded parsnip in the conversation between Rosine and Joel and felt that keenly. Sonny and Masterson were looking at *Penthouse* magazine together on the couch. Margaret was knitting a sweater for the new man who was, in his way, talking to Mary. On this, the 15th day, they were due to set out for Mary's home town; on location, you might say, although even Joel admitted that they had no precise destination. At 10 A.M. Frank had gone to see about an old bus that he had bought second-hand from the police. As the garage hadn't finished bolting the seats into new positions designated by Joel on a scrap of paper, Frank went down to the beach to do some more fishing. The angry relationship between them all by this time vibrated and filled the lounge. A single pulse of the relationship got lonely for Frank and blipped down the stairs of the flat, under the door, out the back garden gate, throbbed through the town's streets, down the cliff path, getting weaker and weaker until it went across wet sand like tired footsteps. The pulse reached Frank at the edge of the tide and at once surged into the movement of a fisherman's cast, speeding up the fishing rod until, no longer a weak pulse, it screamed across the water 50 yards and disappeared modestly into the sea. Under the waves, 12 feet down, a hook with a piece of ragworm on it, cocked up and looked at the fish. Remnant of the lost pattern isolated in idea swarms. Back in the lounge, Jerry was jealous of this pulse leaving the room and brooded on Frank and Mary. After all, it wasn't much of a life for Jerry just going in to Mary at breakfast time. So when Mary got off the arm of the new man's chair and said, 'What's that little white cupboard in the wall, right up there by the ceiling?' Jerry was only too ready to look. First someone had to say, 'There must have been a boiler here once; it's only an old flue door.'

'Go on, Jerry; you look; go on, you're taller than me.'

Some items of knowledge are so meaningless that they become really dangerous in the wrong hands. They are the small fry that we pay very little attention to until we suddenly realize how coherently they can be made to swim. Jerry stood on a chair and pulled at the door which opened very much as you might think. Inside were the three old letters formerly stolen from Uncle Richard, and a small ivory box.

The ivory box was soon opened. It contained a few non-safety matches and Jerry put it on a walnut-topped table left beside his chair from teatime.

Then he began to read the letters in his slow, boxer's voice:

'About 70 members and mentally-handicapped persons travelled by coach to the game. The weather this year was the opposite to last year. . .' read the first letter. 'By the time the afternoon was over the rain had stopped and a ride home in the fine weather was enjoyed . . .'

The second letter said: 'In the ferry for the Isle of Wight an abominable Hell's Angel dressed in leather sat next to Mr Smith and they both drank tea, neither looking at each other.'

By the time Jerry read the third letter they were all quiet: 'We are always talking and thinking what Aubrey's reactions might be to life in general. I have had a most wonderful weekend at the Tacuarembo Hotel, what used to be Conway Manor under County education. That American company has hardly altered it at all so far: I think you'd recognize most of it. My bedroom, shared with Barny, had two double beds, bedside lamps, two armchairs, a carpet on the floor which was stone, and then in a small nook behind a curtain, which amused us both, was a washbasin and toilet. It all seemed so fantastic how they had managed to make the hotel so comfortable, and not spoilt anything of the manor house atmosphere. Because of Barny's stomach, we had a special health food supper at 9 o'clock that evening in the ballroom, soup, cheese salad, whole meal bread, home-made.'

Rosine did not think she had ever heard such wonderful, comforting words. If you do not live your life alongside a person, with what will you love them? she asked herself. The sense of sharing, of warmth, of concern for Aubrey. The top of the head squashy with concern. Hope at night-time, learning from each other during the day, heady praise for some third party at meal-time, someone known to both of you; your love full enough to nurture other people within it.

It is possible to say at this moment of sincerity that Rosine was a fine, tall woman, who was now sitting down. She had red hair, of course, a thin nose, was firm-breasted, somewhat anyway, and had the haunches and, without taking the analogy too literally, the brain of a lioness. So this slightly-refurbished Rosine casts her presence retrospectively over the old, and, unless you watch it, becomes a fixity at this point, like that unfinished Liszt Fantasy. As though the size of her breasts or the stretch of her stomach made any difference to your knowledge of her, when you compare these imagined externals to her own intimate internal view of her own stomach as a gassy area held in with lean strength or of her breasts falling and then drawing her onward half-heartedly, of her mouth as rushing forward in a pucker, reining back resignedly, then opening to allow in a little air.

The incipient love within her for the letter writer rose within her body and glistened on her lip.

This was too much for Joel, who impatiently got up and seized the ivory box.

'The people who own the Tacuarembo Hotel support the capital-ist military government in my country,' he declared.

He removed the matches from the box and handed one to each person, saying, 'Keep it in your pocket.' When, about 8 P.M., Frank at last parked the bus outside the flat and came upstairs to ask, 'All set?' Joel gave him a match too.

The upshot was that, as they went downstairs with their cases, Jerry had the sense of responsibility. Joel had the sense of bringing off a joke which should have been Jerry's, for the boxer had intended merely to burn the letters, not anything mentioned in them.

13

The Windows Move

The navy-blue bus waited under a street lamp whose light was energized by darts of rain. The first things they noticed were chicken wire over all the side windows and iron bars inside the rear window. Difficult to know whether they were in a prison or a vehicle. They could have been Babeuf and followers arrested in Paris, mid-1790s. 'The cage is an acrid travelling show and its prisoners/storm the wires of their acid history.' But Frank modernized the occasion: 'All these bars put there by the police heroes for their paddy wagon,' he said. The phrase, born in ironic intentions, grew up into a wilful adult in five seconds flat and soon made the bus itself heroic. So the vehicle became, like politics, the spirit of daring among people: it could sweep the ground from under your feet. Another gesture from the bus that thwarted Frank's irony was that its engine had already been started into fragments of a senseless, brave life, whereas Frank had thought it afraid and silent. As they listened, the engine shuddered with the phrase, 'We love from the heart and we hate from the heart.' For all his pretended revolutionary fervour, Frank couldn't understand it. He climbed the steps and looked in. An old man, wearing a peaked cap and white linen coat sat in the driver's seat, just a bit of white-haired identity creeping from under his black cap. The driver kept his mittened hands on the shaking wheel and did not turn round.

Frank glanced back at Joel: 'But I could've driven . . . And isn't that Uncle Richard?'

Joel gave him a knowing smile.

'Proceeds to Mencap,' Frank argued weakly.

'The driver comes free,' Joel answered cockily. 'I hijacked him.'

They all mounted the bus steps and looked down inside to discover that, if the bus had sneaked a heroic stature, many heroes have a very hollow interior, full of bad, internalized feelings. They placed their suitcases on the floor and stood in a lonely bunch, which was quite possible. The diagram with Joel's seat arrangements was passed around. It looked like this:

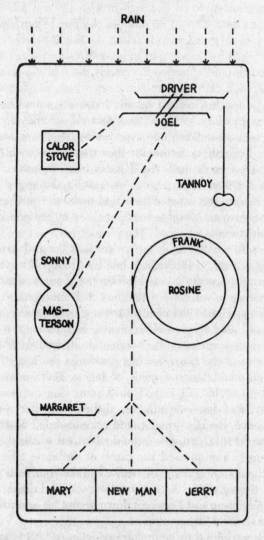

Joel was going to sit facing inwards just behind the driver. To his left, a small, portable stove (in case they couldn't get into a/the hotel that night). Behind the stove, a double seat for Sonny and

Masterson, facing inwards. Opposite, behind the driver, a double seat for Frank and Rosine. At the back, the original rear seat of the bus, with Mary, the new man as a bone of contention, and Jerry. And Margaret stuck on her own in a single seat facing forwards. 'Well, she's deaf. There's no point in chatting to her,' Joel had said. (And who could guess what function she might play?)

In fact, Joel had made part of his motivation clear but not all. It was a diagram of the endocrine glands, he said, but mainly he just liked the look of it and wouldn't say which gland was which. It seemed he wanted the bus interior to be like a body, not a prison: if so, democracy of bodily organ appeared lacking, for why did he control the heat and the driver the brainy functions? And hadn't he just said he'd hijacked the driver anyway? And what about the impoverished example of true decency, old Margaret, isolated, cut off from her ineffectual lover, who sat in the shitty part of the vehicle? In the perfect person acting perfectly shouldn't there be harmony between the glands? Hmm . . . at least Joel's prophecy about the rain was brilliant.

As they stood looking at the diagram and comparing it with the bus, Rosine began to think Joel had borrowed his motivation from a very primitive organicism whose language was usurpation, diverting of intention, violation of intimacy, and moral harm. Weak roof lights led backwards to primitive regions between the sparse seats. Mostly, the floor was full of bolt holes, a reminder that controls on conduct had been altered. Rosine felt heart cramp at the new imputations of harmfulness which swarmed down the feeble darkness. She could see the areas of secret theft, magical poisons, spying and profanation, and could sense the desperate need of telepathy, the back seat rounding off the whole effect very nicely.

All at once, the bus driver's aged voice sounded distantly halfway down the far side, just above the double seat which was to be hers and Frank's. She guessed the cause of the eerie effect: only one side of the tannoy system still worked. 'Take your seats please.'

They stowed their suitcases on the racks and dispersed to their places. As Rosine and Frank sat down he put his arm round her and already she felt a bit surrounded.

Within a while, they were halfway down the street and bless my gonads there was the park behind them, shrinking like a purply-green face flannel being pulled through a dusky tube. The town fled along the chicken wire on either side of them with enough noise to waken the dead. All that mattered was the shaky interior in which they were being radically displaced. The yellow light and dark blue walls oppressed their tired eyesight. It had been a strenuous fortnight, doing nothing all the time. In this yellow lighting, all the colours were extraordinarily angry; Mary's lips were horror-film red; Masterson's hair, orange crepe paper; Margaret's green, candy-striped dress, a prison inside this prison that she could not escape.

On Jerry's swarthy skin the pustules came out to welcome the dark at the back of the bus. That was the only colourless happening. At the front of the vehicle, the arabic silver of Joel's harmonica flashed as it slid from his pocket like a hip flask. They all sat facing the interior of the bus and breathed high in their chests with a neurotic energy the far side of exhaustion. The harmonica wheezed experimentally between Joel's lips. The sound had the same potency that was beginning to trouble all of them.

Joel had on a white shirt with red dragons crawling over it, consummate in their fixity. He wore dirty white trousers with blue dragons over them, gasping for their lives. Accidentally, Mary's customary tweed suit was this time in dog-tooth pattern, which might prove quite vicious.

The bus engine had a new note added to it. With difficulty, Rosine distinguished that Joel was humming, the harmonica for the moment held like an unwanted sandwich just below his mouth. The humming and the bus engine throbbed with dirty dragons. Loosely bolted, the seats enjoyed themselves. Sonny and Masterson, sitting, uniformed as always, side by side, heard the voice as rasping. Masterson felt in his pocket where his revolver was and Sonny felt in his own pocket. When they sat next to each other like this the facing sides of their uniforms were usually shiny. So a tiny shiver ran down between them. Across that excitement they kissed. It was war-time. The Germans were searching the next room. But they kissed. There was a pressing need for sentiment.

Joel began to croon one of the songs they loved so well, slow and sentimental all right, as the electric bulbs in the roof glowed and faded, glowed and faded. 'For you and I have a guardian angel, on high with nothing to do . . .' He seemed to will that inactivity on the angel and his continuation to the part where the angel doled out true love to the happy couple was most reluctant.

The new man, sitting between Jerry and Mary on the back seat, was accidentally wearing that old brown suit of his as though he were ready to dive head first out of an anus. The love was so true that he did dive backwards epileptically, but Mary and Jerry rescued him before he did himself any damage against the bars. Frank did his best to protect his own companion, tightening his arm round Rosine's shoulders, but that too was a menace far removed from song and becoming steadily removed from Bing Crosby too.

As Joel sang the 'True Love' song his sallow face came creeping out of his long, black hair. A tortoise head emerged. He savagely adopted the grin of a satyr, as he sang about giving to you, giving to me. Fiercely, he beamed the song home to their hearts, the words of love the scalpels that lay bare their chests. It was as intrusive as burglary. Talking of burglary, Frank's arm, round Rosine's back, all at once sent a hand nipping round the corner to press her left breast, moving the green cotton of her long dress upwards in a mass, and giving then taking away a lop-sided epaulette. Every time the epaulette disappeared Rosine thought it had been robbed from her; but she did not wish it back.

The crooning snaked through two major towns and four villages.

At last the arabic of the harmonica took up its role as paltry occult. Joel raised it to his lips and drank in coloured sound. Harmony crept into his mouth like a net of flaming wires. He breathed it out again in greenish chrysolite streaks, and other sparks of it darted along pathways to their hearts. The slowness of a train, bird song, Doppler effect . . . the sound was a résumé of certain past events but changed and harmonized in the manufactured chords of the instrument.

The love trio on the back seat joined in the singing, while Margaret whispered an imaginary knitting pattern to herself, having forgotten her brown paper bag with all the wool and needles. She was thinking of making a sock, but because her pictorial ability was weak it was rather a fish-shaped set of instructions that issued from her lips.

Sonny and Masterson clung and pressed the shinyness close between them, trying to kiss away sound, but it floated in their ears, stabbed through their backs, and united them in coloured hyphens between their bodies. The hyphens struck through a silver sheet of arabic metal between them. Then the metal shook them in thunder as the bus drove on.

Thin rain freckled the front windows and rays of outside light periodically entered the tunnel in which all their movements jerked.

Inside Rosine's womb Frank's hand poised with its fingers loosely pointing upwards. 'Do you know what this is? A dead one of those.' His hand turned downwards, a crab walked feebly into an old joke.

Rosine looked down at her dress, now assembled over her knees in the drawing of a single hair as it enters the scalp. It was only Frank's hand taking root. She was quite dispassionate about that; or rather, her eyesight was as wide as the bus and Frank's harmful actions were a minor lurching compared with a total harm which could theoretically seat 42 persons – and so was ample for only nine of them. The bus entered the tremendous event of the New Forest. Frank's hand temporarily paused, ashamed of that idea rhyming: the forest as dress or scalp, the bus as his hand or hair.

Above their heads, the tannoy crackled and the driver's thin voice said exclusively to Frank and Rosine: 'Do either of you remember the play, *Outward Bound*?'

They thought of the driver's arm inside the white coat: horsehair, a grey bone spiking through.

Rosine shouted, 'Yes'; but the driver did not look round. Frank did not withdraw his hand and she could not have asked him to without missing the point.

'OK, Mary,' Joel called out.

On the back seat, Jerry and the new man were now sitting straight forward. Mary was diving about, pulling something sand-coloured from the bucking luggage rack above Margaret's head, while the dog-teeth of her skirt patterns simultaneously snarled at the poor old woman and creased in self-worry up Mary's stockings.

An inset suddenly: deep cracks in Joel's face scarred the eye that experience had hacked but not bloodied. The eye in its hammock of black net was leading their actions into a time scale where they didn't all want the actions to go.

The eye as unsmiling as the compound surface of an insect's. 'The café was on the street level, and by the number of its windows looked like a cage open to all regards.'

The eye implying a willingness for a brief life. Implacable in that, not responding to them, nothing to say, everything to sing, its own decision frozen into black ice years ago.

Past the eye a fibre of smoke.

Joel sang about Margaret's green, candy-striped dress, the one she had worn in the hotel stillroom and was now wearing in this . . . moving room.

Of course, she couldn't hear.

'Grave Mary, my organum,' sang Joel.

At this, Mary's voice joined in, singing at a one-fifth interval below Joel's plainsong. Mary's contralto told of the crumpled shadows of Margaret's dress, unexplained lumps across its front, of the moveability of the dress, the knowledge of golden kippers swimming under the green sea, the fat ocean. The two of them must have been learning the song for the previous fortnight.

The motion of the bus created centrifugal effects in the singing. It also threw Frank's lungs to one side and bulked the air in that direction. Then it hoisted him back, catching his gulps by surprise as the air packed into his stomach. For once, it was Frank who was dizzy and queasy, trapped in his love for Rosine as in a swaying bus that mastered him. The snags in the song's breathing were the same expression of dishonesty he lived with daily, showing the mirror his unworried journalist's face. If the mirror was to distrust him, that too had to be acted.

Across from him, Sonny traced the outline of a penis on the misted window behind him, trying to copy a photograph in the book he and Masterson were sharing. Chicken wire spiked all round the shape. Within those limits the sexual symbolism was clear enough but the symbolism of wire was more intense.

Then nine human beings were caught up in the howl of the harmonica as in a Blakean stream of bodies. The bus was of uncertain size. The burglary inside Rosine continued. Mary was fighting with a live, foam mattress that snaked from her arms and panted on the floor. She stepped back gracefully and smoothed down her suit. From inside, her chewing gum flesh had never felt more appetizing to others or more durable. From outside, her figure was a neat tree of hate. Joel's foot stamped hard on the floor as he sucked at the harmonica's black windows.

He was their supreme theomachist, critic of manners, arch-informer.

They stopped looking back on their former selves with joy and tenderness. The present was ornamented by the wailing music, the arabic pattern, and the grotesque work of their faces. An innumerable multitude of small voices.

Within each of them a certain amount of heat was rising; the bus windows were weeping with acid.

Joel's voice floated down the bus.

'Where now, Margaret? The ocean?

'You've got

'that pain again . . .

'slip

'down the sand

'slip

'down . . .'

aaah-hoooh, aaah-hoooh, breathed the harmonica.

Margaret was the eternal plaintiff; no wonder she shrank in her seat hoping she was safe behind the bars of her dress. Persecution wobbled on all sides.

In that alien transport, British Railways Sonny stood up. Mary was still standing. There could be nothing between them except what Joel had to say.

The harmonica finally left Joel's mouth in a sound of wonderment, drifted left and fell to his knee, his hand wandering downwards on his wrist-end like an ostrich eating silver.

Ill will rang a bell for Jerry and he stood up. Crisp white shirt, charcoal grey flannels, his best. He lent some of his charcoal colour to Joel's voice.

'We haven't done much,' said the burnt voice of Joel. 'But there's a sort of story and we'll get the play out of it.'

Autumn was beginning in the New Forest as he continued: 'So far, we only impress each other in pairs. We're going into areas of surgery where that changes.'

Masterson stood up, nodded his red hair in complicity at Joel, and went on doggy tiptoes down the bus, trod over the foam mattress in the centre aisle, squeezed past Mary and stood at the back beside Jerry. The new man still sat on the seat between them.

'We're beginning to know who we are. Just beginning,' said their ambiguous lecturer, smoothing back his locks with a coquettish hand. He could have eaten them in the way a tortoise eats a piece of meat. Choking a bit, but with iron contentment.

Tiptoe, tiptoe went Sonny, sidled past Mary and stood in front of Masterson. Sonny was a bald ornament amid so much hair. The new man still sat stoically on the back seat.

'We have the right to take the old like this,' said Joel. He broke an imaginary frailty in his hands – except that one hand, of course, most untidily came away with the harmonica, so that you had some image difficulties in comparing the movement with breaking a wishbone. Something had broken though.

'Let's throw nothing away. Do you hear that, Rosine? We need every emotion you've got.'

Rosine felt still. She heard Joel's voice calling an ugly softness out of her body, as if she were taken up in a cruel enthusiasm of a crowd. The stiffness was in resistance to that, the stiffness that genuine rectitude has sometimes, yes, it really has sometimes. Frank's hand left her rigid breast. Her left shoulder stayed on the upgrade, though the epaulette had degraded itself.

'Some of us are naturally prepared for this moment,' said Joel. 'I'm proud of Mary, proud of Sonny and Masterson and Jerry. Such a change in consciousness. Proud of you, Frank.'

As it surged onwards, the bus itself trembled, ready for a compliment that never came.

A journalistic hand slowly left the internal Rosine and began drawing her personality from under her dress. By opening a clutched fist Frank shamefully disclosed her privacy to the others. She ruffled her green silk furiously to distract attention but that was just so much libel action. It was too late.

'Others are learning about themselves,' said the inexorable moralist in front of them.

Frank blew Rosine a mock kiss across that same hand's palm but did not return her private personality with the breath.

Joel stood before her. It seemed to Rosine the whole field of dragons was in motion, red mouthing blue. Gently, Joel raised her past the bruise area of his trousers into the red, arterial levels of his chest. Frank squeezed her hand as he rose with her. Rosine dreamwalked ahead of Frank to the back of the bus. As she came to the foam mattress she felt an impulse to break sequence by lying down on the sand. For all she knew they might rape her. She was encouraged to go in turn past Mary and stand with Frank in the crowd at the rear. Jerry and Masterson hauled the new man to his feet. The driver, like 'Don't shoot the pianist', didn't even turn round; he was in no position to join them. The coach sped onwards through upright bars of trees.

A forest of hair and breathing. The food they had shared at tea lay at the same level in their bodies.

Only one head was left at belly height. Margaret's. She turned to smile at them. Trying to be clever, she pathetically opened her heart showing the row of broken teeth, one gold.

The old woman felt the stirrings of her next move, trying to please. Mary bent forwards over the back of her seat, reached a hand to Margaret's left shoulder and pressed it in hard sympathy, nudging movement through the weighty body until it was difficult to say if outside or internal motion had the mastery.

'This needs the greatest kindness,' said Joel starting towards the rest of them. 'Margaret is a very sick woman. Until my diagnosis tonight only her doctor and she herself knew just how sick she was. Now she has to lie down and be cured.'

It was a spoof. No ear heard Joel's concern for Margaret, which was no more than a matter of pose. Each of them heard different sentences in which the word, 'revulsion', basked. But Margaret, being deaf and none too bright, saw the sureness of Joel's movements, the sureness of a lover who swayed down the bus towards her. What he had said about lying down on the sandy foam mattress was being coaxed in her as a reciprocal movement by Mary's hand. The old woman apologetically half turned in her seat to the others; her hand spread outwards in a helpless gesture which admitted: 'Only my doctor and myself knew about my illness . . .' She was the most healthy person there.

The new man began to sing a part of the Creadores song he had always felt was specially his:

The new men swell like bees with honey
Seize the hive and seize the money . . .

The fat woman's body was persuaded to slide out of the seat and Mary lowered it, face upwards, to the sand. The green stripes of the dress washed over the sand. Margaret's personality was dwindling. No need to bother about knowing that old-fashioned individuality which was retreating inwards and diminishing rapidly. Her illness was now quite enough to know instead. You can joke with an illness instead of with its victim, as the history of bedside manners teaches us. Margaret's small personality disappeared into the huge wave of her body and might have remained suspended in the water, a wilful baby sand-eel, had not Joel treated her so brutally now. He knelt beside her and looked and spoke so coldly that the affrighted personality shrank even more within the wave to the size of a mere fishy egg. Round the egg, the sea was getting colder, the grey hair of the old woman stopped moving on the sand. Joel was talking in a low, hypnotic monotone. The rise and fall of the woman's body was no longer noticeable. Her face grey and peaky. The last vestige of herself was shock, which drained slowly. Joel snapped his fingers. She was in a trance. The final light went out within her. The gas ring of her breath had already turned out and sunk to the bottom like a coral. The cheeks of the illness were grey as the sea under a darkening October sky. The wind was keen. Frank, practised fisherman as he was, shivered. Joel's strong fingers descended to Margaret's throat, paused at the top button of her dress, did not open it, travelled down and opened the second button; carrying on downwards, he opened all the other buttons to the waist. The stripy wave forever turned and crested under the bleak light. Joel held the dress front together with two fingers of his left hand and with his right reached to one side, to the seat Margaret had formerly occupied, which now held Joel's surgical instruments. He brought a pair of manicure pincers over to the body and opened the dress. Seven heads craned forwards to see what they could see, but there was deft management from Joel, who held the dress so that it looked dark and cavernous inside the old woman's body. Joel put his hand in; it searched about among the internal liquids Margaret had carried there through all the years. The surgeon's tongue poked into the side of his cheek and his smile was slow and languorous. Seven pairs of eyes tried by glances to enter the dialogue of facial expressions between Margaret and Joel, Margaret's expression dead and Joel's living. Despite that, colours were exchanged between the two faces; grey transmitted from Margaret's cheeks to Joel's and patchy red from Joel's to those of the entranced woman. Mary, kneeling at the body's head, caught hold of its hair and forced the sightless eyes to regard the tremors in Joel's lids. Margaret was without sound, without her human whisper. She lived in a fragment of her being. Her dry lips were parted, the lower snagged by a stained tooth. Rosine, in her warm haven among the spectators, watched Joel's arm reaching into the dress and thought how lightly by comparison she had been tested, to suffer Frank's hands, one of which still rested, a warm face flannel, on her buttocks. The seats they had been occupying kept their arrangement and the lines of force which had run between them remained; but the tension was also expressed as potency over the whole bus. There was only one quiet body and that was the objectified mound in which steel pincers searched, dangling above the sea bottom, ignoring drifting seaweed. The bus was an expanse of inky yawn, but the green stripes and the sandy square on which that wave held steady were the emblem of the past, established as specimen without real concern for its inhabitants. The pincers plunged downwards through the water into sand. They closed over a red object, lifted it, emerged from the dress, bearing with them a small piece of ragworm.

'There's the illness,' said Joel triumphantly, holding the red fringe out towards them.

It was a good joke.

The ragworm must have been previously buried in the foam mattress and perhaps Mary had slit Margaret's dress at the back as she helped her down to the mattress, a little stagey trick. They all sighed with relief, although Joel still looked as if he understood all pattern and order whatsoever.

'Here, I can use that,' said Frank. For another joke, he took the ragworm, and pocketed the harm.

Joel snapped his fingers and Margaret awoke. Seawater covered the bus floor: her dress had leaked like a paper bag.

'A case of steatopygia,' Frank wisecracked.

The hypnotist hands stretched out and framed Margaret's watery face.

'Can you hear, Margaret?' asked Joel.

Within the sourd-muet deadness thoughts began to revive and if Margaret couldn't hear it was as if she could. The sea, going out across the ribs of sand, left a distant roar, an almost-decipherable broadcast from a walkie-talkie set.

'Let us be of the Creadores . . .' sang the new man, as usual only almost decipherable himself but as happy as a transistor radio. He had temporarily forgotten he loved this piece of old deaf government, kidnapped by hands still imprisoning her face.

'I've an idea for a second operation,' Joel announced finally, releasing Margaret. 'We want to do our best for you.'

('Now whoever offered a sacrifice for having good desires?' Margaret's danger seemed not over.)

Joel snapped his fingers; the old corruption of fat yielded to its crack of doom; Mary caught Margaret as she again sagged and fell into position on the foam.

Among the spectators the only live figure was Rosine.

She felt warmed by an inexplicable unintelligence that imposed a god-like space between herself and the intelligent cruelty of Joel's joke. The space was an area of no-harm, the primary selfishness that simply knows how to love, not how to separate ourselves from others. Against the blackness of a hurrying bus window the new geniality came into focus like the reflection of her own face. The bus engine gurgled. No. The flat, white face in the reflection was not hers. The eyes were too soft and mild, the cheeks too rounded.

'Look!' screamed Rosine, pointing at the window. 'Uncle Aubrey!'

Joel jerked round in alarm. The others looked just in time to see a face vanishing as though under water.

'Stop the bus,' ordered Rosine.

The new man's heart melted. His whitened lover's eyes were drawn to the divine beauty of his deity abased on the mattress and he could bear to hurt no-one.

'Yes,' he shouted. 'Sturr it at once.'

'Ahimsa,' said Frank.

The bus stopped.

They were outside the hotel.

Stepping over the water that still leaked from Margaret's body, they filed out of the vehicle and walked in the rain towards the building.

The Tacuarembo was the manor house of their yesterdays, guarded by an entrance like a dilapidated sentry box and a grey stone wall, which enclosed a long, triangular garden. The part of the wall nearest to them was bright yellow in the floodlights of the entrance; the wall's middle was swathed in night; and at its far end, down the road they had come, an isolated light gleamed at the apex of the triangle.

'Ah!' said Frank, and took Rosine's arm firmly. He led her round the puddles to the sharp corner of the garden, 50 yards away, where a neon bulk gloated as it lit up a signpost saying 'Tacuarembo Hotel'. The sign looked over the dark garden wall like a baby over its cot.

'There's your Uncle Aubrey face,' said Frank, pointing upwards.

Rosine shook her head. 'The bus was going too fast and the face held still. Then it sank backwards,' she said.

The noticeboard showed the hotel had just been taken over by Americanized Latin ownership because under the main sign it read: 'The Tacuarembo Hotel is people.' Joel had said: 'Those owners are meat merchants who co-operate with the American investors in Uruguay to keep down peasant wages and then come over here to invest their money in case our revolution wins.'

Frank and Rosine went through the garden gate and began back to the entrance. Lights set in the flower beds shone over hundreds of cut marigold plants. The plants were a lesson that even overall brightness of personality may be temporary and needs at least yearly renewal. The cut stems were not the worst of the garden's unsatisfactory traits. One day it might fail you completely or suddenly go dead in one corner. Rosine's brain locked into a plant phase, a set grin, a straight path of packed earth through the flower beds. Plants clasped together like green crabs. Such tight foliage patterns are known at many brinks of despair. Luckily, no-one ever has to stop there. If you have will-power you can walk right through on to the lawn. Worn holes in the grass showed where the swing had been; half the clock golf numbers had been stolen; the big elm tree had a bare spot on its main branch where a climbing rope had hung. The rope now lay in a sodden heap on the grass. It's pointless to stay in the neurosis of lynchings when we should remember other people with kindness, thought Rosine.

'The other day I wanted to make a list of hotels I had stayed in and what had happened to them,' she said, stopping on the wet grass under the hotel's dark side walls.

'Why didn't you?' asked Frank.

'Well . . .' said Rosine, shrugging off the whole issue she had just raised.

It was to have been a simple list, just quick paragraphs. Hotel X was closed after the public health inspector's complaints. Hotel Y was taken over by a large hotel chain and modernized with an underground car park. Hotel Z was now an evening class centre . . . The list was to be at least four pages long. As Rosine began, she could not bear the creative responsibility she was assuming over all the people involved: to act like a totalitarian novelist reshaping these lives into her personal form. Also, her own personality fluctuated too quickly in the distortion of years passed in review. Each hotel name was a claw stuck in a thin, resinous surface and she was worried that some of those amiable buildings were really sinister when even the recital of their names jerked at the soft resin and threatened to tear it. Even with people, she had never met anyone so gentle she could write a single sentence about them and get it true. She repeated these sentences to herself: 'We are always talking and thinking what Aubrey's reactions might be to life in general. I have had a most wonderful weekend at the Tacuarembo Hotel . . .' If only she could herself talk in such gentle rhythms . . .

Back at the doorway, the rest waited for them. As they arrived, the new man said: 'Here! What about Margaret?'

Joel had to go back to the bus and wake her up from her new trance.

Areas of roof and gable that none of them could see properly. By the time their eyes had worked out what part of the hotel roof looked like, their visual memory of previous parts had faded. By weak floodlighting, the hotel's porch may have seemed crumbling, but it was crystal clear. Above that light, a non-architectural shape was established in the obscurity. Their eye focuses extended and contracted along the presumed contours of the upper building and its surrounding trees until this artificial shape was constituted mathematically from the mechanics of their eye adjustments. An extremely complex outline of sawn-off logs and pencil points. Then, as the group mind became stilled, this weird hotel-form was tremulously achieved. The mathematical form held steady above the black digits of the ballroom windows until it obliterated any notion of the real hotel's corrupt neo-Gothic. Inside the tortured Gothic body, added to by greed and so deservedly wasting away, was this other hotel of perfect potential. The ideal hotel would regain perfection when the manor house's charred rafters were hens' feet stiff against a morning sky.

Margaret reached that broken frontispiece, the hotel entrance. The group's idea hotel-form closed over them as they went through swing doors and into the foyer. As soon as they were inside it, the idea form went out of control and multiplied to infinity round the safely-known area of foyer. Then the hotel was like a love you find, which seems quite habitable at first, but, once stayed in, expands shapelessly round you. In the apparently infinite complications of a long-lasting love are all kinds of rooms whose particulars may be boring or garish. Unless you see that the way love has thinned out is proof of its huge size and complexity, you become bored with the rooms you live in, destroy the wondrous emotion in some desperate way. You go away to find someone new with whom everything can become small-time and intense again. Not to keep the old love fresh is to promote death rather than life because hunting for new experience all the time is at best an artificial way of keeping young. At the age of 60 we must join hands as we walk down the street.

For similar reasons, you must say without irony that the hotel foyer – as familiar as a copy of the Mona Lisa – is marvellous, with its reception office, sign saying 'Restaurant and Ballroom', corridors behind a rear archway, and a wide sweep of staircase by the lift. (And never mind the red plush lampshades and comfydays sofa.) Anyway, do you feel how cosy that pair of brackets is? Here's a less cosy pair, for instance: (die . . . can this be a mere coincidence in our relationship with time?). Unfortunately, the hotel's new arrivals were not living in the freshness I'm recommending, and found that the foyer created deadness at the foot of the brain and numbness there, which produces alienation, distant reactions, poor sense of direction and bad memory. It should have been, on the contrary, the art of contemplation that arose, the introduction to cosy love, the dawn of endless adoration. If only we could offer such things to our hotel guests! Such adoration can be glorious, though so idealized that its god's qualities include both excellence and sadness. Alas, you look away from the altar, where you have been standing with bowed head, and intruders hurry towards you, perhaps in welcome, perhaps in sham rage, perhaps in murder in the cathedral.

The hotel manager, a lean man of sham rage and spurious welcome, at this point drew attention to himself. He began swimming about behind the glass of the reception office until he froze into an advertising pose with the slogan, 'Certain diseases overcome our century.'

Then he distinguished himself at the door of the office. Under his streaky grey hair, a pair of black eyebrows; he wore a light blue suit, black shoes, a tie knot that jerked forward from his collar, and if I said Shah of Persia that would be quite unfair. To the manager.

This 'worthy', for whom the mildest stimulus was enough to trigger rage or welcome, hurried to them furiously and caught Jerry by a shirt sleeve.

'You haven't thought much about me for the past three weeks, have you? Forgotten you work here or something? We've had to make do with two down there . . . I'm not sure I want you all back . . . Oh, go on then for God's sake, off to the stillroom you three and make it snappy . . . and what in the world have you been doing, Margaret? You're soaking wet. There's no good shaking your head and whispering at me, my girl.'

'We had a bit of a jacquerie back there,' said Frank.

No-one understood him.

'Good evening, sir, can I help you?' said the manager, dismissing the others with a wave of the hand. 'Have you booked?'

Joel said: 'No. We want rooms for one, two, three, four, five, six – you'll put up the three workers, I suppose – and the coach driver, seven. He's seeing to the luggage.'

'I'm afraid I've only got singles,' replied the manager. 'We wear ties for dinner,' he added pointedly. 'Normally, you'd be too late, but we've got a supper dance and discotheque tonight, plus a visiting pianist.'

'That sounds a lot all at once,' said Rosine.

'It would be if the pianist had arrived,' the manager told her with his disease-of-the-century smile.

He handed them a key each, explained that there was no night porter these days as the last one had left rather suddenly, said 'Do mind the step' and indicated the entrance to the labyrinth of corridors and stairs. Clearly, what with the broken-down hotel entrance and the original plush red of the foyer, the new Latin American ownership had not had time to do much with their money. Even the internal archway leading to the labyrinth still had a widow's peak topped with Ariadne's diadem. When you added the original manor house together, the one that existed before money began talking, the result was a sort of obsolete personage, deaf but lovable. But when you added the greed it became not lovable at all.

Margaret led the other two workers towards the kitchens while the guest section of their party mounted the stairs.

In the thorax of the hotel was a small triangular room without windows. It was beside an old chimney that central heating had made redundant. Without that room the arrangement of corridors would have differed. The unused triangular room lent purpose to the entire hotel but had none itself. Among these dozens of occupied rooms this should have been the area of no-harm, an architectural leaving. In fact, it was an ambush.

Rosine's room was next door to the triangular cell. With no-one to guide her she went an unfamiliar way.

Entering the first corridor, a blackbird sang in an elm tree.

The second corridor, a sound of mint being chopped in the hotel kitchen.

The third corridor, a sound of flowers dropping into a vase.

The fourth corridor, a laugh.

The fifth corridor, she charged herself to make no noise.

The sixth corridor, it was almost as if Uncle Aubrey stirred in her arms.

Entering her small, square bedroom she felt her back grow warm, and her front grow cold.

Some nights nothing will keep the curtains open. Guiltily they close, and never mind whether it is dark or not. And if it is so much the better, thought Rosine, as she crossed the six paces of the room and pulled the fragrant material over the shiny window. The room overlooked the front road and between the dunno curtains she saw one or two people loitering by the garden wall as though in a theatre queue.

Hearts of women beat within the crumpled clothes thrown aside in other rooms. The throb of women was still inside blue and red dragons. Rosine doused her green dress on the green coverlet of the bed. Protectively, the coverlet began to change to a pale red; then because that was over-reacting reverted to washed-out green. The ashamed bed crept even closer to the wall, pretending that Rosine hadn't given it a shove with her knee.

She had scarcely brushed the talc under her armpits when Frank came in.

What she would really have liked to say was: 'You're not much to feel sorry for.'

What he really said was: 'Give us a knock as you go by and we'll go down together.'

On the principle, believe the mouth before you believe the eyes, she trusted him, though what he had really said was more like: 'Give us a knock as you go by and we'll both come back to your room after dinner.'

'Don't be too long, eh?' he said, and left.

Rosine put back on her long, green dress and the coverlet sighed with relief. She gave a last look at the single bed, the wallpaper covered with wavy blue lines, the sporting little sink; but she knew it was not, unfortunately, farewell. Essentially red hair and green dress again, she robbed the room of her colours, went into the pastel blue corridor, musty carpet, and closed her bedroom door with a discreet cough. Then it was past a locked door (the triangular room), past a bedroom door which had a 'Don't disturb' notice hung on the handle, and she came to Frank's room, knocked sharply; and so their first descent that night began.

In hotels such as the Tacuarembo it is with leaden pride that guests acquire the weight to descend to the grand rooms; just as it is by the wings of humility that they will eventually regain their bedrooms. They come downstairs with a stately tread and go back up with a sense of departed grandeur. Imagine that inexorable law of snobbish snakes and ladders going on all over a hotel.

So a very proud group of six people – two British Railways, Mary, Joel, Frank and Rosine – sat round the table Joel had chosen in that remarkable ballroom. Actually, it was hardly different from many a hotel ballroom. Nevertheless, considering the population problem, the solar fire, the problem that plastic bags present world-wide, new ways of talking and moving, new internal sensations of the body that have arisen in the last 10 years, any hotel ballroom is very remarkable indeed. To begin with, all the circular tables are set out as though certain human beings needed feeding with special care. Then there's the revolving ball of faceted mirrors, as though it were not enough that electricity conquers darkness but human beings have to crow about it. (Anyway, Joel had lit the candle on their table.) Also, there's the continual supply of plastic bottles containing spa drinking water. And the kind of old-fashioned movement that went on: an excuse-me waltz, waitresses moving from table to table, and the stable arrangement of the tables themselves – very poor analogies, those, for nucleic structure, radioactivity or maybe magnetism. The whole hotel philosophy was so badly worked out it was difficult to tell which.

As for Max Soupir and His Orchestra. Well!

When did you last attend a hotel dance? If it was recently, you have no part reading this book. If it was a long time ago, you should submit your name to the publisher for verification.

The waitresses' uniforms implied that the hotel management was particularly crude in distinguishing between the status of one individual and that of another. Certainly the waitresses had little in common with the British Railways uniforms that Sonny and Master-son staunchly wore; the black dresses seemed to disdain the black suits. When service industries clash it depends who is currently serving. The two railmen felt snubbed every time the waitresses went through their door marked 'private'. Having entered the world where Margaret, the new man and Jerry were already hard at work, the waitresses bounced back again, hurrying like black sparks through the nuclear tables. They dumped plates of smoked salmon before Joel and his group so noisily that for an instant six pairs of eyes had their focus limited almost exactly to outlines of the green-rimmed plates before them.

Very willingly, the conversation – 'I wonder if Margaret's got any more worm in her', 'Didn't it rain, though?' – stopped. The band went off. As the dancing finished, the so-called 'Crowded Dance-floor' was revealed as eight elderly couples who quite rightly went back to their tables. Roast beef/or lamb arrived. The 'de Sotas party' sorted out the vegetables as the sound of a piano playing elderly rhapsodies created momentary imagery of peas and spinach.

Mary was the first to notice,

'It's our coach driver,' she said.

The old man sat at the grand piano on the stage. His back was to the audience and he still wore his white coat and peaked cap.

'A bit of a hasty stand-in,' said Rosine.

'The principle is watch the hands before you watch the eyes,' said Joel, voicing a strategy similar to Rosine's *modus vivendi* with Frank.

'The trouble is you can't see his eyes from behind and you can only see his hands when they play outside his body. It's rather a secretive way of playing, because so much music is played normally within the keyboard's stomach area,' she replied.

Even Joel's tie had dragons on it – both red and blue.

'I shant get near your breath,' Masterson told Joel, and at the same time he nudged Sonny into the dragony humour.

'Shant you?' said Sonny.

Joel said: 'You've got to speak with apostrophes here.'

No-one understood.

They ate their meat course in silence, absolutely bolting down the food, and drank a harsh Beaujolais Villages. Mary took out her make-up case, looked at herself in its mirror, and was so entranced she hardly ate a thing after that but toyed with her food, concentrating hard on doing that. They had Poire Belle Helène for dessert. Anyone would think the hotel wasn't trying. The piano went on with a persistent Hungarian theme.

Here is what they did with their matches when the cigars and cigarettes were produced.

Rosine lit Joel's cigar.

Mary started to light her own cigarette but her match went out and she said, 'Damn!'

Rosine's match was still burning; so she lit Mary's cigarette.

Joel had already used his match, lighting the candle.

Sonny lit Masterson's cigarette and his own cigar.

Masterson lit Rosine's cigarette.

Frank felt in his jacket pocket: his match was still there, but he said, 'No thanks; I won't smoke at the moment.'

The coach driver had not been given a match.

In the stillroom the washing-up group paused in their work:

Jerry used his match to light a cigarette for the new man.

Margaret struck her match to light the cigarette of one of the two strangers in the work-force but the match-head broke off and fell into the dishwashing machine.

The new man found his match had not enough phosphorous tip and he threw it away.

The two strangers used a cigarette lighter.

Just inside the hatchway lay a tray of dirty dishes that Jerry had set aside. Now he wiped his hands on his new grey flannels and looked at the tray again. One plate had almost a full meal of beef left on it. Round the plate-rim was a scrawly message in lipstick: 'Tuck in. Love Mary. x x x'. Apart from the old question, should guests in the dining room fraternize with stillroom staff – and every decent hotel management knows that fraternizing with waitresses is OK but stillroom staff are not to be approached – it was the crudeness of the message that worried Jerry. After all, he knew his own weakness: greed. It was as though one of the sirens had all at once stopped singing to his hesitant galleon and had stood up on the rock, waved her arms and shouted: 'Coooeee, we're over here.'

Jerry withdrew the piece of beef from cold gravy and looked at the dripping object as it dangled from his fingers. The blood-red message on the plate repelled his lips from the beef; the heavenly song of Bisto drew them near.

The new man, who had been filling the machine's rinse tank with clean water, reattached a piece of rubber hose to its mounting on the machine and came to Jerry's side. Not for the first time, he tried to give Jerry good counsel: 'Nor irrn't dr go trrr . . . crrdrr stomach anneye drrnt norr whtlse.' He couldn't be plainer than that.

Faced with such kindness, Jerry was dumb. He looked into the whitened eyes that he had injured and saw there his knowledge of Mary. He threw the piece of beef into the slops bin. If only he could cure his future actions so easily; but it was a start. He patted the new man on the shoulder, leaving a gravy mark on the frayed shirt. Together they cleaned the plates off and Jerry started up the dishwashing machine again.

Out in the ballroom the party of six arose. A despairing mutual glance went round that out-of-date arena. The piano played remorselessly. Rosine gave a goodbye wave to the back of the pianist. Frank gave Rosine a special bedtime glance.

When they had returned to the foyer the possibility of an hour spent perched in the cocktail bar cast an irresolute moment into their company until Joel said: 'Well, I suppose we're all tired.'

British Railways could hardly wait to get some shuteye, and the two railmen led the humble movement upstairs, before unexpectedly splitting off from the ascent at the nearest bathroom. Most of the dispersal was unexpected like that. Mary ambled off along a corridor that did not lead to her bedroom. Joel went into a lavatory. Frank and Rosine, bound to the discipline of an earlier set of actions, made together for Rosine's room.

The stillroom quintet had finished nearly all the dishes and decided, against hotel rules, to leave the rest for the following morning.

The piano kept playing.

'What are you going to do when all this is over?' Frank asked.

With that question, the bedroom became so dark it could well have been the blitz. Rosine imagined that outside was not the hotel wall and a suburban end of a seaside resort but a road through the New Forest. Across that forest road was a small grocery store in a thatched building. Of course, the store would be closed at this time of night.

'I thought of going mushroom picking in the New Forest, if it's still the season,' she said. 'If only Uncle Aubrey could be with us. We could let him wander into the trees while we picnic by the car.'

'You don't mean "we"; you mean you-and-Don.'

She was silent.

'"Those who have lost an infant are never without an infant child,"' Frank quoted.

She did/not begin to cry.

'I still want to be beside all kinds of weak people,' she said.

(In Frank's bedroom, three rooms away, a shadowy hand dipped into the pocket of a sports jacket hanging on the door and stole a piece of ragworm and a match.)

'We could have bought a whole chicken,' said Rosine.

'Pretty damp in the forest after the rain.'

Knock, knock, knock began the knocking.

'Bring me a saddle of lamb dressed with turkeys,' a female voice quoted.

'What's that from?' asked Frank in surprise.

'I think it must have been the pillow quoting.' And Rosine laughed harshly, her head on the pillow on the narrow bed.

Knock, knock, knock went the knocking.

The red-haired girl put an arm across Frank's shoulder and dragged herself close to him until her stomach full of roast lamb was just touching his stomach full of roast beef. After the interval of lips kissing and nibbling, after the interval of angelic hands, the roast beef at last mounted on top of the roast lamb. At first, the two stomachs wrangled, pushing each other indiscriminately out of shape and stressing the sphincter muscles which kept the food in the leathern bags. Quite soon, the roast lamb relaxed as the weight lifted and Rosine's stomach surged back into normal shape, before being most cruelly flattened again. Back to shape; flattened again.

Knock, knock, knock went the knocking.

Air pressure built up beneath Rosine's heart as her whole abdomen grew taut and rose towards a premonition of eventual withdrawal and her desperate stomach lay deathly still, the dinner lay still, as she waited for the gasp of air released from her throat, her head against cobwebs, and who cares about an organism when there's so much else to think about? When the orgasm came it was above average, for reasons which Rosine to this day has never fathomed. For all that, the fuck was one of those necessary bitters thrown into the cup of humanity.

Knock, knock, knock went the knocking.

'What's that knocking?' asked Rosine.

'A burglary.'

Rosine replied: 'This is the burglary. Next door to this is a small, triangular room. The hotel manager told me. In it is a disused chimney. The burglars have climbed down the chimney from the roof and have made themselves a little den in that room and there they are, eating sandwiches and waiting for everyone to go to sleep.'

'Anyway, with a building as old as this, people sometimes want to carve their initials on the wall,' said Frank, remembering a dream he'd had once.

(In the bedroom next to Frank's a shadowy pair of hands had nailed a piece of ragworm to the wall which had the triangular room on its other side.)

'Anyway,' said Frank again, 'it sounds more as if it's coming from the bedroom next to mine, the one with the notice on the door-handle, the one on the far side of your triangular room.'

(A shadowy hand struck a match and lit the end of the ragworm like a fuse.)

The fire burnt through the wall and into the triangular room. Then, with growing confidence, the fire crackled in the 'Please believe me' message of the assassin, its gold-shod feet shuffled along the floor, down the line of an obliging trickle of petrol. Once the fire had learnt this murderousness, it endowed the hotel with the organs of savage birth. The door of the triangular room was now open, ah! the horrible tobacco of a burning mattress, and a skirt of flame whirled momentarily into the corridor as if its owner had just whisked into the small room and was waiting there like a mad woman.

Downstairs, an elderly pianist selected his notes as an embroideress selects gold threads among white cottons. Upstairs, the corridor began to fill with milky smoke of yellow origin, born in the yolk of the fire.

In room 48 Mary was telling Joel that it was in his will she found her love of matches. Once she had told a more courteous lover that it was in his will she found her love of watches. Now she as eagerly stood the 'w' on its head as Marx had eagerly reversed the Hegelian dialectic. She opted for Joel's combustible chemistry of time, against the longer time-scales of a gentler, logos-ridden dialectic.

Joel's hands, that had only lit one candle the whole evening, paused on her shoulders.

'Before you bribe anyone, bribe him to tell no-one else,' he said.

Joel's lies remained between them as a thick, billowing ache. In their nostrils came the smell of cruelty that was wreathing smokily through the hotel corridors. Lips that could so painlessly have kissed curled back distastefully as their nostril-emotions became acrid.

In the triangular room the phrase, 'He has greatly suffered for us,' was a hideous note of charity in the heart of the flames.

That room cracked like a match-head. The time experience burst open and the springs of a mattress tumbled out. With a roar of fury the punishing flames lolloped out of the doorway, dealing old-fashioned slaps at the walls. The bedroom doors were frightened and flew open to receive the smoke. '*Ah-ha!*' said the flames at the single fault of open doors.

Frank flung their room's door open and found the air white with his worst suspicions. Because the smoke had gone so well ahead of the flames no-one could tell the direction of the fire, which became an occult danger.

Some residents were dupes and ran to receive the flames on their chests, where the scars ever after remained.

(From the middle of a blank page an infant boy ran into the smoke. Being mentally-retarded, he did not return.)

The furnace ron-ronned, swallowed obstacles, licked each open door in dog-like gratitude, and, with lavish anger, tackled the dry traditions of flooring. Out of the smoke rushed a roaring shadow, the black centre of the fire, the body of a gorilla, the body of a premonition, which escaped. Frank stood in the doorway, and, as he saw the shadow pass, between the stripes of his pyjamas came the sound of shivering from fear. Rosine's cold hands pushed at his back. It was not an admirable stage of their relationship. 'Keep close to the ground; avoid the middle of floors,' Rosine called down the corridor to the other guests. At last people began running from their doors in the right direction, meeting with warm, panicky bodies. They all began stumbling alongside walls until the stairs opened before their feet in mesmeric revelation. At that bottleneck was a communion of pyjamas. The fire gripped the walls, as light as a fairy, yet surely chained there for the moment. Hosiery and lingerie were melting in the corridor's middle rooms. Within a noisy song the hive was melting, so far three cells in the honeycomb gone. A fault in the age-old flooring gave way and half the corridor broke through to the first floor. The staircases, so lately declensions of pride, shuffled frantically with humility, and the whole snakes and ladders snobbery ethic was reversed. 'Yes, oh please hurry.' The sound of jissom ended between Sonny and Masterson in their bathroom. In another room, by the kitchen, a kipper was hastily thrown into a hotel wastepaper basket. As the new man and Margaret stumbled into the foyer the wurra-wurra noise from the milling crowd reached crescendo. But the guests' panic started to leave them as soon as they came to stairs that gave a view of the swing doors. Above, extinction was beginning, asphyxiation coughed from room to room, disappointed for lack of victims. One unintelligent infant wasn't much to go on.

Unintelligence burnt hilariously; not for days would that hilarity die down, though the fire would be burnt out long before. In the striation of flame, though a baby's face distorted, it was still kind.

The guests, by now all in the foyer, waiting their turn to leave through the swing doors, heard the lift start. Through the heart of the blazing upper storeys the lift dangerously travelled down as a meniscus down a glass tube in a chemistry experiment. The lift doors slid open. Joel and Mary stepped out fully dressed. Up the stairs, the fire was a red glow flickering above a layer of smoke that could not, with that updraught, descend. Jerry was among the still-panic-stricken of the escapees overcrowding the exit. He was sooted, exhausted, pathetic; his swarthy blackish face, his boxer's gangling arms. In the night-clouds, a window shattered, sounding an abortive fire alarm. Who could tell which rooms were now sweeping up armfuls of fire and carrying it farther on? Here, in the exit queue, it was 1880–1890, the spiritualist years, when blue haze was in the drawing rooms, the ectoplasm was ready in the hidden bucket, and people looked older than they were. The hotel manager was there, trying to count up to 51, but only reaching 49. 'Oh, for Christ's sake, everybody, get a move on.' So far, the hotel residents had been acting in caricature; now they steadily calmed and saw the fire as no special danger for them, more the way of all flesh, the angelic shadow on the bones. The disaster was terribly beforehand; it was next year's special offers come this year; it was only eat meat with discretion. As Rosine at last entered a cell of the swing doors and went outside, for her, the comedy of people ended and the comedy of the building remained. She looked back. The hotel was practically empty. Fire escapes in silhouette. Wet lawns said to bare feet, 'It's all right; it's all right'; gravel paths said, 'Never mind the present discomfort; you have a history still to live.'

The hotel had been placed over an existing fire that it was too small to contain adequately, some of the onlookers mistakenly thought.

Fire reddened the atmosphere. Internal hotel walls collapsed, segments of flooring sagged and gave. House lights were blazing round a stage whose proscenium arch was, more's the pity, blazing too. The whole damned play had gone up in smoke. Hotel windows were a beltane farce, winged with stagey flames of the change to winter. A wintery poverty united all the hotel guests as they crowded together on the drive. The 'de Sotas' group had thrown up the profession of phony-revolutionaries, of mere actors, and, appalled, had joined the audience; but they had forfeited a major part of their wages.

Rosine felt that these reminders of the dramatist's art had become symbols, not entirely coherent in their meaning but symbols linking her past life with today's curious fire.

The fire engines arrive.

The Wry-Tup

The fire engines arrive and the brigade starts to tackle the blaze.

One of the firemen is McFarlane; Joel has disappeared.

Piano playing is still heard from the hotel ballroom.

A figure from the crowd dashes into the building to try to rescue the pianist.

The would-be rescuer is Jerry, whom we have observed just beginning to repent his greed.

The first floor gives way.

Neither the pianist nor Jerry come out again, but the piano playing stops.

Donald reappears in the crowd now that Joel has gone and McFarlane strolls up to him as fire fighting continues.

'I hope you'll give my rescue attempt a good wry-tup.'

Now the story cannot end there, neither can it be resolved at this level. It could be partly resolved by reference to the driver of the second train, the one that towed both McFarlane and Donald away from the rail crash. 'Somewhere, ahead of the fiercest person you know is another engine, pulling you and the person who masters you . . .' etc.

We'll let McFarlane die (cancer of the trachea?) in favour of this wider context which develops as Donald and Frank investigate the Scotsman's activities. His small-scale slum landlord activities perhaps lead to a Sunday colour supplement story on 'seaside slums', this to a wider journalistic campaign protesting at lack of care for the disadvantaged, and so on up to widest governmental responsibility and concomitant hard-heartedness in electorates.

However wide the new context we, of course, know that it would still hold many contradictions; so for the sake of making things only apparently clearer the context is not worth supplying.

The new man marries Margaret.

The story, incoherent as it is, becomes complete. And then it relates to our real lives. I'm talking to you. You were Rosine all along; you knew that. I love you. I'm sorry Tom died.

I'm asking all of you who have read my book this far to send a donation of some kind to Mencap, 123 Golden Lane, London EC1. That's where this part of the author's profits is going, though the text has nothing to do with that society and no real persons are represented in its pages.

(If you are reading the book for the second time, please send a second donation – and don't say you weren't warned I'd ask again.)

No slight is intended against British Rail.

16

Illustration of a Thought from Scheler

The story about 'seaside slums' didn't stand up. The following month, Frank and Donald climbed through the broken window of a semi-detached house scheduled for demolition. They had to be careful of broken floorboards, scattered glass, rubble, cardboard boxes and other rubbish. A boxroom, halfway up the stairs, had been used as a lavatory by dossers. At the top of the house was the bedroom where McFarlane had lain. No bed left now and the brown trunk gone too. A grubby mound of newspaper and magazine cuttings swelled up from all round the skirting boards into a hill two feet high in the centre. They picked up a few damp cuttings: five photos of the lower halves of female nudes, cut off just above the buttocks. They found hundreds similar. None of the bodies had upper halves. And a new genre: film magazine pictures from the 1940s. In most, the man was giving the female star a vampire-like kiss. Vampire kisses, buttocks, legs, feet dominated the room's mound of frozen ideas. 'The man who thinks historically and systematically approaches ideal and exact images better than a man impelled by tradition.' However, Scheler says nothing here about women or about cruelty.